WINNER

DUTTON ANIMAL BOOK

AWARD

THE POND

ROBERT MURPHY

Illustrated by Teco Slagboom

THE OVERLOOK PRESS
NEW YORK, NY

This edition first published in paperback in the United States in 2013 by
The Overlook Press, Peter Mayer Publishers, Inc.

141 Wooster Street
New York, NY 10012
www.overlookpress.com

For bulk and special sales, please contact sales@overlookny.com,
or write us at the above address.

Catalog-in-Publication Data is available from the Library of Congress

Book design and typeformatting by Bernard Schleifer
Manufactured in the United States of American
ISBN 978-1-4683-0372-8
1 3 5 7 9 10 8 6 4 2

In memory of my father

The Virginia road was a morass, a continuing and apparently bottomless mudhole; anyone familiar only with modern turnpikes and good roads would have found it incredible. It ran between the pine woods and the sandy cornfields and occasionally passed a wooden house that had long since lost whatever paint had been on it and now stood weathered and gray between the road and a muddy barnyard where there was always a mule or two standing with hanging head, ears drooped forward, and an air of dejection and boredom. There were old Model-T Fords standing in some of the yards, so covered with mud and red clay that their original black paint was invisible, and the houses all had a bleak, utilitarian air because their owners had neither the money nor the energy to do more than just live in them. It was a poor country, between Richmond and Norfolk; the day of commercial fertilizers in any quantity hadn't dawned yet, and the land had long since been farmed out. The farmers who hadn't given up and moved somewhere else scratched a thin living out of it, and that was about all. A good deal of the land, between the fields where the corn was turning brown and the second-growth pine woods, had gone back to brush, greenbrier, scrub oak, holly, honeysuckle, and small struggling trees. There was a little autumn color but not much; most of the trees had lost their leaves except the oaks, which were brown or a somber deep red, and soon what color there was would be leached to a wintry gray against the dark pines.

There was another Model T with two boys in it zigzagging down the road, its high running boards awash. Two fans of mud and water curved up from beneath the wheels and descended like waterfalls on the sides of the road. The Model T bucked and pitched like a destroyer in a heavy sea, and the boy driving it, tall, blond, rather thin, and about fourteen years old, fought valiantly with the steering wheel to keep it on a straight course. He was accustomed to such driving; once out of town in Virginia in 1917, most of the roads were like this one; but this was a particularly bad stretch and he was completely concentrated on getting through it. He knew that if he didn't keep enough momentum the roaring engine would stall and they would be bogged down, in which event one of them would have to wade ashore and find a farmer with a mule to pull them out.

The other boy, stocky, with red hair and freckles, of about the same age, was half standing in his seat, holding on to the windshield. His eyes were on the road too, but farther ahead. It was his job to pick out the least dangerous-looking parts of the road and direct the driver. It was a mutual enterprise; nobody could watch ahead, swiftly estimate the probabilities, and keep an eye immediately in front at the same time.

"Left, now, Joey," the red-haired boy, Bud, said. "Left till you get to that rock, then quick right."

Joey swung, the Model T yawed, slid a few yards sideways, and came back on course again. Joey swung right at the rock, and forty yards on the road rose a little and grew drier.

Joey stopped, pulled on the emergency brake which also put the gearshift pedal into neutral, took his hands off the wheel, and stretched his arms.

"Great day!" Bud said. "You reckon any more of them will be worse than that?"

"I reckon not," Joey said. "That was always the worst one. My father got stuck in it the last time we came down. He didn't tell anybody, but he did. I told him to go left but he didn't go and he had to take off his shoes and roll up his pants and go get a mule."

"We're better than he is."

"Cost him a whole five dollars. He gave me an extra five dollars in case we got stuck too."

"Can we spend it now?" Bud asked. "I got a idea."

"We can't spend it. We got to get back through it coming home, anyhow."

"We'll make it all right," Bud said. "We made it this time, didn't we?"

They grinned at one another, having accomplished something that a grownup had failed to do. They were exhilarated by this rare triumph, and by being on their own for the first time. Several months past, Joey's father and three of his friends had bought the place where they were going as a hunting and fishing camp; it was an old farm, with a house and a lake on it, and this was the first time that Joey had been able to talk his way into going there alone. He had asked his friend and neighbor, Bud, to go with him. It had taken several family councils before their fathers, who were in favor of letting them go by themselves, had been able to convince their mothers that nothing lethal would come of it; the fact that there was a caretaker on the place helped.

"Let's go," Bud said, after they had sat there a little longer savoring their success. "Let's go, so we'll have time to get some fishing in."

Joey started the Model T again. The road, although very muddy and badly rutted, was better now; there was a gravel bottom somewhere under it most of the way. They had two more dubious-looking stretches, but these had been improved by some local farmer who, tired of being stuck in them, had cut poles and laid them across the road. The poles had sunk into the mud, but they did furnish bottom. The Model T bounced across them, and presently they came to a village named Chickahominy Forge, which consisted of three houses and a store with a gasoline pump in front of it. This was the place where they turned off the main road to make their way eight miles back into the country, and they had been told to check in at the store. They stopped the Model T near the gas pump and got out of it and went in.

The store was dim, unswept, and in a state of monumental disarray. A back-country store, it carried everything, and carried it piled up and scattered in all directions. The counters and shelves looked like a cyclone had struck them; besides the things all over the floor, horse collars, boots, steel traps, and hams were hung from the ceiling; there were more variegated smells than in an Oriental bazaar. Two or three old black men were sitting around the stove in the middle of the floor, eating sardines from cans, and when the two boys came in, pausing a moment to accustom their eyes to the gloom, one of them got up, went over to the kerosene barrel in the corner, and pumped a little kerosene over his sardines. The boys looked at one another and made faces, then walked to the end of the room where the storekeeper, Ed Pitmire, was selling another man a bottle of liniment. Pitmire was a bear of a man with a barrel chest, a long nose, and four days' growth of black beard. He looked as unswept as the store.

Pitmire turned his attention to the boys. "Your father wrote me y'all were comin' down," he said to Joey. "Y'all should have come in the train and let me take you over. There's a bad place up the road a piece. You could have got stuck in it."

"We came through it," Joey said with pride. "We made it. You getting ready for wild turkey season?"

"Sure. Plenty of turkeys this year. Y'all need anything?"

"I reckon we do," Joey said, and got out his list. His father usually bought some supplies from Pitmire, who was the only point of contact in the vicinity and therefore a man to be considered; Pitmire also would meet the single daily train and drive them to their destination in his Model T when the roads were too bad to drive from Richmond. "We need some beans and some corned beef hash and bacon and pancake flour and syrup and some eggs. You got some eggs this week?"

Pitmire nodded, and began to pick canned goods out of the confusion and stack them on the counter. "Two each?" he asked, and gave them two each at Joey's nod. The eggs went into a paper bag and would have to be watched out for. "You ought to take Ben some eatin' tobacco," he said, and produced three packages of Beech Nut. "That all?"

"I reckon it is," Joey said. "Can you charge it?" He had been told to charge the things and felt pretty grown-up when he said it, but, as usual, wasn't convinced that it could be done. His own transactions were always in cash, for penny candy or milkshakes, and he didn't understand how merchants got their money from charge accounts.

To his relief Pitmire nodded, scrawled some figures on a dirty sheet of wrapping paper, and stuck the paper in a drawer. "Y'all gonna do some fishin'?" he asked. "Fishin' ought to be good, it ain't rained too much. Ought to kill some squirrels, too. Season starts tomorrow. Y'all got licenses?"

The two boys looked at each other and their faces fell. They had forgotten about licenses; there had been too much else to think about. Their double-barreled twenty-gauge guns, which they had been carefully taught to manage over the last two years, were in the car; now they were useless. They were too disappointed to say anything; they glumly shook their heads.

"Y'all go ahead and shoot," Pitmire said. "The warden comes around, I'll tell him you'll have 'em next time."

The faces lighted up again.

"We'd sure appreciate it if you did that."

"Yes, sir. We sure would. You reckon it will be all right?"

"Leave it to me," Pitmire said. "Y'all can bring me a fish when you come back."

"Yes, sir. Would you like two fish?"

"One's enough. Liza and me, we can't eat but one fish. I'll get a mess of squirrels, anyhow."

"We sure thank you," Joey said, and picked up as many cans as he could carry and took them out to the Model T. Bud followed him with the rest, carrying the bag of eggs by holding the top of the bag in his teeth. He could always think of a precarious way to do something.

"Be careful," Joey said. "We better put them in the front seat."

"I'll put them on the back seat," Bud mumbled between his teeth, and the bag tore. He dropped the cans he was carrying and just managed to catch the eggs on the way down. None of them broke; he put them carefully on the back seat and picked up the cans. They finally had the provisions stowed, climbed into the Model T, and looked at one another. They were on the last lap, they were nearly there, and excitement began to take hold of them. In their minds' eyes they could both see the lake on the place, always called "The Pond," and themselves on it catching huge bass, unsupervised, free as birds, masters of their lives. It was a delectable vision; they grinned at one another and Bud cranked the engine.

Three hundred yards down the road they turned off onto the sandy track into the woods and settled back. The track got little traffic and was much better than the highway; hardly anyone ever went in the direction they were going now, and few people came out very often. The natives were self-sufficient in the main, butchering their own meat or shooting it, raising their own corn and vegetables, supplying their own needs except for such things as kerosene, matches, and a few canned goods and notions they could buy at Pitmire's store or other articles they couldn't buy from Pitmire and got from the "mail order." The Chickahominy Swamp, which ran off into the Great Dismal Swamp, contained them to the south, and the poor land which had been largely deserted stretched around them in the other three directions. The land rolled a little, but not much. It was like an island, cut off from the world and forgotten by it. There were not over a dozen families on the eighteen miles of the road which wandered about and ended up in an abandoned pasture, and not half of them had cars; many of them were poor black people who were lucky if they owned a mule.

The boys passed the first cabin, set back a little in trees, within a mile; three ragged young children playing in front of it waved and gave them wide white smiles. There was one more such cabin four miles farther on with more smiling children. They knew when they passed it that there were only three more miles to go; the excitement built a little higher, and without realizing it they both sat forward on the seat.

They came over a hilltop and dropped down, turned a corner, and stopped on the little bridge that went over the spillway of the dam. Water roared softly beneath them, and a few feet off to the right the Pond, their future kingdom, lay quietly in the sun. It was roughly rectangular, and they were near the end of one of the long sides; it curved away from them, lined with old, tall cypresses with their feet in the water. The needles that were left on them were brown, so their color was reddish and rather somber; the road ahead was lined with them too, big trees three feet or so in diameter, reddish and feathery. They were surrounded by cypresses, which didn't grow in Richmond or any place else that they knew. The feeling descended upon them, as it always did when they came to the big cypresses, that they had entered a different world. Joey turned off the engine and silence fell, a sort of waiting and mysterious quiet, and they looked at one another and grinned with delight.

"Boy!" Bud said.

They sat there for a little while, savoring the quietness and the thought that all this, and the Pond and the fish in it and the squirrels along the shore, were theirs for three days to run about in and explore, catch and shoot at.

Bud stirred on the seat finally and brought into the open a question they had both been secretly thinking about when they had the time. "You reckon," he said, "that Mr. Ben will be all right?"

Mr. Ben was the caretaker. He had come from one of the best families in Richmond, but he had been a black sheep. In his younger days he had had grievous scuffles with the bottle; he had had the habit of getting himself into cheap rooming houses and staying there for a week or two completely out of touch with his family and too drunk to get out of bed, or if he could get out of bed he would wander around the Richmond streets and disgrace himself by falling down in the most public places. It had finally got so bad that they had made a sort of remittance man out of him; they paid him an allowance so long as he stayed a long way off, out of sight and out of mind. He had wandered for years all over the United States and finally, God knows how, had found this obscure place and come to rest with the farmer it had been bought from. He had stayed on as a caretaker, and although his passion for the bottle had long since burned out, the boys were in awe of him; they had heard their parents' talk, about his misadventures, which their youthful imaginations had enlarged to monumental proportions and considerably overcolored.

"I mean," Bud went on, "will he . . . ?"

"Oh, he'll be fine," Joey said, hoping that he would. "My father wrote him we were coming. He wouldn't do anything my father wouldn't like."

"You reckon he wouldn't? You sure?"

"Why, sure I'm sure," Joey said stoutly, trying to convince himself. "You think he's a wild man or something? What would he do, for gosh sakes?"

"How do I know what he'd do? We'll be there all alone with him, won't we? He might get drunk and chase us with a knife or something."

"Good Christmas!" Joey said, with as much disgust as he could muster. "What for?"

"Because he's found a bottle or something."

"Shucks!" Joey said, but he wasn't too vehement. His own imagination, which he had managed to keep fairly quiet, was warming up under Bud's encouragement. A silence fell between them; they sat and stared out over the Pond. A few feet from shore four cypresses grew in a cluster in the water, and something fell out of one of them. As it hit the water a huge bass rose in a shower of spray, engulfed it, and fell back with a tremendous splash. The two boys forgot Mr. Ben and a possible bottle and being chased with a knife; they forgot everything except the bass, and were galvanized to instant life.

"I vench on him!" Bud shouted. "I vench on him! Let's go!"

He jumped out to crank the Model T, while Joey sat there and turned the ignition key and felt cheated. Bud had shown more presence of mind than he; to vench on anything first was to have first go at it, as every boy knew. It was a law as unchanging and unbreakable as the laws of the Medes and Persians, and there was no appeal. The Model T started, Bud jumped in, and they tore along the road, up the hill, through the gate, and around to the back of the house.

It was a sound wooden house with five rooms on the first floor and two on the second, standing between two great black walnut trees. There was a porch along the back of it, half of which was roofed and screened; the other half was unroofed and the kitchen door opened on it. It needed paint. There was a small old barn about fifty yards away that wasn't used any more except to store junk in. The boys stopped the Model T between the house and the barn and looked around. Although the house looked as bleak as the rest that they had passed, it didn't seem as bleak to them; it was their headquarters. There was no one in the yard. The boys grabbed their cased bait-casting rods out of the back of the Model T and ran through the house as they tried to put them together. There was no one in the house either; Mr. Ben was out somewhere. Outside again, they calmed down long enough to set

Teco—

up the rods and reels, assemble their gear, and grab a paddle and landing net from the back porch, and then took off on the wooded path that ran down the hill to the boat landing.

The small wharf faced out upon a little cove; a very large cypress grew in the water a few feet in front of it, framing a view over about a quarter of the Pond, the sunny water and the distant, close-growing rank of trees on the opposite shore. This small view was somehow a friendly one, an introduction to the rest of the Pond which opened up without a house or a sign of man's handiwork when you got into a boat and left the cove. There was a large, half-sunken wooden box with wire sides on one side of the wharf to keep fish alive in until whoever caught them was ready to take them home, and two rowboats and a bateau, flat-bottomed and double-ended, were tied up on the other side.

Joey usually paused on the wharf and looked out from it for a moment or two, feeling that he was meeting the Pond again and getting ready for the pleasures of being upon it, but he didn't do it this time. The big bass was in his mind, hurrying him. He unwrapped the old trap chain hooked to a nail that kept the bateau from drifting away and jumped into the stern. Bud got into the bow, and they shoved off and headed out to cross the Pond.

"Faster!" Bud said, in a fever of anxiety. "Faster! He'll be gone."

Neither of them even looked up the Pond.

"Faster!" Bud said again. "Go *on*."

Joey didn't reply; he didn't have the breath for it. He dug the paddle into the water, and the bateau skimmed along until they got to within fifty yards of the group of cypresses where the bass had jumped. Joey stopped paddling and the bateau coasted along, losing way; then Joey began paddling again, very carefully, and they sneaked up on the spot. Bud raised his rod and brought it forward. He was too anxious; the reel ran over, and he had a backlash. The line snarled and the plug swung in a short wild arc and smacked the water beside the boat.

"Goddamn!" Bud said. He sat down and began frantically to strip off line in order to untangle the bird's nest caused by the backlash, shaking with anxiety and frustration, tangling it more.

"Give it to me," Joey said, beginning to shake himself. "You're messing it up. Give it to me, damn it!"

He couldn't sit still; he half rose and started for the bow, and the bateau began to rock. He sat down quickly again, almost frantic himself with the urge to get at the reel and fix everything; he'd never seen such a butter fingered performance as Bud was putting on. "Give it to me!" he shouted. "Let me have it, you clumsy ox!"

Bud looked up. "Back up!" he snarled. "Back up! You've let us get too far; we'll scare him!"

Joey looked around and saw that Bud was right. He reached for the paddle, but it wasn't there. In his excitement he had let it slide into the water, and it floated mockingly twenty yards away.

"Back up!" Bud snarled again, not looking up. Joey didn't say anything. "Back up, will you?" Bud said, and raised his head. "What are you waiting there for? Back up!"

"Bud," Joey said.

"Yeah, yeah."

"The paddle's out there."

Bud put the rod down and stared. Joey pointed.

"Oh, *damn!*" Bud said in complete disgust. "Now you have messed it up. How are we going to get it?"

"We'll have to paddle with our hands."

"Good Christmas! And you calling people clumsy oxes."

"You started it," Joey said, stung. "Getting a backlash when I put you in the exact place. The first cast."

"I guess you got paralyzed and just dropped the paddle, huh? You sick or something? You got a temperature? You see a man get a perfectly natural backlash and can't—"

"Oh, shut up!" Joey shouted.

They sat and glared at one another from opposite ends of the bateau and presently, seeing that they weren't getting anywhere, made peace by silent mutual consent. They rolled up their sleeves and paddled with their hands. It was a long and tiresome process, and wouldn't have worked if there had been any wind. They finally reached the paddle, and Joey picked it out of the water.

"You reckon you better tie it to you?" Bud asked.

"You reckon it's my turn to fish? You sure messed that up. You better get that backlash fixed before we move from here. We'll have to go somewhere else; we'll never catch him now."

"I'll fix it," Bud said. "But I get to fish until I catch one."

Joey could hardly quarrel with that, after having lost the paddle. "Okay," he said. "We'll go around the shore and try him again on the way back."

Bud got the backlash fixed finally, and Joey rowed back across the pond and started to paddle slowly along fifteen or twenty yards offshore while Bud dropped the plug along the shoreline and reeled it in. They had both practiced their bait casting for long hours in their backyards and were surprisingly accurate; it was a pretty thing to see the plug drop into the center of the little three-foot openings between the cypress butts and start wiggling its way back toward the boat.

There was almost a dreamlike quality about this kind of fishing, gliding slowly and silently over the dark cedar water with only an occasional dip of the paddle. The paddler watched the fisherman and the shore, where an infrequent squirrel was surprised as it foraged on the ground or a bird flashed into view and out of it again; the woods were still, the cypresses brooded almost over their heads, and the fisherman cast and reeled in, concentrating on his work, with a slow and steady rhythm. Neither of them spoke. A series of water drops fell from the paddle as it was retrieved from a leisurely stroke, the plug splashed when it hit the water, and there was no other sound except the distant rattle of a kingfisher as it flew from tree to tree far ahead of the bateau.

Presently the quiet was broken when a bass darted out from shore, hit the plug, and jumped into the air when it felt the hook. The broken water flashed in the sun, the bass gleamed as it curved, shaking its head, back into the water again, and Bud played it until it gave up and was netted and put into the live box amidships. They both moved in to admire it as it sulked in the live box, a good dark fish of two pounds or so, and then they changed places.

Joey didn't get a strike until they came to the first long cove where a great dead oak lay half submerged and partially blocked the cove's entrance. The bass came out from under the sunken trunk; he was a big one, Joey had gone a little dreamy, and the strike was so hard that it took the handle of the reel out of Joey's fingers. The reel spun backwards, and the fish ran down into the tree and tangled the line among the sunken branches and got away.

"Ah!" Joey said. He tried to reel in and couldn't. "I'm tangled up," he said in disgust.

"Why didn't you hang on to him, for gosh sakes?" Bud demanded, and swung the bateau. They each took hold of a branch and Bud poked about with the paddle. They had to roll up their sleeves again and feel about under water until the line was free again. It took a long time, a deal of amateur profanity, and a soaking to the shoulders for both of them; by the time the plug was free the sun had sunk so low that they were in shadow and chilly. They looked up the cove, which was lined all around the shore with trees, and decided to go back and try the fish they had seen from the road again before they quit.

"I get to catch him," Bud said, as they started across the Pond.

"You caught one. It's my turn."

"You'd had one if you hadn't gone to sleep. Anyhow, I venched on him."

It was a problem. He *had* venched on him, and even if he'd had a backlash Joey had lost the paddle. Joey realized that he didn't have much of a case, but he tried anyhow. "If you hadn't had the backlash—"

"I venched on him."

"Okay, gosh hang it. Catch him, then. Only, I get to fish until we get there."

"Okay," Bud said, and they went across the lake. Joey worked the shore until they neared the cypresses without raising a fish, and they changed places in the bateau. They crept up to the place, scarcely breathing, and Bud cast his plug. They both stared in fascination as it returned through the water. Nothing happened. Bud tried several times more, bracketing the spot where the monster had appeared, but the monster refused to be drawn out. Finally they gave him up for that day, and headed for the wharf, sliding across the lengthening shadows on the water, shivering a little in the gathering evening chill, but at peace with one another now and content.

CHAPTER TWO

They caught the fish in the net and dumped it in the live box by the dock, hooked the bateau's chain on the nail, and went up the hill. It was twilight by this time and they were hungry; they were both thinking of Mr. Ben again, but didn't mention him to one another. They had had a good afternoon and were looking forward to the warmth of the house and food, and somehow the old man didn't seem quite so dubious any more.

When they got to the clearing at the top of the hill there was the smell of woodsmoke in the air and they could see a light in the kitchen. They reached the back porch, closed ranks, climbed the back steps, and went in. The kitchen was warm; there was a roaring wood fire in the stove, a kerosene lamp was burning on the table, and Mr. Ben was just dumping an armload of wood into the woodbox. He heard them come in and straightened up and turned around. He was in his late sixties, lean, of medium height, and a little bent and lantern-jawed; his hands were gnarled and slightly misshapen by "the rheumatism"; he trapped muskrats in the winter and this kept his hands in cold water a good deal, but he had a good, friendly face and was still lively enough. He had about three days' growth of beard, upon which the lamplight cast a silvery sheen.

They spoke together. "Hi, Mr. Ben."

He made what once might have been a courtly bow. "Gentlemen," he said, "good evening. When I saw the car and you weren't here, I thought the alligators might have made off with you."

The boys looked at one another. "Alligators?" Bud said. "There aren't really alligators, are there, Mr. Ben?"

"Well, I didn't see any today, but it was a little cool."

"I never saw an alligator when I was here with my father," Joey said, looking at Bud. "When it was warmer."

"They're shy," Mr. Ben said, "with grown people. It's different with boys. Yes, sir, Chickahominy River alligators are mighty careful."

The boys looked at one another again, and Bud said, "We better bring the things in."

"I reckon we better," Joey said. "Excuse us, Mr. Ben."

When they got to the Model T, Bud hissed, "We better be careful. Anybody talks about alligators . . . What's he trying to give us? You think he's making fun of us, or what?"

"He never tried to make fun of me before."

"Maybe he was always too busy talking to your father . . . or something. You smell anything?"

"Smell anything? Smell what?"

"Whisky or anything."

Joey stared at him. A fair amount of the time Joey was a dreamy boy; he was a great reader, and some of the phrases he encountered conjured up pictures in his mind that dulled his ears to the exterior world and turned his eyes inward for a while. He would get out of this world and into one of his own, but except when this fit was on him he had surprisingly practical moments. He had a better sense of reality than Bud, who was inclined to embroider a situation and then be caught in the embroidery, letting his imagination run away with him. "Shucks," Joey said. "I think you're making too much of it. He's not going to do anything silly. He's not going to do anything. He likes it here. He hasn't anyplace else to go, anyhow."

"You reckon?" Bud asked. "What's he talking about alligators for, then?"

"I think he's trying to kid us," Joey said. "You thought so yourself a minute ago."

"I . . . okay. Maybe he's trying to kid us, but I'm going to watch him just the same."

"Okay," Joey said, and picked up as much as he could carry and took it into the house.

Bud followed him in with another load. Besides the things they had bought at the store, they had brought two cakes baked by their mothers, two cooked chickens, four loaves of home-baked bread, half a dozen cans of soup, and three jars of home-made raspberry jam. All of these things were piled on the kitchen table and then stowed in the kitchen cabinet. Mr. Ben's eyes lighted up at the sight of all this plunder; living alone, he seldom cooked very much except eggs and cornbread, side meat and a fish once in a while.

The boys then brought in their clothes and gear. Joey lit another lamp, and as the guns always went into the living room and stood in corners, they took their guns in there and stood them up. The living room was rectangular; it had a sheet-iron wood stove with a fire in it against one wall and a table covered with blue-figured oilcloth that was used to eat upon on the other wall. The room had been plastered and painted a long time ago and it was hard to say what color it was any more; there was a window in each short wall, one of them giving out on the back porch and the other looking out over the fields in the front. The front window had a somewhat sagging couch in front of it; most of the furniture had been left by the farmer owner and had been supplemented by old, worn-out things that Joey's father had sent down.

Joey left the lamp on the table until they got their clothes, and then carried it into the bedroom. There was no stove in there, and the room with a big brass double bed and an old bureau and several chairs in it had a graveyard chill. They didn't stay there long. They went back to the kitchen, leaving the lamp in the living room again, and stood watching Mr. Ben put more wood into the stove.

"What will we eat?" Bud asked. "Chicken?"

"Chicken and beans," Joey said. "Would you like chicken and beans, Mr. Ben?"

"I would indeed," Mr. Ben said. "Perhaps a little soup first? You have soup, don't you?"

"Yes, sir."

"You both got a little chilled, and soup warms the cockles of the heart."

"The cockles of the heart?" Joey repeated. He liked the phrase; he could see in his mind's eye the cockles of the heart, whatever they were, expanding and gently waving to and fro in the soup's savory steam.

"Joey," Bud said, after a moment.

"Huh? The cockles of the heart."

"Oh, *come* on. Open the soup while I open the beans."

"Open them and give them to me," Mr. Ben said, setting two saucepans on the stove. "Then you can set the table while I get them ready."

They opened the cans and gave them to Mr. Ben, then set the table and put the chicken out. Bud sliced some bread, opened a jar of jam, and they stood in the kitchen door watching Mr. Ben at the stove. He shook one saucepan and then the other; he had removed the lids from the top of the stove to hurry things along, and every time he raised one of the pans, a little of the firelight glowed on him. In the dim kitchen, lit by the single lamp, he looked somewhat like an old stooped alchemist trying to transmute some unimaginable mixture into gold. "Soup's hot," he said. "Get the plates."

Joey got the plates and put them on the table, and Mr. Ben poured the soup into them. He put the lids on the stove again and set the beans back to keep warm, and they all picked up their plates and took them into the living room. Mr. Ben brought the other lamp and put it on the table and they all sat down and Bud picked up his spoon.

"Just a minute," Mr. Ben said, and bowed his head. "O Lord, we thank Thee for what we are about to receive," he said, and attacked his soup. He sucked in a spoonful with a sound that could only have been equaled by a powerful suction pump. "Ah," he said. "Splendid! Splendid!"

The two boys looked at one another out of the corners of their eyes, and had a difficult time not to laugh aloud; it had been dinned into them that one ate soup silently. Mr. Ben was completely concentrated on his soup. They all finished it, the boys took out the plates and brought in the beans, and Mr. Ben cut up the chicken. No one said anything until the beans and chicken were gone, for the boys were still a little wary and Mr. Ben was enjoying himself too much to be distracted; then Joey brought in one of the cakes and they each had a quarter of it.

Mr. Ben pushed back his chair. "Gentlemen, sir," he said, "that was real fine." He belched. "Yes, sir, real fine. I'll wash the dishes. My hands get chapped and the dirt gets into them, and the hot dishwater takes it out." He got up and took his plate into the kitchen, and they could hear him pouring water into a

kettle. They took their own plates into the kitchen; neither of
them was concerned with his hand-cleaning procedure. It would
have horrified their mothers, but the boys rejoiced because they
had no dishes to wash. He gave them dish towels and they dried
the plates and knives and forks as he got through with them and
put them away. He concentrated on his work; the kitchen was
quiet except for a subdued rattle of dishes. An after-dinner peace
descended upon them all, and the boys, having watched Mr.
Ben with the soup and the rest of the meal, felt better about
him. He began to seem almost like other people, and by the
time they went back into the living room Joey was relaxed
enough to remember the chewing tobacco. He went into the
bedroom and brought it back.

"We brought you this from Chickahominy Forge," he
said, and handed Mr. Ben three packages.

"Well, that was real neighborly. Thank you both. I was
just about out." He went out to the kitchen, brought in a few
sticks of wood, and put them into the sheet-iron stove, which
began to roar almost at once, and turned the draft down.
They pulled up chairs in a semicircle around it.

"Mr. Ben," Bud said, "you reckon we could shoot some
squirrels tomorrow?"

"Squirrel? Why not? If you want, you could borrow
White's dog."

They both looked at him, trying to decide whether he
was making fun of them again or not. They knew of the
Whites, who lived five or six hundred yards up the road; the
water came from there, carried over in buckets, for there was
no well at the house. It had fallen in, and hadn't been fixed
yet. Both their fathers were quail hunters and they knew
about bird dogs and beagles, but neither of them ever had
heard of a squirrel dog. Squirrels lived in trees, and what

could a dog do about that? A sudden constraint fell upon both of them.

"A squirrel dog?" Bud asked, carefully.

"His name's Charley."

"Yes, sir," Bud said, and his eyes slid toward Joey. Nobody named a dog Charley. He, Bud, knew a man who had a horse he called Polka Dot, but the man was often away in a "home"; he wasn't quite right in the head. There was a silence.

"He's a right good squirrel dog, if you can keep up with him," Mr. Ben said.

"Yes, sir," Bud said again, and moved in his chair.

Joey thought it time to take a hand. "What does he do, Mr. Ben?" he asked. "Does he point up trees?"

"Why would he point up trees? He runs around until he finds one on the ground and trees him, and then he stands there and barks."

The air cleared; both boys smiled. It sounded like a wonderful way to hunt squirrels. They had gone with their fathers and watched them shoot quail, but had never tried it themselves. The two or three times that they had tried to hunt squirrels before they had still-hunted them, sitting in one place without moving in the hope that sooner or later a squirrel would appear. No squirrel had ever done it, at least within range; they hadn't been able to sit still long enough.

"You reckon Mr. White would lend him to us? Doesn't he want to hunt squirrels himself?"

"No," Mr. Ben said. "When I was over there today for water he said he wasn't going to. The boys won't, either. They have to go to school, to make up some work."

"Maybe he would loan us Charley, then," Joey said. The more he thought about a squirrel dog the better it sounded;

excitement began to take hold of him. "How would we get him, Mr. Ben?"

"I'll go get him for you in the morning, or I'll go over there with you. That would be best. After that you can go yourselves."

The boys looked at one another, pleased and reassured; Mr. Ben seemed to be turning out pretty well after all.

"Yes, sir," Joey said. "Thank you, Mr. Ben."

"Or, better than that, when we get him over here we might feed him. They don't feed him much over there. If we feed him once, he'll come back himself as long as you're here."

He grinned at them, and they grinned back; suddenly there was a warm, conspiratorial feeling among them. Bud visibly relaxed in his chair and then sat up. "What will we feed him?" he asked. "We haven't got any dog food or anything like that."

"I've still got the dishwater," Mr. Ben said. "I'll stir up a pan of cornbread with it before the stove cools off." He got up and went into the kitchen, then stuck his head back into the living room. "That dishwater will be real nourishing," he said. "It'll fill him up good."

His head vanished and the boys grinned at one another again. They felt fine now, for with the cornbread under way all their doubts began to recede; Mr. Ben was no longer an object of apprehension and doubt; he was doing something for them and they accepted him completely. All at once they both began to feel drowsy, a healthy, relaxed weariness from the drive from Richmond, the afternoon on the Pond, and the relief they felt about Mr. Ben. A vast desire for sleep suddenly came over them, a little confused with their anticipations for the morning and its adventures with the squirrel dog, and they both stood up. They looked into the kitchen where the old man was putting the pan of cornbread into the oven.

"Good night, Mr. Ben," Joey said. "We sure appreciate your trouble."

"We sure do. Good night, Mr. Ben."

"Good night," he said, and shut the oven door.

They took off most of their clothes in the warmth of the living room, ran into the freezing dark of the bedroom, put on their flannel pajamas, and jumped into the bed. It took them into its dank, chilling embrace; but they got their backs together, presently their teeth ceased chattering, and they began to get warm. They each thought drowsily of the day, of conquering the mudholes and being on the Pond, of being free and on their own, and of the surprising friendliness of Mr. Ben.

"He likes us," Bud said. "Mr. Ben, I mean. He's not at all like I thought."

"You see?"

"See what? You weren't sure about him yourself."

"He's even better than being home. He didn't tell us to wash our faces or anything. And he's going to get us the dog."

Bud began to laugh and then he made a sucking sound, imitating Mr. Ben's enthusiasm with the soup. Joey began to laugh too. They snuggled closer together, still laughing, and almost at once were asleep.

They were awakened by Mr. Ben throwing wood into the living room stove and lay for a few minutes whispering together until they thought the stove was going well and the night's chill would be off the living room. Through the window beside the bed they could see that there was a light frost on the ground, and when they blew out their breath it produced a little vapor in the room. They waited a little longer, warm and wide awake now with anticipation, and then jumped up and ran into the living room and dressed in there. They decided to have pancakes for breakfast. They got out a box of prepared pancake flour, stirred it up with water, and greased up the skillet. The pancake-mixing was a serious enterprise for a while, and then they began to experiment. They flipped them into the air, as cowboys were supposed to do; some of them landed on the edge of the skillet, several landed on the floor, and before they were through they greased the top of the stove and cooked the pancakes on that. They would have been run out of the kitchen at home if they'd tried such maneuvers, and at first they weren't sure that the same thing wasn't going to happen to them here; but Mr. Ben just watched them for a moment or two, grinned to himself, and let them alone. He merely said that he never had much appetite. In spite of this declaration he got away with a surprising number of pancakes, but the boys left him far behind. When they couldn't hold any more they surveyed the kitchen. It was a mess, but by silent mutual consent, because of the unusual freedom Mr. Ben had allowed them, they set to work and cleaned it all up. Then they all set out for White's, each carrying an empty bucket to bring water back in.

"There's something I ought to tell you," Mr. Ben said as they walked up the road. "They got a boy named Horace. They don't talk about him much, because he's got a head so big one of these buckets won't go over it. He's afflicted."

They both stopped and stared at him, feeling all of the distaste, which was almost a horror, of the healthy young for an abnormality. They didn't want to see the boy; their own mental pictures of him gave them each a crawling feeling in the stomach; but they didn't want to turn back and leave Mr. Ben. They were beginning to feel a sense of loyalty and good will toward him.

"He won't be up yet," Mr. Ben said. "It's too early and too cold. His feet aren't on right, he sort of has to walk on his ankles, and so he goes around the yard in a little cart when the weather's good. I wanted to tell you, in case you see him you won't be surprised."

"Is he . . ." Joey began, "is he . . . crazy?"

"No, he's a right nice boy, but he's different. If he saw you today he could tell you five years from now what the date and the weather was and what you said to him. Word for word." He realized they were all standing still. "He won't make any fuss, if that's what bothers you. But like I said, he won't be out of bed yet."

Joey swallowed; it sounded safe to go. "Okay," he said, and they started to walk again. Bud, who hadn't said anything, stood still for a second or two longer and then caught up with them. They reached White's gate without saying any more, and turned into the sandy, rutted lane.

The house was on the left side of the lane, a hundred yards back from the gate. It was a wooden house, like most of them in that country, and the paint had mostly disappeared from it; the barn was on the right. The well was a little in front of the house, boxed in with lumber and having a wheel above it for the rope which held the bucket to run through. There were three big oaks around the house; the whole group of buildings, weathered and gray, looked rather desolate and bleak against the dark pine woods that grew behind them.

They had nearly reached the well when a man came out of the barn and waved at Mr. Ben. He met them at the well. He was thin, of medium height, dressed in dirty overalls and hip boots manured to the knees; his thin face, like Mr. Ben's, had three days' beard on it, and his eyes were too close together and strangely remote.

"Morning, Sam," Mr. Ben said. "This is Joey and this is Bud."

"Good morning, sir," Joey said, and Bud echoed him.

"Hi, boys," he said. "Nice to meet y'all." He smiled at them, somehow managing to give them the impression that he saw them not as boys but as inanimate portions of the landscape. There was nothing hostile in this; it was even vaguely friendly; but it was evident that his mind was on something else, and they both felt that it usually was. He turned to Mr. Ben. "New schoolteacher's here," he said. "Crenshaw helped move her in."

"That's fine," Mr. Ben said. "Crenshaw, he's too young to be lonely all the time."

An odd, secretive expression flitted across White's face. Both boys saw it and wondered at it. "Reckon you're right," he said. "Well, I better get back."

"If you're not going to use Charley," Mr. Ben said, "we'd like to borrow him."

"You go ahead." He turned, put two fingers in his mouth, and gave a piercing whistle.

They all stood there for a moment, and a big black dog trotted around from behind the house and came up to them. He was thin and his ribs stood out. His lines were mostly those of a foxhound; he had the long hound ears and the foxhound bone and head and carriage, but only his ancestors knew what varieties were in him. He stood there quietly looking from one of them to the other, self-contained and undemonstrative. He had never learned to be demonstrative. He was a back-country farmer's dog, and the farmer had four children and played-out land and little money and wasn't a demonstrative man. No one had ever made much of Charley, and he had accepted that; he was a working dog, in the same class as a mule, and a good deal of the time he had to shift for himself. No one had ever got very close to him or tried to. Joey leaned over and patted his head.

He accepted the gesture, looked at Joey with an expression of faint surprise, and moved off a step.

White turned to him. "You go with them, you hear?" he said to the dog, and turned back. "I hope you get some," he said, and went off again toward the barn.

They filled their buckets and started back again. The dog went with them, walking several steps to the rear of Mr. Ben.

"He sure is a quiet dog," Joey said, after a moment. He was a little puzzled by Charley; all of the dogs he knew made much of people, wagging their tails and thrusting their heads into a hand to be patted. "You think he likes us, Mr. Ben?"

"You think he'll mind us?" Bud asked.

"He'll tree squirrels," Mr. Ben said. "When you knock one out of a tree he'll grab it and kill it and maybe run around with it, but you catch him and take it from him."

"He won't bite if we do that, will he?" Bud asked. "He's a pretty big dog and he don't seem very friendly to me."

"Don't worry about that. You do what I say. If he'd ever tried to bite anybody Sam White would have taken a shotgun to him and he knows it."

"But he doesn't wag his tail or anything."

"He don't tree squirrels by wagging his tail. Nobody in that house ever wasted time making him wag his tail."

They got to the house; the boys went in, put on their high-top shoes, and got their guns and shells and hunting coats. Mr. Ben took the pan of cornbread out of the cold oven and gave Charley half of it while they stood and watched him eat. "You stay somewhere near the Pond, if you can," he told them, "and then you won't get lost. If you do get away from it and can't figure where you are, find a creek bottom and follow it back to the Pond. You don't know the country very well yet."

"Yes, sir."

"You go up this side of the Pond first."

"Yes, sir."

They started out. So long as they were in the big field that surrounded the house, Charley stayed near them; when they got to the edge of the woods, he disappeared. They didn't know whether to call him or not; he was somewhat of a mystery to them, too self-contained, and they didn't feel any assurance with him. Behind the cypresses that bordered the Pond the country was full of old oaks, maples, and hickories mixed with beech and holly and a little underbrush; there was not much pine in this vicinity. The boys walked along scuffling the fallen leaves, wondering whether they were doing the right thing.

"You reckon that Charley's gone home?" Bud asked presently.

Joey was just about to reply when they saw the dog, a hundred yards or so ahead of them through the trees; he was running, and as they watched he jumped high in the air. He did this to listen, to see if he could hear a squirrel running about in the leaves on the ground, but the boys didn't know this and were puzzled. When he came down he turned to the west and put on speed; shortly they heard his long hound's bay.

"He's got one!" Bud yelled. "Come on."

They started to run, dodging trees and brier tangles, stumbling and panting. They found him presently; he was standing beneath a huge oak, looking up into the top of it. They were scratched and blown, and when they looked up the tree could see nothing. A vast disappointment took hold of them.

"Shucks!" Bud said. "There's nothing up there. Come on, dog."

Disappointed and feeling that they had done something wrong, they turned away. As the dog saw them start off he ran around the tree and bayed again; his voice, urgent and deep, vibrated about them and echoed back, rounded and diminished, from across the Pond.

"He thinks it's still there," Joey said. "We better go back. Maybe it hid up there when it heard us coming."

They returned; one of them got on one side of the oak and one on the other. They stared up until their necks grew stiff, carefully looking along all the branches. They were ready to leave again when a little breeze came up, and high in the oak, near the top, Joey saw a flicker of movement. The squirrel had flattened itself against a limb and its gray color, so much like that of the bark, had made it almost invisible; the flicker had been its bushy tail, blown a little by the breeze.

"I see him, I see him!" Joey shouted. He raised his gun and shot.

He apparently dusted the squirrel, for it jumped from its hiding place and began to leap swiftly from limb to limb and run about the tree. It was a difficult target, small and quick and never still. Joey fired his second barrel; Bud fired both of his. They were too anxious and excited to be cool about it; seven shots were fired before the squirrel came tumbling down. Charley had watched it moving, and was right beneath it when it fell; he grabbed it and ran about. The boys yelled at him, dropped their guns, and chased him around the woods until they caught him.

"Give it to me!"

"Drop it!"

"You, Charley!"

It was their first squirrel and they wanted it so badly that they forgot to feel a little apprehensive about the dog. Bud got his arms around him, and Joey pulled his jaws apart and took the dead squirrel out. He allowed it. As soon as the squirrel was taken away from him he accepted the situation and started off to find another one.

The two boys sat down, still shaking from excitement and the chase to catch Charley, and admired their prey. They smoothed its rumpled fur, patted it, and finally put it into Joey's game pocket. They looked triumphantly at one another; a new and enthralling world had been opened up.

"Boy!" Bud said.

"Great day! That's sure more fun than still-hunting."

"Whew!" Bud said and wiped his sweaty face. "It was sure hard to see, though."

"He's a good dog. He's sure a good dog. He knew it was up there all the time."

"Yeah, and we were going to leave him."

"I'm sure glad Mr. Ben thought of him. He wants us to have a good time, and he doesn't holler at us to dry the dishes or wash our faces or anything."

"Listen!" Bud said.

They sat listening, opening their mouths a little, concentrating. Far off, mellowed by distance, there was a long, rolling bay. Both boys jumped up as though an electric current had gone through them. They ran about and found their guns and took off in a wild and heedless scramble through the woods.

CHAPTER THREE

A little after noon they got back to the house and laid four squirrels on the edge of the porch floor. They were scratched and weary, famished and happy; they had never had such an exciting time. Charley had returned with them and lay down near the foot of the steps. Mr. Ben came out of the kitchen and grinned when he saw the squirrels.

"I was about to call out the militia," he said. "It sounded from here like somebody started a war."

"We shot up almost a whole box of shells," Joey said. "They're hard to hit, but we sure had a swell time. Mr. Ben, you reckon we could keep Charley here? You reckon my father could buy him?"

"Maybe my father would put in some money, too," Bud said, "if they wanted too much for him. We could be partners."

"Sam White wouldn't sell him," Mr. Ben said. "He's too handy to have around. He'll run a rabbit if he comes on one, and they hunt possums and coons with him at night. We'll give him the rest of the cornbread after a while, and tonight I'll make some more. That'll keep him around. You better have some lunch."

They all went into the house and began to get together a lunch of more soup and beans. Joey poured a little water into one of the agate basins on the table near the stove and started to carry it out onto the porch to wash his hands. When he reached the door he stopped and stared. Charley was on the porch and the four squirrels had disappeared; the tail of the last one was just vanishing down his throat. Joey's exclamation of dismay was so tragic that Mr. Ben ambled over to the door beside him, and Bud came after him and looked over his shoulder.

"Mr. Ben!" Joey said in anguish. "Mr. Ben, he's eaten them all!"

Mr. Ben grinned. "Dang if he hasn't," he said. "Hides, tails, and whiskers. It was my fault. I forgot how hungry they keep him, and I should have put them out of reach."

"But they were our first ones," Bud wailed.

"Plenty more where they came from. In another hour or two you can go out and get some more. Eat your lunch, now."

With a last, reproachful look at Charley, Joey turned around. Bud had gone back to the stove and had already poured out the soup; he was putting the beans on the plates. They looked at one another, trying to be mad at Charley; suddenly they both began to laugh.

"Tails and everything!" Bud said. "You ever hear of a dog eating squirrel tails?"

"He looked like he was just swallowing his own whiskers," Joey said. He laughed again, and then a disturbing thought occurred to him as they sat down at the table. "You reckon he'll get a bellyache now and won't go this afternoon?"

This thought sobered them; they wanted nothing so much as another wild scramble like the one of the morning. It had been the most exciting thing that had ever happened to them.

They looked at one another apprehensively.

"You reckon he will?" Bud asked. He got up from the table and ran into the kitchen. "Mr. Ben, you reckon Charley will get sick and won't go?"

"Get sick from what?"

"From eating squirrel tails and everything. We want to go again, and if he gets sick . . ."

"Take more than a little fur to make him sick," Mr. Ben said. "That dog could digest two ax heads and an armful of wedges and holler for more. His stomach hasn't had much practice, and it's as good as new."

Bud ran to the door and looked into the yard. Charley was back at the foot of the steps again; he bulged a little, but seemed otherwise unchanged and in good working order. Bud went back to the living room.

"He looks all right," he said. "He looks like he could go." He sat down and attacked his beans. "Hurry up, Joey."

"I am hurrying up."

"You both take your time," Mr. Ben said, poking his head through the door. "Squirrels have more sense than people; they take a nap in the middle of the day. You have an hour or two yet."

They slowed down obediently, finally finished their lunch, and went out and sat on the back steps. The time went by on leaden feet; within ten minutes they had both asked Mr. Ben if they shouldn't start out.

"I'll tell you when," he said, and went into the house.

A few more minutes crawled by; Joey stared at the dog. He had dropped his head on his forelegs and seemed to sleep. Joey continued to stare at him, half hypnotized; a series of mental pictures, in which he and Charley roamed an endless forest, drifted through his mind. They became increasingly fond of one another; Charley grew more demonstrative all the time, looking at him soulfully, returning from his forays to be patted and made much of, sleeping beside him at night, going out of his way to please his master.

Joey had never had a dog; he had never really wanted one before, and now he longed for Charley's affection. The experience of the morning, so new and exciting, had a good deal to do with it; in his well-sheltered life he had never got near his primeval hunting ancestors before, and now that he had, a change was beginning to take place within him. The other things that he liked would be less important. The new feeling was going to influence him for a time and shift and deepen, but at the moment it was focused on killing, the fierce joy of holding his gun on a living creature and pulling the trigger and seeing the creature fall. There was a feeling of guilt mixed up in this, for the evils of violence, killing, and destruction had often been impressed upon Joey, especially by his mother; but the guilt was unrecognized and therefore unadmitted, though it brought with it a sense of loneliness, vague and undefined, and made him turn to Charley, who had started it all, as a friend and support. He got up and walked over to the dog to pat him on the head, but Charley got up, moved out of reach, and sat down.

Joey, feeling rebuffed, looked toward the porch. Bud had fallen asleep sitting up; Mr. Ben had come out again and was standing there watching him.

"Doesn't he want to make friends?" Joey asked.

"He might, in time," Mr. Ben said. "He's just got to get it into his head that somebody wants him for more than yelling at, taking a kick at, or shooting over. You keep working on him, boy."

"Yes, sir," Joey said, and felt a grateful warmth toward the old man. "You reckon it's time to go now?"

"I think you could start persecuting them again."

"Yes, sir," Joey said, and went over and shook Bud.

Bud waked up, yawning and stretching. "I vench on him," he said muzzily, and got his eyes open. "Joey? What . . . ?"

"It's time to go," Joey said. "Come on."

Bud looked around, collecting himself, and saw Charley. He stared at the dog. Something had happened within him while he slept; there had been the beginning of a sorting-out of preferences in his subconscious mind. He had been caught up in the excitement of the hunt, but now he wasn't so sure that he wanted it again. Despite his interest in guns and shooting, he remembered with something like remorse the first dead squirrel and its small paws curled under its chin. "I'm still tired," he said. "Maybe we ought to go and try the fish again."

"The fish?" Joey asked, nonplussed. "Good Christmas, what do you want to go fool with the fish for? Squirrels are more fun than a fish."

"Not that fish," Bud said.

Joey didn't know what to say. Bud's change of heart confused him and seemed almost like a betrayal; they had always wanted to do the same things together before, and had been practically inseparable. Dissension had suddenly appeared between them, and Joey didn't know what to make of it. "Aw, come on," he said finally. "Come on, Bud."

Bud shook his head. "I'd rather go fishing," he said.

"Gosh hang it, you can fish all the rest of the year. You can't hunt squirrels that long."

"I don't want to hunt squirrels," Bud said, and because he didn't want to be thought a sissy, added with a defiant air, "I don't like them when they're dead."

"Oh," Joey said. It was all he could think of to say. He understood, finally, as he hadn't understood before, that he had lost his friend—or, at least, he had lost him except for fishing. This didn't make him angry—he acknowledged Bud's right to his preferences; it made him lonely and sad. "Okay," he said.

In the face of this acceptance Bud's defiance disappeared. "I'm sorry, Joey," he said. They looked at one another unhappily, almost in grief. "I'm sorry," Bud said.

"Okay," Joey said. Then he brightened a little. "Look," he said, "you can't fish by yourself. You'll have to paddle, and when you quit to cast the boat will turn around and everything. If you'll go with me awhile, I'll go fishing with you after that."

"Okay," Bud said, anxious to make amends. "I don't have to take my gun, do I?"

"Not if you don't want to." He went into the house and got his gun and came out again. They called the dog and started out. Charley didn't seem too enthusiastic, but he followed them. When they got to the edge of the woods he trotted off, but they walked for quite a distance and didn't hear anything out of him. Joey saw him once, far ahead, but the enthusiasm that had informed Charley during the morning wasn't in him now; he was just trotting around and didn't jump high in the air to listen. They kept on for a while longer, but nothing happened; finally Joey stopped. "Heck," he said, "he's not hunting. Gosh hang it all, he ate too much." Feeling deserted all around, he gave up. "Let's go back."

"Okay. You reckon we ought to call him?"

"No," Joey said. "Let him go on and take his darn walk."

They returned to the house, put Joey's gun in a corner of the living room, got their casting rods and a paddle and net, and went down to the wharf. The small breeze of the morning had held; on the part of the Pond that they could see, the ripples glinted in the afternoon sun. There was a moment of constraint when they unhooked the old trap chain, for they both wanted to try for the fish and they each wanted to give way to the other, now that they had had their trouble.

"You catch him, Joey," Bud said finally.

"Heck, no. He's your fish."

"I want you to catch him."

"You venched on him."

"Joey—"

"I don't want the darn fish! You catch him, or I won't go."

"Okay," Bud said, and climbed into the bow. "What you reckon we ought to try him on?"

"The wiggler that's spotted like a frog, maybe."

"I bet he *would* take that one," Bud said. "Only thing is, I haven't got it. We didn't bring the tackle box. I got this red and white one; he wouldn't look at it before."

"You better go up to the house and get it then."

"Okay," Bud said, and climbed out on the wharf again and ran up the hill. He had the tackle box when he came back, and put on the spotted wiggler.

Joey paddled across the Pond; the small waves slapped under the bow of the bateau. He stopped paddling as they neared the group of cypresses, and the bateau coasted almost to a stop. Bud cast, very carefully; the spotted wiggler began to return through the water, and suddenly, right beside it, a monstrous bass materialized. He looked as long as the bateau was wide; he was a fearful and wonderful fish. Both boys stared at him, and their jaws dropped; Bud forgot to wind his reel. The wiggler stopped in the water, the bass turned and slapped it contemptuously with his tail, and vanished as suddenly as he had appeared. Bud sat down as though his legs had been cut out from under him. "Oh!" he said. "Oh, Joey!"

Joey managed to speak. "Go on!" he hissed. "Don't just sit there! Try him again."

Bud stood up and tried him again. He tried a dozen times, but the monster had seen enough, and finally Bud gave him up. "He's too smart," he said. "He's gone. Oh, Joey."

"Gosh! You ever see such a fish? Great day, he was as long as the paddle."

"Maybe in the morning. Maybe we could try him again in the morning. We don't have to go until right after lunch. You try him then. If I hadn't stopped reeling in . . ." Bud was very downcast; he looked as though he was almost ready to weep.

Joey had thought that Bud's failure to keep the plug moving might have spoiled everything, but he wasn't going to say so now. "Aw, he wasn't going to take it," he said. "If he was, he'd have smacked it right away. Maybe we'll get him tomorrow," he said. This fish had been so big that he'd forgotten the squirrels for the moment. "Well, let's fish."

Bud moved back to the stern. They crossed the Pond again so that the fisherman would be facing the shore correctly, and spent the rest of the afternoon fishing. Taking turns, they caught five fish by the time the sun had dropped to the tops of the trees, but none of them even approached the size of the one by the cypresses. They had had a good afternoon, however, moving silently along the wild shoreline that was unbroken except for half a mile on the eastern side that had been lumbered long ago and was open and covered with brush, stumps, and decaying treetops left by lumbermen. They had fallen into a half-hypnotic state which was only broken occasionally by the strike of a fish. The ranked and close-growing cypresses brooded above them; as the sky took on color they headed for the wharf in the encompassing silence, each thinking of frontiersmen paddling their lonely way far from civilization and looking for a place to camp for the night.

The big fish was the main topic of conversation during dinner.

"Maybe he was what I was thinking about when I asked you about alligators," Mr. Ben said with a twinkle in his eye. "I remember now I was over there one day and that fish came up for a frog with his mouth open, and I thought he was going to swallow the boat. He scared me. Took me the rest of the afternoon to get over it."

"You scared us with the alligators," Joey said, sure enough of Mr. Ben now to tell it. "We thought you were . . . We didn't know if you were trying to kid us or what."

"I bet if we had a frog we could catch him," Bud said. "You reckon we could find a frog, Mr. Ben?"

"Not now. They're all down in the mud for the winter."

"How could we catch him, then? I'd sure like to take him home. My father never caught a fish that big."

"Mine either," Joey said. "We got through the mudhole he got stuck in, and if we could catch the fish too I bet he'd sit up and take notice, and think we were really something."

"I imagine he thinks so already," Mr. Ben said.

"He doesn't show it much. He's always telling me to be careful of the car, and to study harder, and quit eating so much butter and everything. He doesn't seem to think I've got much sense."

"He let you come down here by yourselves," Mr. Ben said.

"Yes, sir, and we didn't wreck the car and we got through the mudhole. How do you reckon we could catch that fish, Mr. Ben?"

"Just keep trying. It would be better early in the morning or late in the afternoon when there isn't much light and he can't see so well. Fish gets as big as he is, he's smart. He's not going to take hold of anything he doesn't look over first. We better get the dishes done." He stood up.

Bud stood up too. "Will you wake us up early, Mr. Ben?" he asked. "Real early, so we can get over there?"

"I will." He picked up his plate and took it out into the kitchen, and Bud followed with his own plate. Joey started to do the same thing, but noticed a Sears, Roebuck catalogue on the shelf behind the stove and stopped to look at it. He put his plate down and picked up the catalogue. It opened to the fishing-tackle section, and there before his eyes was a wonderful thing: the Kalamazoo swimming frog, sixty-eight cents. "In pulling the frog through the water," he read, "the legs kick backward with identically the same motion used by a live frog."

Stout Cortes upon his peak in Darien was not filled with wilder surmise than Joey at that moment; he forgot to breathe. He read the paragraph about the frog again, more slowly this time, and a shiver went up his back; in his mind's eye he saw himself casting the frog out and the explosion of water as the huge bass smashed at it. "Great day!" he whispered. "Great day in the morning."

Bud put an end to his rapt contemplation by coming through the kitchen door. "Joey?"

Joey started, closed the catalogue, and turned guiltily around. He made his decision upon the instant; he was going to keep his discovery to himself.

"What are you looking that way for?" Bud demanded.

"Like what?"

"What's that book?" Bud asked, and walked over and looked at it. "I bet you were looking at the ladies' underwear, that's what." He picked up the catalogue and it was all Joey could do not to snatch it out of his hands.

"I was not! I was not!" Joey shouted, terrified that the catalogue would fall open again at the frog. "Give it to me, damn it!" Mr. Ben stuck his head in the doorway at the uproar and looked at them askance; Bud hastily put the catalogue down and they both busied themselves clearing the table.

The dishwashing began in an atmosphere of constraint. Bud was baffled by Joey's performance, and Joey was even more baffled at himself. The vehemence and the variety of his emotions startled him, as well as the speed with which they had taken hold of him. He knew that he had done a mean thing when he decided to keep the frog for himself and tried to rationalize this meanness as a natural result of Bud's decision not to kill any more squirrels with him. It wasn't very successful, and left him with a lingering feeling of guilt, but despite this he was grimly determined to have the fish. Several hours ago he had been willing for Bud to catch it, but that time was suddenly past; he had to have it now.

Mr. Ben washed the dishes and said nothing; Joey saw Bud look at him several times out of the corner of his eye. Joey avoided the glance and wondered how to get the catalogue out of sight; all sorts of schemes went through his mind. The long and uncomfortable silence that threatened to hold the house until bedtime was suddenly broken by footfalls on the porch. The door opened, and a tall, muscular man, about twenty-five years old, came in.

He was carrying a lantern and was dressed in overalls and a ragged gray sweater; his head was bare and his thick dark hair looked as though it had been cut with hedge clippers. He was a powerful man, but there was an odd diffidence about him. "Evenin' to y'all," he said, in a mild voice.

"Hello, Crenshaw," Mr. Ben said. "This is Joey and this is Bud."

"Hi, Mr. Crenshaw."

"Hi, Mr. Crenshaw."

Crenshaw nodded, smiling shyly at them. They looked back at him with interest, for he was the man who had moved the new schoolteacher in.

"Blow your lantern out," Mr. Ben said. "We're about finished up in here."

Crenshaw raised the glass globe of the lantern with the lever on the side, blew out the flame, and put the lantern on the kitchen table. They all went into the living room; Mr. Ben put more wood into the stove, and they sat down around the table.

"You get any squirrels today?" Mr. Ben asked.

"I got five," Crenshaw said. "I went down to see if Sam wanted Charley, but y'all had him." He smiled shyly again at the boys. "I had to still-hunt. Did y'all get some?"

"We got four," Bud said, "but he ate them after we came home."

Crenshaw shook his head. "Yes, sir, he'll do that if he can. Seems like they could feed him."

Although a part of Joey's mind was still moving around the catalogue and what to do about it, the rest of it fixed upon Crenshaw.

"Schoolteacher all moved in?" Mr. Ben asked.

"Yes, sir. Her name's Mandy. She came from up yonder around Blackstone, somewhere. I reckon she feels sort of lonely. It's the first time she's ever been away from home."

"You'll have to help her get over that," Mr. Ben said.

"Yes, sir, I reckon I'll try."

He smiled shyly again, and suddenly Joey began to like him. He was obviously poor and worked hard for what little he got; he seemed unaggressive and diffident compared to Joey's father and his enterprising friends; but somehow there was a feeling of trustworthiness and decency about him.

"How did your crop turn out, finally?" Mr. Ben asked.

"Not very good, I reckon," Crenshaw said, and several lines appeared on his forehead. "I worked hard at it, but seems like my land's just gettin' too poor for much."

"My potatoes aren't any better than they ought to be, either," Mr. Ben said. "Nobody did any great shakes, the way I hear it." He added, encouragingly, "Well, maybe next year will be better and we'll get more rain."

"I sure hope so," Crenshaw said, and looked toward the kitchen. He had heard something, and then the others heard it. There were footsteps on the porch, the door opened and closed, and two boys appeared in the living room doorway. The oldest was a year or two younger than Joey, and the other a year younger than that. They were both small for their ages and not very clean; the eldest appeared to be wearing his father's cast-off clothing to which the other had fallen heir in his turn. They stood in the doorway for a moment, waiting. They both bore a resemblance to Sam White: the eldest had his thin face and close-set eyes; the other's face was rounder and softer.

"Come in, come in," Mr. Ben said, a little impatiently. "Odie, Claude. This is Joey and Bud."

The four boys looked at one another with careful appraisal, trying to be casual; only the eyes of Odie and Claude indicated a wistful envy as they noted the good clothes of the other two. They walked over to the sofa against the window and sat down, and became as immobile as two rabbits crouching in their nests. Only their eyes moved.

The two men took up their interrupted conversation,

paying scant attention to the four boys. Their voices rose and fell; Crenshaw was so diffident that Mr. Ben had to keep asking questions to keep the conversation going. Most of it seemed to be agricultural, and Joey's attention wandered from it after a while and moved to the White boys. He became aware that they were not quite so immobile as they seemed. They communicated with small twitchings and an almost imperceptible poking of elbows; Joey realized that they would stop even that if they caught him watching them, and pretended his interest was elsewhere. By their movements they seemed able to direct one another's attention to the guns in the corner, the clothes hanging on hooks in the wall, or anything else that interested them. They would frequently turn their attention to Crenshaw, and when they did this the twitchings would increase; once or twice secret half-smiles crossed the face of Odie, the older one.

Crenshaw finally said something about turkeys, and Joey's attention immediately fixed on him again. A turkey meant a wild turkey, a fabled bird, so shy, elusive, and clever that it was the ultimate goal of every hunter. Joey had heard a lot of turkey talk from his father and his father's friends, and although he was sure they would be too smart for him for a long time to come, he had, deep within him, an intense secret longing to get one. The White boys heard the word too; they became completely immobile again, listening.

"You saw them, then?" Mr. Ben said.

"Yes, sir. It was a right big flock. They were—"

Mr. Ben, glancing at the White boys, interrupted him. "I'm glad there are some around," he said. "You better see if you can get a shot at them before somebody else breaks the flock up or scares them out of the country."

Crenshaw, a little belatedly, got the point. "I reckon that's right," he said. He looked ill at ease for a moment, and then stood up. "I better go along," he said, and smiled at Joey and Bud. "It pleasured me to meet y'all."

They stood up and smiled back at him. Mr. Ben got out of his chair and went into the kitchen with him; they heard him light the lantern and go out the door, and Mr. Ben came back into the room. "Well, now," he said to the Whites, "what have you two been up to?"

Their eyes slid toward one another and the small one, Claude, said in a deep voice, "We reckoned they might want to go coon huntin' tomorrow night." By "they" he meant Joey and Bud, beings from a different world; the deep voice, coming from such a small boy, seemed incongruous and funny. Joey and Bud, caught unaware, almost laughed at it.

"Thank you," Joey said, "but we won't be here. We have to go home." Not knowing what else to say, the four boys stood looking at one another; Joey suddenly remembered that they hadn't eaten the other cake yet. "Do you want some cake?" he asked.

The eyes of Odie and Claude gleamed; Joey could almost see them licking their lips. They nodded, and Joey went out to the kitchen, cut the cake into fifths, put the pieces on plates, and brought the plates in on an old tin tray. Odie and Claude could hardly wait to get hold of it; their hands started to come up while Joey was still in the doorway, but they remembered their manners and let the hands drop again. Everyone sat down at the table and began to eat. The two country boys licked the rich chocolate icing first, and looked at one another; thereafter they ate with intense concentration, and didn't look up until all their cake was gone. They both sighed, wiped their mouths with their sleeves, and reluctantly stood up.

"Reckon we better go," Claude said. "Sure was good cake. Maybe you can go next time."

"I'd like to," Joey said. "Next time I'll bring another cake."

Odie and Claude exchanged a swift, hopeful glance, and Claude said, in his deep voice, "I hope it's real soon."

The other poked him with an elbow, he winced, and they both bobbed their heads, murmured what must have been a "good night," and, turning quickly, went out. Mr. Ben and Bud went out after them; Joey stayed in the living room, for a plan had suddenly formed in his mind. When the other two came back in he said, "They sure seemed to like the cake, didn't they?"

"It was nice of you to think of the cake," Mr. Ben said. "I wonder how long it's been since they had any." He shook his head slowly. "It's too bad, it's just too bad."

"Do you think they'll tell their father about the turkeys?" Joey asked.

"Not them. He'd beat them for not finding out where they were, so they won't mention it. They have to be pretty careful. Did you see them nudging one another? They've had to develop a language of their own. Now you've seen them, maybe you can see how lucky you are."

"Yes, sir. If you'd let Mr. Crenshaw tell where he saw the turkeys, you reckon Mr. White would go after them?"

"Why, he'd have been out there before light."

"But they were Mr. Crenshaw's turkeys, weren't they?"

"They'd be Sam White's if he could find out where they are."

"You reckon I'll ever get a turkey?" Joey said.

"Maybe. If you ever run into a flock and break them up, you come right in here and get me. Turkeys call to one another when they get scattered. I've got a turkey call, and we'll get where they were and see if we can call them to us. You better go to bed now. That's where I'm going." He took one of the lamps, waved at them, and went out of the room.

They undressed down to their underwear, took the other lamp, and went into the cold bedroom. They put their pajamas on, and Bud jumped into bed. Joey acted as though he was going to do the same thing.

"Oh, heck," he said, taking up the lamp as though to blow it out. "I forgot to leak."

He saw that Bud was not going to get up again, and taking the lamp he went into the dining room. Walking softly, he picked up the catalogue, took it into the kitchen, hurriedly found the page with the Kalamazoo swimming frog on it, and tore out the page. He crumpled the page and put it into the stove; there were a few embers left, and the page caught fire and burned. He stood there a moment, took the catalogue back into the living room, put it where it belonged, and went into the bedroom again. Bud didn't stir; he was already asleep, hunched up on his side of the bed, and Joey raised the lamp a little and looked at his sleeping face. It didn't look happy; there were lines across the forehead, as though Bud was worrying about something in his sleep. Looking at it, Joey suddenly felt unhappy too and confused. He didn't want to feel that way; he blew out the lamp and crawled into the cold bed.

~ CHAPTER FOUR

Mr. Ben woke them early the next morning, as they had asked him to do, and they emerged reluctantly from sleep. It was dim in the room, and the world outside seemed gray and one-dimensional, still shadowed by night. "It looks like rain," he said. "You better go do your fishing and then come back for breakfast. Maybe you'd better start home right after that. If that road gets much rain you'll be in trouble."

"Yes, sir."

They got up and dressed silently in the living room, collected their gear, and went down to the wharf. The first streaks of color were coming into the sky, dyeing the overcast; they both felt half-awake and a little remote from the world, as though they were still dreaming. Although it had got a little warmer during the night, thin wisps of mist came off the water and thickened and trailed languidly over the Pond, giving their surroundings an unsubstantial and faintly eerie air. Neither of them spoke. Bud took the paddle and got into the stern of the boat.

"You fish," Joey said.

Bud shook his head.

"You venched on him."

Bud shook his head again, and Joey climbed into the bow, picked up his rod, put the spotted wiggler on his line, and sat down. The seat was wet from the night's dew and soon soaked through his trousers. They shoved off and slid silently through the trailing mist; presently the clump of cypresses materialized fragmentarily through it, Bud stopped paddling, and Joey cast. The excitement that he should have felt wasn't in him, and he wasn't surprised when the big bass didn't appear. He cast mechanically several more times and laid the rod down on the bottom of the bateau. The whole thing had been an anticlimax, without savor, and he wished that he hadn't come out. "Let's go back," he said.

"Okay," Bud said, and paddled back to the wharf.

They caught the fish in the live box, strung them on a small tree branch, and took them up to the house, wrapped them in newspaper, and put them into the Model T. They cooked breakfast, ate it, and packed up. They said so little to one another that Mr. Ben looked at them searchingly several times but didn't say anything. They had lost touch, Joey because of his scheming about the frog and Bud because he felt that something was wrong between them and couldn't define it, and he wasn't going to ask. They finished their packing, stowed their gear into the Model T, and shook hands with Mr. Ben.

"Maybe you'll see the alligators next time," he said, grinning at them. "What will I tell Charley when he comes over for breakfast?"

"Tell him I'll . . . we'll bring some dog food next time," Joey said. "We sure thank you, Mr. Ben."

"Yes, sir," Bud said. "Thank you very much."

Mr. Ben stood on the porch watching as Bud cranked the Model T, and waved as they turned the corner of the house and went out the lane. At the gate they saw Charley trotting down the road; he stopped when he saw the car, watched it come through the gate, and turned home.

* * *

They stopped at Pitmire's store and left a fish, and after a muddy but uneventful trip got to Richmond. It began to rain as they reached the city limits, so they decided to leave their gear in the Model T until after it had stopped. Joey dropped Bud at his house, which was close to Joey's; their parting was a quiet one.

"Thank you, Joey."

"Okay. I'll see you."

"I'll see you."

Joey drove around the block to the alley, put the Model T in the garage, picked up the fish and walked through the long backyard to the kitchen door. The maid, Mary, a small, skinny black woman whose age no one had ever been able to guess, let him in.

"Hi, Mr. Joey. Your maw's been worryin' you get stuck in them roads and fall in the lake and get lost in the woods. You do any of 'em?"

"Not any," Joey said, and put his package on the table.

"What's that? You got fish in there? You gon' mess up my kitchen with fish?"

"I have to clean them. One's for Bud."

"You ain't goin' do any such thing. Lawd, Lawd. Fish scales an' fish guts . . . No, suh. Anybody cleans 'em I cleans 'em. You go on, now. Your ma be home presently."

She shooed him out of the kitchen. He went into the dining room, with its big, glass-domed, fringed lamp hanging over the center of the golden oak dining table, pausing to throw the wall switch rapidly six times to see the opalescent colors of the glass. Mary stuck her head in the door.

"You quit that, you hear? You had any lunch? You better

take a bath. I bet you ain't washed your face since you been gone. You take a bath, and I fix you some lunch."

"Okay," he said, and went through the living room and up the stairs, into his father's "study" at the rear of the house. It was a disorderly room crowded with overstuffed chairs, a big leather-covered couch, bookcases, a flat-topped desk, and a gun cabinet; the closet was full of outdoor clothes and fishing tackle and the desk and bookcases were piled with sporting magazines and catalogues. Joey's father was in the insurance business, but his heart belonged to the quail, the ducks of lower Chesapeake Bay, and all fish that showed spirit. Joey rooted about until he found the Sears, Roebuck catalogue, opened it to the page showing the Kalamazoo frog, and placed it in the middle of the desk. Then he went to his own room and changed his clothes; he wet his hair, washed his face and hands with a minimum of water in the bathroom, and went downstairs again. The fish had disappeared and his lunch was ready; he sat down at the kitchen table and ate it.

He was just finishing it when his mother came in. She was a pretty woman, tall and fair; there was an air of quiet good humor about her, and she smelled good when she kissed him. She had been downtown, and had on a big flowered hat and the suit that Joey liked; her umbrella was wet. "I didn't expect to see you so early, honey," she said. "Are you all right?"

"Yes'm. Mr. Ben thought we'd better come back before it rained too much on the road."

She put her umbrella in the sink. "I'm glad he thought of it. Were you polite to him?"

"Yes'm."

"I hope you got enough to eat."

"Yes'm."

She glanced at Mary and shook her head with humorous

resignation; she had long since given up any hope of getting more than a very bare report of his activities from him.

"I tole him to take a bath," Mary said. "He comes in smellin' like coal oil and smoke an' I don't know what, but he jus' wet his hair an' thought he fooled me." She snorted.

"I don't need a bath," Joey said. "How could I get dirty down there, for gosh sake? We didn't even have to wash the dishes. Mr. Ben washed them, because he had dirt in his hands and the dishwater takes it out."

Mary cackled. "Miz Moncrief, you hear that? He been washin' in dishwater when he wash at all. Ain't no dishwater get very dirty from *him*, I reckon."

"Take a bath, Joey."

Joey saw that the battle was lost. "Heck," he said and went upstairs again. He undressed, ran the tub full of water, and stretched out in it. Presently, lying quietly in the warm water, he fell into a semi-somnolent state and lived over again the excitement of the squirrel hunt and the first attacks on the bass, and moved on. In the reverie that engaged him there was nothing unpleasant like his falling-out with Bud; Bud was forgotten, and didn't even appear. As his reverie progressed only he and the splendid things he was going to do in the future were in it; for now that he had been to the Pond without grownups and got an intimation of what it could hold for him, his reaction to the world about him was changing, or had already changed.

He fell asleep in the warm water after a while, and only waked up when his father came into the bathroom and gently shook his shoulder.

"Wake up, boy," his father said. "You'll drown in all that water if you're not careful."

"Hi, Dad. Dad, can I have a Kalamazoo frog?"

His father, tall, lean, dark-haired, and ruddy, looked at him in puzzlement. "A what frog?"

"Kalamazoo, Dad. It only costs sixty-eight cents. It kicks when you pull it." His father still looked puzzled. Joey stood up in the tub, reached for a towel, and began to dry himself. "Wait a minute," he said. "I'll show you." He finished drying himself, ran naked into the study, and came back with the catalogue. "Here," he said. "This is it."

His father looked at the frog, and read about it. "I couldn't figure out what you were talking about," he said. "Do you think it's any good?"

"Yes, sir. Could you get it tomorrow?" He began to put on his underwear.

"Get some clean underwear."

"Yes, sir." He ran into his bedroom, grabbed a clean union suit from a bureau drawer, put it on, and came back to the bathroom again. His father wasn't there, so he went into the study and found him sitting at the desk. "I can have it. Can't I? Please, Dad?"

"What's all the rush, Joey?"

Joey squirmed. "It's a sort of a secret," he said. "I want to go down again soon, and I have to have it. And a hunting license. We didn't have hunting licenses."

"Did you hunt?"

"Yes, sir. Mr. Pitmire said it would be all right. Mr. Ben borrowed White's squirrel dog, and we hunted with him."

His father regarded him for a long moment, recalling his own youth, and his estimation of the whole situation came close to the truth; he suspected a very large fish in the background, and thought he knew what was going to happen about catching it sooner or later. He didn't want to inquire too closely, for he knew that Joey would have to work things out for himself. He remembered the secrecies, the aspirations, the fumblings, and the discoveries of his own boyhood; he wished that he could talk to Joey about these things and help him, but he knew that he could not. "All right," he said finally. "I'll get you the frog. It might take a few days, but you won't be going down for another two weeks, until Thanksgiving vacation."

"Yes, sir," Joey said, immensely relieved. "Can I stay longer this time?"

"If you want. Did you get any squirrels or any fish?"

"Yes, sir. We got four squirrels, but the dog ate them. They don't feed him, Mr. Ben said, so we'll feed him next time and put the squirrels where he can't get them. We got some fish, too. Mr. Ben's nice, Dad."

"Mr. Ben's all right. You mind what he tells you."

"Yes, sir."

Joe Moncrief stood up, and laid his hand on Joey's shoulder. He was a little envious of the boy, just starting out. "If you need anything else before you go, you tell me. You'd better get ready for dinner now."

"Yes, sir. Thank you, Dad."

"You're welcome, friend. Maybe I can get down for a day or two while you're there."

"It would be fun if you could," Joey said, and went off to his room to dress.

The time crawled by, and Joey thought it would never pass. He rode his bicycle to school, played sandlot football in the afternoons, and did a modicum of studying in the evenings; he was often dreamy and absent-minded in class. His father brought home the license and a new belt knife, and, after a few days' delay, the frog. It was a wonderful thing, made of rubber and realistically spotted; he kept it on his bureau and tried to make it work in the bathtub. The bathtub was too short, but he got an idea of how he would have to manage it; after he got the frog the time went by at an even more reluctant pace.

He saw Bud every day; their relationship was friendly but lacked the warmth and interest in each other's doings that it had formerly had. Although Bud mentioned the Pond several times, Joey didn't encourage talk about it; he had decided that he wouldn't ask Bud to go with him at Thanksgiving, and didn't mention that he was going himself. They weren't in each other's houses all the time, as they had been formerly, and Joey's mother asked him about it.

"Have you and Bud quarreled, Joey?"

"No, ma'am."

"He's not here any more."

"He's sort of busy, I reckon."

"His mother asked me what had happened to you."

"I've been sort of busy too, with my frog and everything."

"Joey, are you sure . . . ?"

"Yes, ma'am, I'm sure."

"Well, that's good. I'd better talk to his mother about your Thanksgiving trip."

There was a silence, and Joey's toe dug into the Brussels carpet. "Mom," he said finally.

"Yes, Joey?"

"Mom, he . . ." He paused; he had almost said that it was Bud who didn't want to go, but at the last minute decided to tell the truth. "Mom, I don't want him to go."

"Oh, Joey. I thought there was something. What is it, Joey? Tell me."

"It isn't anything," Joey said. He didn't want to tell her that Bud had no desire to shoot squirrels, and about the frog.

It was a private thing, one of the privacies that grownups were always prying into for no reason that he could see. "Mom, it isn't anything. It *isn't.*"

"You're sure you haven't quarreled?"

"No, ma'am. We're playing football together this afternoon."

She looked at him for a moment, with love and a little melancholy, acknowledging that this mysterious masculine performance showed all too clearly how he was growing up, growing away from her. "All right," she said. "But we'll have to ask your father. He may not want you to go alone."

"Okay," Joey said, puzzled in his turn as to why it had all become so complicated. "Can I go play football now?"

"Yes," she said. "Kiss me."

He kissed her quickly and a little sheepishly, and went out.

He wanted to be home when his father got there, but a quarter of a mile from the lot where they played football he had a puncture in his front tire and had to walk his bicycle the rest of the way. Further tribulations caught up with him two blocks from home, in the shape of a boy named Jerry MacDonald, who was in charge of the Christmas bonfire. Practically every Richmond family kept their trash for weekly collection in wooden barrels at their back gates; and every group of neighborhood boys— "gangs" as they called them-selves—stole these barrels for a month before Christmas, hoarded them somewhere, and burned them on their favorite corner for three or four days during the holidays. These fires were kept burning day and night by details who were appointed far ahead of time; parental permission for the details was obtained early; it was the most important event of the year. A gang was respected for the splendor of its fire, and the gang members sat about on boxes, set off firecrackers, and discussed matters of interest while their parents visited one another and drank eggnog and ate fruit cake. These were ancient customs, the origins of which were lost in the mists of the past.

Jerry hailed Joey from his front porch, and came down to the street. "I just finished making my list up," he said. "You reckon you could be at the fire the night after Christmas? Early in the morning, I mean."

"I reckon so," Joey said. "How early?"

"From four to eight, maybe?"

"Why do I have to get up that early, for gosh sake? I'd rather be there from seven to ten."

"You were there from seven to ten last year," Jerry said. "You had it easy."

"You had it easy yourself. You were there in the daytime. I bet you're going to be there in the daytime this year, too."

"All right, I am, but I have all the work to make up the list, don't I?"

"I don't think it's fair," Joey said, passionately, and saw his father's car stop before the house. "I got to go."

"You can't go until you tell me about the fire."

"Gosh hang it, I don't *want* to get up at four o'clock in the morning."

"The only other thing I've got is two turns on the last day."

"I'll take—" Joey began, and caught himself. He might want to go to the Pond then, he thought. It was three days after Christmas, and they might let him go by that time.

"I can't be there then. I might go away." He began to move his feet restlessly. "I got to go, I tell you."

"You've got to take the first one, then," Jerry said, and grinned like a possum at him.

"Okay! Okay!" Joey shouted and trotted off, pushing his bicycle, scowling, and grumbling to himself over the heaviness of his social obligations. He was still grumbling when he reached home, and then forgot the encounter in the uneasiness he felt over his coming interview with his father. He took his bicycle through the passageway beside the house and left it in the backyard and looked down at himself. His knickerbockers were dusty, his hands were grimy, and one of his long black stockings was torn, so he went in through the kitchen, up the back stairs, and changed his clothes before he went to find his father in the study. Joe Moncrief was looking through a gun catalogue and glanced up as Joey stopped in the doorway.

"Hi, Dad. Dad?"

"Hi, Joey. Come on in."

Joey went in and stood in the middle of the floor. "Dad, did Mom tell you . . . I mean, I reckon you talked with her."

"You mean about Bud?"

"Yes, sir," Joey said in apprehension.

"What's it all about?"

"I wanted to go by myself."

"Why?"

His father's eye was on him, and he knew that he would have to come up with a reason this time; he squirmed. "He just doesn't want to shoot squirrels," he blurted out. "He just wants to fish all the time."

"And there's only one Kalamazoo frog?" Joe Moncrief asked. His original estimate of the situation was working out as he had suspected it would.

Joey didn't say a word; he looked at the floor.

"Well," his father said, after a bad moment, "I think it's all right. I don't want you driving alone, though. I'll write Ed Pitmire and have him meet you and take you over."

Joey breathed again; a great smile appeared on his face. "Thanks, Dad," he said. "Dad? He'll just be for you and me, huh? I mean, if I don't . . . I mean . . ."

Joe Moncrief smiled at him. "Sure," he said. "Don't rush it now. Big fish are smart. Take your time."

CHAPTER FIVE

Ed Pitmire's driving technique was simple; he pulled the throttle lever all the way down when he started to go somewhere and never touched it again until he arrived. The engine roared, knocked, and rattled, the mud flew and the car swayed, bucked, and did its best to hurl its passengers over the semi-opaque windshield or over the side. Joey hung on to anything he could reach and enjoyed himself. Pitmire presided over the uproar with an Olympian calm, with most of his attention on the woods; once he stopped, reached down for the shotgun beside him, blasted away at a squirrel, jumped out and retrieved it, threw it in the back of the Model T, and drove on. Occasionally he would shout something unintelligible and Joey would shout back affirmatively.

They tore across the spillway, roared up the hill, turned in the gate, and stopped behind the house. Pitmire killed the engine; the silence was like the silence on the first day of creation, profound and almost unbelievable. Joey looked around, delighted to be back. Mr. Ben came out of the house, and as he walked toward the car Joey reached into the back and came up with the package his mother had given him.

"Hi, Mr. Ben," he said, handing him the package. "My mother sent you this."

Mr. Ben grinned and opened the package; a dark blue sweater, heavy and warm, was in it. "Why, thank you, Joey," he said, pleased. "It's real nice to be remembered. I'll write your mother a letter. Come in awhile, Ed. I've got something that will pass for coffee."

"I've got to get back," Pitmire said. "Some people are doin' their shoppin' today and Liza don't feel so good. I'll help you unload." He got out of the car and hoisted a big can out of the back. "I didn't know you'd gone in the dog business."

"Dog business?"

"Got twenty-five pounds of Spratt's dog biscuits in here. Mr. Moncrief had me get it."

"Oh," Mr. Ben said, and grinned again. "Joey and I went into partnership awhile back. Just put it on the porch." The three of them unloaded the car, piling a small mountain of food and gear on the porch, and Pitmire waved at them and left, almost taking the corner of the house with him. As they listened to his headlong progress down the hill Mr. Ben shook his head. "He's wasted around here," he said. "The Roman chariot races could have charged extra to see him."

"Yes, sir," Joey said. "It was a pretty wild ride, but we got here. I reckon I better put the things away." He began to carry the things in and stow them. When he unpacked the frog, he took it into the living room and showed it to Mr. Ben.

"It just might work," Mr. Ben said, examining it. "Nobody's thrown anything like it at that fish before, that I know of. You wait until almost sundown, and then try it." He handed it back. "You've a visitor outside."

Joey went to the porch window; Charley was sitting near the bottom of the steps, looking at the kitchen door.

"Great day!" Joey said, vastly pleased. "He knows I'm here." He went out, and when he got to the bottom of the steps extended his hand. "Come here, Charley. Come see me, boy."

The dog cocked his head; his tail stirred a little, but he remained where he was. Joey's disappointment showed in his face; he stood there for a moment and then recalled the dog biscuits. The can was still on the porch and he went back and got two square, thick biscuits out of it; returning to the foot of the steps he held one of them out and spoke to the dog again. Charley licked his chops hungrily but didn't move; only his eyes showed how much he wanted the biscuit. Joey was puzzled; he had never seen a hungry dog act in such a fashion, and didn't know what to do next.

"Put it on the ground," Mr. Ben said from the porch. "Nobody ever handed him anything before. If they did, likely it was to get him close enough to kick."

Joey dropped the two biscuits on the ground and joined Mr. Ben on the porch. As soon as he was there Charley got up and came over to the biscuits, bolted them, and sat down again.

"Take him one, now," Mr. Ben said, "but don't try to get too close to him."

Joey did as advised. Charley watched him approach, and half stood up to move away. Joey squatted down and extended his arm full length. The dog looked at him for a moment, ready to jump aside, and then stretched his head forward and took the biscuit daintily in his teeth; then he moved off a little and ate it.

Joey returned to the porch; he was disturbed by what he had seen. "Mr. Ben," he said, "how could they treat him so mean that he acts like that? They're cruel to him."

"They're not really cruel," Mr. Ben said. "Or they don't mean to be. It's just the way they are with animals; lots of country people are like that. An animal to them is sort of like a machine or a plow or a shovel. If it does something they don't think it should they bat it one. Besides that, Sam White's got such a nasty temper sometimes he's rougher than most. He's got a mule over there he's pounded so much it'll turn around and kill him one of these days. Don't you ever get near it."

"No, sir."

"You remember that. That mule's smart. He stores up all the whacks he's had, and he waits for one real good chance to get even. He knows he's not going to get more than one. He hates the whole human race. You stay away from him."

"Yes, sir, I will. Charley did take the biscuit from me, though. Maybe he's beginning to know I like him."

"You take it slow and easy with him. He'll come to you presently."

"Yes, sir. I reckon I'll go squirrel hunting now." He went into the house, put his gun together, and changed into his hunting clothes. The bedroom, bare but clean, was chilly; it would get colder all winter, and Joey wondered fleetingly whether he would be comfortable in the bed without Bud to help him warm it up. Now that Bud wasn't there he missed him, but he didn't dwell on this or even acknowledge it. His mind was too full of anticipation, of killing squirrels and being there and free to do as he wished. He went outside and whistled to Charley and started off for the woods.

The dog came after him as before, and moved out ahead of him when he came to the trees. He knew what he was about now; it wasn't like the first time, when neither he nor Bud knew what they were supposed to do. When he paused to listen for Charley's voice, the woods around him, so silent and still, suddenly seemed to be full of a brooding mystery; a feeling came over him that the woods withheld from him, just beyond the compass of his eyes and ears, a secret that he couldn't penetrate. It was like standing before a closed door and not knowing how to open it. This was a feeling that he was going to have again and again when he was alone: a waiting and a reaching-out to know and be merged with the mystery, an exaltation and a yearning. Many woodsmen have had it and are only completely happy when they are lost from the outside world and on the edge of it. It drove the mountain men of the early American West into the silence and loneliness of the Rockies and still sends its acolytes far into wild places where they can be alone.

When the dog began to bay in the distance Joey, who had been standing in a trancelike immobility, shook his head and stood for a moment collecting himself. He was a little shaken by his first exposure to an experience as mystical and moving as the experience of religion, or the more universal but equally mysterious one of falling in love with one woman. To put it simply, he had fallen in love with the woods; like every lover, he would make many fumbling mistakes before he understood his love.

He found Charley at the base of a very tall cypress near the water. The squirrel was curled around the tip of the trunk, and seemed halfway to Heaven. In Joey's mind it was already in his game pocket; he raised his gun and shot, but the squirrel didn't move. It was so high and its hide was so tough that the shot didn't penetrate it.

Joey had a rather hazy notion of the range of his gun, and he couldn't believe his eyes. He shot again. The squirrel was stung and stirred a little, but stayed where it was. Joey fired at it twice more. Finally he realized that he just couldn't reach it, and gave up. He called Charley, but Charley sat with his eyes on the squirrel and refused to leave it. Joey couldn't move him and presently went off, and then the dog gave up in his turn and ran away to hunt again.

Their erratic course, during which Joey killed three squirrels with great expenditure of ammunition, took them the length of the Pond to the head of it where the country flattened out into a big swamp. The dark, slow branches of the stream that fed the Pond meandered through it and cypresses grew thickly in the water, many of them bearded with long gray streamers of Spanish moss. It was a dim and ghostly place, featureless and silent. Joey had never been into it, but as he skirted the edge and looked down the dim, watery aisles between the cypresses he determined to come back in the bateau and explore it. It was the wildest-looking place he had found so far; it looked as though no one had ever been in it, and he wanted to penetrate it and move about and see what was there.

The prospect was exciting, and as he thought about it he decided that he had killed enough squirrels for the day; besides, the afternoon was getting on and his mind turned toward the bass. He didn't know where Charley was, but he whistled and yelled for him, waited a little while, and went back; when he reached the house the dog was waiting for him in the yard. Mr. Ben was on the porch, he had apparently been out on the Pond, seeing to his traps, and had three muskrats that he was skinning. "Any luck?" he asked.

"Yes, sir. I got three." He watched as Mr. Ben made three careful cuts around the muskrat's tail and working from them turned the animal's skin inside out over its head without cutting again except for the legs. "Gosh," he said. "Isn't that

something? Mr. Ben, how did Charley know I'd quit? I was up there calling him and he just came home."

Mr. Ben got up and went and picked up a flat board, about as thick as a shingle and narrowed toward one end. He put the skin over this so that it was stretched a little, and hung the board up in the screened part of the porch for the skin to dry. "I don't know how he figures it out," he said, coming back and starting on another muskrat. He threw the skinned one to Charley. "Some people eat muskrats," he went on, "but I'm not hungry enough yet. Maybe we'd better ask Sharbee how he knows. Charley I mean. I have to go see him pretty soon, and you can go along and ask him."

"Who is Sharbee, Mr. Ben?"

"His name's not really Sharbee. It's Shaw B. Atkinson, but everybody calls him Sharbee. He's an old black man who lives back in the woods, up the road a way. If anybody knows how an animal knows anything, Sharbee's the one. You just wait and see."

"Yes, sir. You reckon I have time to skin my squirrels before I go out on the Pond?"

"I think so."

Joey took the squirrels out of his game pocket, picked one out, laid it on the porch, and took out his new belt knife. So far, so good; but he didn't know what to do next. He turned the squirrel over and over, and finally, seeming to recall that one started to skin animals (with the exception of muskrats) by cutting a slit along the belly, made a tentative slice at it. The skin was tough and had apparently been put on the beast with glue; he hacked and sawed and made a mess of it. Finally, covered with blood, hair, and confusion, he looked up and found Mr. Ben quietly laughing at him.

"I'm not very good," he said.

"Give me one of the others," Mr. Ben said, "and watch."

Mr. Ben took the squirrel and made a slit on each side of the tail and cut through the tailbone. Then he stood on the tail, and taking the squirrel by its hind legs gave a steady pull. The squirrel peeled out of its skin like a man peels out of a sweater, leaving only a little skin over the shoulder, head, and chest which Mr. Ben peeled off over its head. Then he gutted it. "A nice young one," he said. "We can eat it for breakfast. Give me the other one and I'll skin that. You better go fishing."

"Yes, sir," Joey said, and handed over the other squirrel. He had watched Mr. Ben's expert performance with great interest and wanted to try it himself, but the sun was pretty well down. He went into the house, put his gun in the corner of the living room, and went into the bedroom and put his casting rod together and tied the frog to the end of the line. Suddenly, as soon as he had finished all this, he began to tremble. He was at last about to try the fish; everything was ready; now that the long-awaited moment had come he had an attack of buck fever. He was deathly afraid that he would do something wrong and ruin his chances to catch the bass for all time to come, and he wished that Bud was with him for support. When he realized he was wishing this he stopped trembling, and suddenly was ashamed of himself for his scheming and the way he had treated Bud.

These various emotions, coming all together, confused him; he laid the rod down on the bed and his face grew hot. For a moment he stood there indecisively, almost making up his mind not to go. He felt mean and sneaky and cheap, wanting to catch the fish and not to catch it. Tears came to his eyes and he rubbed them away angrily and said, "Gosh hang it!" Then he picked up the rod and ran out of the house, past Mr. Ben busy at his skinning, and down the path to the wharf.

He got into the bateau and cast loose and paddled across the Pond. The western shore on his right, one of the short sides, was deeply shadowed now by the hill behind it. The breeze had dropped with the sun, and the long length of the Pond, stretching away on his left, was still, without a ripple. He stopped paddling and cast the frog, jerking the rod tip a little to see if it would kick. It kicked perfectly, and he wound it in and put the rod back on the bottom of the bateau. He began paddling again; he felt that everything was right, but got no satisfaction from the feeling. It was not as he had anticipated it, at all.

When he got to the right distance from the cypresses he carefully swung the bateau, put the paddle down silently, stood up, and made his cast. It was perfect. He began to reel in, jerking the rod tip just enough. The frog had moved only six feet before there was an eruption of water so loud and spectacular in the silence that he jumped and almost lost his footing; he jerked the tip up and was fast to the bass.

A swift, wild thrill of triumph scorched through him, so intense that he forgot everything else, and then he was too busy to think for a while. The bass was crafty and full of power; it made one long blind rush, burst out of the water, shook its head savagely, and went to the bottom. Joey couldn't move it; he was terrified that it had tangled him around a sunken tree. He had read somewhere that when a fish did that, the way to stir it up was to keep a tight line and tap smartly on the rod, so now he drew his belt knife and rapped on the rod repeatedly, and the shocks traveling down the line got the fish into motion again. It ran toward him and, having got some slack, surfaced and threw its head about to shake out the hook. Joey frantically wound in line, almost weeping with anxiety, until he got rid of the slack, and then played the fish until it was exhausted and came in belly side up beside the bateau.

It was a very large bass, and must have weighed between twelve and thirteen pounds. Joey had to lay down his rod and use both hands on the landing net; the bass filled the live box, and after he had got the hook out of its jaw he sat down and stared at it. He was shaking from the excitement and the fear of losing it that had been in him, and now that he had it safely in the box he felt deflated and empty; the emotions that had confused him in the bedroom descended upon him again. He thought of Bud and his own maneuverings, the page torn out of the catalogue, and his face grew hot with shame. He got up stiffly, like a boy retreating from a fight, measured the length and depth of the fish with the paddle and cut notches on the paddle handle with his belt knife; then he scooped up the fish in the net and dumped it over the side. He didn't even watch it lie for a moment in the water and then swim wearily away. He sat down and dropped his head into his hands and drummed his feet on the bottom of the bateau and wept.

They had squirrels for dinner; they were young, tender, and sweet, and Mr. Ben showed Joey how to make lyonnaise potatoes. Joey was quiet and subdued, for the affair of the bass had worn him out. When he had returned from the Pond Mr. Ben had taken one look at him and asked no questions, and Joey hadn't volunteered any information. He was grateful to Mr. Ben for not talking about it.

They picked the small squirrel bones and took care of the dishes in companionable silence and went back into the living room and sat down by the stove. Mr. Ben filled his pipe and lit it, got out a pad, an old pen, and a bottle of ink, and wrote

Joey's mother a letter in a fine copperplate hand. When he had sealed the letter he looked at Joey and saw him nodding in his chair. "Maybe you'd better go to bed," he said. "You're tired."

Joey's head came up. "It'll be cold in there."

"We'll get you a brick," Mr. Ben said. "I meant to get one for myself." He went out and returned with two bricks, which he placed on the flat top of the stove. "Soon as they get hot enough we can turn in."

"Yes, sir," Joey said, and sat looking sleepily at the two bricks on the top of the stove. "You ever killed a turkey, Mr. Ben?"

"Why, I've killed a couple. But that Hosiah Burt, that your father bought the place from . . . gentlemen, sir, he used to slay 'em. He'd find out where they were using, and he'd go there and just stand still for hours if he had to and wait for them to come to where he was. He'd get up against a tree and never move his feet or much of anything else. He'd stand there and move his head slow, looking this way and that, and if they didn't come his way that day, they'd do it the next or the day after that, or sooner or later. He practically turned into a tree, and that's what it takes. A turkey's got the sharpest eyes of anything; one little movement and they're gone."

"Yes, sir," Joey said dutifully. Warm and half asleep, his drowsy mind pictured Hosiah Burt, who Mr. Ben had once said was a tall man with a beard, immobile as a statue flattened against an oak or a beech while a flock of turkeys fed through the woods toward him. Somehow Hosiah faded and Joey took his place; the beautiful birds, slim, wild, dark, gleaming with a shifting iridescence, came toward him scratching and peck-ing in the fallen leaves. One little movement, Joey knew, and they'd be gone, and he was still as a stone. They came closer, and then they were within range. An old gobbler, a great heavy bird with a long beard hanging from his chest, suddenly threw up his head suspiciously and Joey exploded into action. "Bang!" he shouted.

He and Mr. Ben both jumped in their chairs; both of them almost upset.

"Great day, boy," Mr. Ben said, when they had righted themselves, "you took five years off my life." He began to laugh. "I was talking about turkeys, and then . . ."

"I shot a big gobbler," Joey said, shamefaced. "I reckon I was dreaming, Mr. Ben. I'm sorry I scared you."

"I don't mind being shot if you got him. There's no eating like a turkey, and I haven't had one for a long time." He got up and went upstairs, and when he returned he had a little thin-sided box with him. He sat down and scraped the chalked lid of the box across the top of one of the sides. A series of short, clear, yelping sounds filled the room, and Joey's hair stirred on his neck. He had heard domesticated turkeys make the same sounds, but this was wilder and more plaintive; it was a wild turkey itself. He stared at the box in fascination, and Mr. Ben said, "If you ever break up a bunch of turkeys, don't run around and shoot just to be shooting. Don't shoot unless you get one in range. If you don't, keep quiet and come right back here and get me. When a bunch gets broken up they want to get together again, and they stand around and call. You get me, and we'll go and see if we can call one up."

"Yes, sir," Joey said. "I sure will. Could I see the call, Mr. Ben?"

Mr. Bend handed it over. Joey was all thumbs with it, and couldn't get a sound that had any resemblance to a turkey. Mr. Ben grinned at him. "Takes practice," he said. "You can work on it now and then." He took the box back and put it on the mantel behind the stove. "You're too tired to be any good at it now." He leaned over and spat on one of the bricks. It sizzled, and he nodded his head and got up and found an old newspaper in the kitchen cabinet and brought it back into the living room. He reached behind the stove and brought out a wooden instrument that looked like a big pair of pliers, picked up a brick with it, and, laying half the newspaper on the floor, put the brick on it and wrapped it up. "There, now," he said. "Go and put that in your bed and jump in after it."

Joey remembered the sizzle. "Won't the paper burn?" he asked. "It's awful hot."

"It probably will be scorched brown by morning, but it won't burn. I've been doing it for years."

Joey picked up the brick. It was so hot that he had to run into the bedroom with it. He put it into the bed, came back, and undressed and put his flannel pajamas on. "Good night, Mr. Ben," he said.

"Pleasant dreams. Oh, I almost forgot. Odie and Claude want you to go coon hunting tomorrow night. Want to go?"

"Yes, sir," Joey said, and went back to the bedroom again and crawled into bed. The brick was wonderfully comforting; he pushed it around with his feet until all the cold, dank places were warm, and then brought it back to within a few inches of his stomach. It was like a little stove, and as drowsiness overtook him he thought of the turkeys again and then the bass; but this time it was something that had happened long ago, and somehow the meanness had been cleansed.

CHAPTER SIX

The day dawned clear and a little warmer, and there was a boisterous northwest wind; it was roaring in the walnut trees when Joey went out on the back porch to brush his teeth and wash his face with cold water in the enamel basin. Because he hadn't washed his face since he'd left home, he went all out and used a little soap; he felt phenomenally clean and glowing when he came back in again. Mr. Ben was busily scrambling eggs on the stove and had already cooked the bacon. He pointed to the loaf of bread on the table, and Joey cut a few slices and toasted them one at a time on a long fork over the rear eye of the stove from which Mr. Ben removed the lid.

"It's not a very good day for squirrels," Mr. Ben said, as they finished eating. "The wind's making so much noise in the woods I doubt if Charley could hear them very far. He hasn't showed up, anyhow. Maybe Sam took him off somewhere himself."

"Yes, sir," Joey said. Since he'd got up he'd been thinking about the head of the Pond again, and now he had a good reason to go there; he could take his gun along and still-hunt if he felt like it. He decided to go. "I reckon I'll go up toward the head of the Pond in the bateau."

"Keep your eyes open up there," Mr. Ben said. "You might see some turkeys. If you want to go to Sharbee's with me, you get back in the middle of the afternoon."

"Yes, sir, I'd like to go."

"Maybe you ought to take a couple of sandwiches, then you wouldn't have to come back so soon."

"Yes, sir," Joey said, and set about making two sandwiches from canned corned beef. He put them into an old paper bag, got his gun and fishing gear together, and went down to the wharf. The water was rough in the wind, with a running glitter of sun on it, but Joey stayed under the lee of the northern shore and had no trouble. The trees were tossing about in the woods; it was a crisp, cool day of low humidity, with a high, clear sky, that brings a feeling of well-being with it, and Joey sang to himself as he paddled up the shore. He didn't fish; there was enough wind under the lee of the shore to swing the bateau around if he left it to its own devices, and he saw nothing to shoot at. When he reached the head of the Pond he hugged the east shore and turned into the mouth of the stream. He was among the cypresses, and as the swamp was low and under the wind, the silence of the place settled around him.

He didn't have to get very far in before the strange, brooding quality of his surroundings took hold of him; among the close-growing cypresses, gliding over the dark, still water was like being in another and different world. He paddled slowly and silently, listening, not wanting to break it; it seemed to him that he had left the Pond and its familiar, everyday creatures behind him, and that at any moment some unknown creature, unknown and unguessed at, would appear. He followed the winding water farther and farther into the swamp, hearing nothing but the drip from the paddle as he brought it forward and the whisper of blood in his ears.

There was more Spanish moss now, hanging gray and ghostlike from the trees and reflected on the water; no other plant in the world would have been so fitting for such a place. The feeling of almost penetrating the mystery, more intense here than in the sunny woods with Charley, had come upon him again, and at one point he wished that he could stay here forever. He had lost track of time but his subconscious was aware of the tyranny of it; finally he decided reluctantly that he would have to turn back.

He let the bateau lose its forward way and moved to the other end of it. Now that he faced in the opposite direction he realized at once that he didn't know the way out; the waterway that had seemed so easy to follow in its winding course was now only one of several, and there was nothing to distinguish between them in all the water around him. At first he thought only that he would be late to go with Mr. Ben to see Sharbee, and then he knew he might be much later than that. The neighboring Dismal Swamp was well fixed in local legend, and now he remembered stories he had heard of men who had got lost in its gloomy recesses and never got out again, of torch-light hunts for them finally given up. He had forgotten to keep the bow of the bateau steady, and now he realized, as he watched a cypress in front of him, that it was turning slowly; he didn't even know any more in which general direction he should be heading. The surrounding swamp, so fascinating in its difference a few minutes ago, had become a prison that held him with a remote and inimical detachment.

The strange blind panic that takes hold of people lost in the woods and makes them run in circles took hold of him, but here, surrounded by dark water and cypresses, he couldn't run; he couldn't engage in the violent physical action that re-leases the tension of the nerves and leaves the lost one sweating and exhausted but calm enough to think a little. Any violent action here would have him ramming into the trees or capsizing the bateau.

He had a few bad minutes in which panic ruled him so completely that he didn't think of anything, but he was not given to hysterics and presently the panic began to subside. He came out of it sweating and trembling but sensible again, and assayed the situation. At best he would have to stay here until he was missed, probably at the onset of darkness, and Mr. Ben came looking for him; then a few gunshots between them would give his location and the location of his rescuer; gunshots, or even shouts, carried well around the Pond where it was so quiet. It occurred to him then that this water was flowing into the Pond, just as it was flowing out over the spillway; there must be a current, a small current but a definite one. He was excited by this thought and rather proud of himself for having it, and suddenly very hungry. He got out the sandwiches, tore off a small piece of the bag and put it in the water, and began to eat. He watched the floating paper. It moved very slowly, but it moved; by the time he had finished the first sandwich he had some idea of the direction he should be going. If there had been any wind the paper wouldn't have been much use to him, and he realized that.

He wondered what he would have done if there had been any wind, and thought of the sun; but it was the middle of the day and the sun was overhead. He would have to wait for afternoon to use the sun. He didn't intend to wait that long if he didn't have to, but it was a lesson to him. He hadn't thought of being lost before or bothering about direction, but now it would be a part of his thinking.

He waited until the paper was almost out of sight, and

caught up with it and waited until it was almost out of sight again. Presently it became waterlogged and sank and he put a new piece of paper overboard, and so, by very slow stages, he came through the swamp into view of the Pond again.

He had a great feeling of triumph when he saw the open water; he wasn't quite the same boy who had gone so heedlessly into the swamp. He was aware that he had learned something and had had a minor victory, and was very pleased. He looked back into the swamp and knew that he would go into it again and again without fear, for it was a special place to him now, and he picked up the paddle to go back to the wharf.

Before he took a stroke his eye caught a movement at the edge of the stream near the Pond, and he held the paddle motionless and watched it. There was some creature in the water; moving at the apex of a ripple it turned in and came toward him. It rolled and dove and surfaced again, frequently changing direction, seeming to play, moving with such a fluid grace that it fascinated him. It came closer, until he could make out the rather flat head and broad whiskered muzzle. Then it saw him; it stopped, looked at him for an instant, and dove so smoothly that it scarcely disturbed the water. A line of small bubbles appeared as it swam underwater past the bateau and he didn't see it again. He was sorry that it had gone; it had been the most beautiful thing in motion that he had ever looked at. He realized belatedly that he could have shot it, but he didn't have any regret; he was glad that he hadn't. It had been so beautiful in action that it had been more fun to watch than to kill.

Back at the house again he found Mr. Ben waiting for him, and told about the creature he had seen. "It was so smooth and slick it hardly even made a ripple," he concluded. "You reckon it was a muskrat, Mr. Ben?"

"It must have been an otter," Mr. Ben said. "A muskrat has a pointed face and isn't that pretty to watch. Otters are the prettiest swimmers of all, even prettier than seals. They're hard citizens when they're pushed, too. They're rough fighters. I didn't know there were any around; they're rare. They're worth twenty dollars. I'll have to see if I can trap him."

"Yes, sir," Joey said, but he wasn't sure he wanted the otter trapped. "Twenty dollars is a lot of money, but he sure was pretty." Then he added, "Maybe you can catch him when I'm not here."

"I'll wait. Put your rod and gun away, and we'll go along."

When they had walked along the road a way Joey asked, "What are we going to Sharbee's for, Mr. Ben?"

"I want to get some fox bait from him. He mixes up a mess of stuff that stinks like the Devil, but you put a drop or two around a trap and a fox is just bound to come in and roll in it. It works on them the same way catnip works on cats. I don't know how Sharbee figured it out. Maybe a fox told him about it."

Joey grinned. "Maybe he'll tell me a few fox words."

"Some people around here think he really could," Mr. Ben said. "He's the greatest hand with the varmints I ever saw, but he doesn't say much. I think he's more at home with animals than with people."

Joey tried to picture the man in his mind, but he wouldn't come clear; he was too foreign to the boy's experience. He remained faceless and indefinite as they walked up the road.

After they had gone about a mile and a half, Mr. Ben turned off the road into a path through the woods, which they followed until they came to a small, unpainted, weathered cabin in a little clearing.

"Don't talk too much," Mr. Ben said as they approached it. "Sharbee's shy, even with me."

He knocked at the weatherbeaten door, which was hung on strips of dried leather for hinges, and a black man of medium height opened it. He was rather slight, with regular, almost aquiline features, as though some Arab strain far back in his ancestry still persisted. The irises of his eyes were pale, nearly amber, like a wild creature's, and there was the air of a wild creature about him; he seemed ready to retreat to a place of safe concealment and watch from there. Joey found him strange and a little disturbing.

"Morning, Sharbee," Mr. Ben said. "This is Joey. He's staying with me, and I brought him along."

"Mawnin', Mr. Ben," Sharbee said in a soft voice and ducked his head slightly to acknowledge Joey. "Y'all come in?"

"We'll come in for a minute, thank you."

Sharbee stood aside, and Joey followed Mr. Ben in. There were two rooms in the little house; from the one they were in, which held a wood stove, an old table, and three decrepit chairs, which crowded it, Joey got a quick impression of a piti-ful bareness, unpainted and as weathered as the outside. Everything had a worn cleanliness, but Joey was not accus-tomed to such an air of poverty. He was a little startled, but tried not to show it or to stare. They all sat down, and before a word was said, two cottontail rabbits hopped out of the other room, stopped under Sharbee's chair, and became very still. Joey knew enough about wild rabbits to know that no one he had ever heard of had managed to tame one of them, even when they were taken from the nest before their eyes were open. He was still thinking about this impressive fact when he realized that a raccoon, with its little black highwayman's mask, was peering at him around the corner of the door.

He had seen a tame raccoon once, from a distance, and had always longed for one; he didn't know whether to make a gesture toward it or to sit very still.

"Y'all be quiet," Sharbee said, as though he knew what the boy was thinking, "he come in." He turned to Mr. Ben. "I reckon you came for the fox bait," he said. "I got it all made up. I get it presently." He made a chirping sound, and the raccoon ambled into the room and stopped in front of the boy.

It looked him over carefully, glanced at Sharbee, and climbed into Joey's lap; it sat there peering questioningly into Joey's face with its black eyes. It was such an engaging little beast and seemed so intelligent in its regard that Joey's heart went out to it. He forgot the tales of raccoon ferocity in fights with dogs that he'd heard from his father's coon-hunting friends; he smiled at it. The raccoon began to make a low, chuckling sound; it climbed up his arm to his shoulder, thrust its sharp little nose into his ear, and made a series of soft little puffs that tickled. Joey felt its small hands feeling around his ear and examining his hair, very deftly and softly. He couldn't resist any longer; he raised one hand and lightly stroked its fur. The raccoon was very still for a moment; Sharbee chirped again; then the raccoon climbed down Joey's arm, sat in his lap once more, and began to play with one of the buttons on his shirt. It was still chuckling.

"He like you," Sharbee said, in his soft voice. "Most people pat him, he liable to bite."

Joey cupped his hands around the animal in his lap. It was soft and warm, its busy little paws were like hands, and its dark eyes seemed friendly and full of mischief; he loved it. It was not at all what he had thought a wild animal would be like, and suddenly he wanted it very badly. "I'd sure like to have it," he said, looking at Sharbee, and then added in a rush, "You reckon you could sell it?"

"No, sir," Sharbee said. "I don't reckon I could."

"Please sell it," Joey said. "I've got ten dollars saved up, and my father would give me more." He looked at Sharbee beseechingly, entreating him; he had never wanted anything so much.

Sharbee looked at him with his odd, amber eyes, glanced quickly around the bare room, and dropped his glance to the floor. "No, sir," he said softly. "I don't reckon I could."

Joey was about to speak again, to offer more money; he didn't know where he'd get it, but he'd get it somehow. He opened his mouth to speak, but Mr. Ben forestalled him.

"Joey," Mr. Ben said, and having got Joey's attention, shook his head.

"Yes, sir," Joey mumbled, and a feeling of loss, of desolation, washed over him. The raccoon suddenly ceased playing with his shirt button, looked at him with its head cocked slightly, and then climbed up to his shirt pocket and began to feel around in it with one paw, chuckling. This gesture made him want the creature so much more that it almost brought him to the point of tears. He couldn't stay there; he picked the raccoon up, placed it gently on the floor, and went outside. He walked a little way down the path and stopped; as he stood there a feeling of protest welled up in him and the woods around him blurred a little on his sight.

He leaned against a tree and got control of himself. He was suddenly aware of his tears and then ashamed of them and wiped them roughly away, but his longing for the raccoon was undiminished. He had to have it, and Mr. Ben would have to help him. When the old man came along the path he fell in beside him. "Mr. Ben," he said. "Mr. Ben?"

"Yes, Joey?"

Teco

"Mr. Ben, he has rabbits and everything, and he could get another coon. Why couldn't he, Mr. Ben?"

Mr. Ben walked a few steps without saying anything. "I guess," he said, finally, "that he loves that one. He's pretty lonesome there alone, and poor, and not many people like him. They're a little afraid of him, maybe, because he does things they can't do, and because he's different."

"He could love another one," Joey said, "just as easy. If you went back and said I'd give him thirty dollars . . ."

"We won't do anything like that," Mr. Ben said. "Thirty dollars would seem like all the money in the world to him, and it wouldn't be fair. I won't let you tempt him like that. You've got so much and he's got nothing but that coon, and I won't be a party to getting it away from him."

Joey stopped, and Mr. Ben stopped with him. "But I *want* it," Joey said, and tears of frustration threatened him again. He was angered by this; it made him feel like a wailing child, and to cover this feeling he became a little defiant. "If you won't help me," he said, "I'll bring my father here and he'll get it for me."

Mr. Ben stood there quietly looking at him, and under the old man's steady regard the defiance leaked out of Joey as air leaks out of a punctured balloon. He stared back at Mr. Ben for a moment and then dropped his glance; in another moment he began to squirm. The things that Mr. Ben had said, the things he had heard and ignored, came back to him now; he began to realize what Mr. Ben had meant about Sharbee having nothing in his poverty and himself having so much. He realized dimly, and for the first time, that there should be an obligation upon the fortunate of this earth. He was ashamed, and when he recalled how the old man had let him go his own way he was more ashamed still. He stared at the ground and dug into it with the toe of one shoe. He still wanted the raccoon passionately, but he knew now that he couldn't have it and why. He looked up. "I'm sorry," he said.

"That's better," Mr. Ben said, and they started to walk again. After a few steps Mr. Ben said, "I'll ask him to get you a little one in the spring."

"Yes, sir. Thank you, Mr. Ben. I reckon I was sort of mean, wasn't I?"

"A little one would be better. That one grew up with Sharbee; it would want to go back to him after a while."

"Yes, sir. I didn't have to be as mean as that."

"I know how much you wanted it," Mr. Ben said. "We all want things a lot sometimes, and it twists us around a little."

"Yes, sir," Joey said. He almost told Mr. Ben about the bass, and decided not to; that, on top of the raccoon, wasn't very pleasant to think about. He looked at the old man. Lantern-jawed, stooped a little, and with a three days' growth of beard, he wasn't a very heroic figure to the casual eye, but to Joey he had emerged considerably enlarged from the fracas just finished. Mr. Ben turned his head and looked at him; Joey smiled, and Mr. Ben smiled back. They were friends again, better friends than before, and there was a very pleasant feeling between them as they walked down the road.

After they had finished their dinner and washed the dishes Joey remembered that Odie and Claude were coming to take him coon hunting. He had never been coon hunting, and the prospect was exciting—so exciting that it didn't occur to him that the object of the hunt was to kill the cousins of the creature that had so enthralled him only a few hours before. In his mind they were, in fact, different animals; Sharbee's raccoon, which lived in a house, was set apart from the feral creatures of the woods. Wild things were to shoot and tame ones were to cherish, and that was the way it was.

He had taken off his hunting shoes when he got back to the house, and now he put them on again. He got out his heavy sweater, gloves, and the hat with eartabs on it and laid them on the table, and then waited impatiently. Time crawled by; it seemed as though the two boys were never coming.

"Mr. Ben," he said, "you reckon they've forgotten?"

"I doubt it. Probably Sam found something for them to do. He usually does."

More time went by and Joey wandered aimlessly about; he had almost given them up when he heard their footsteps on the porch and they came into the kitchen. Odie was carrying a lantern and Claude an ax, they were wrapped up in a weird collection of threadbare sweaters, old coats, and jackets, and both of them had stocking caps pulled down around their ears. Their eyes went first to the kitchen table and found it empty; they looked with a quick disappointment at one another and then at Joey, trying to hide their regret.

"I'm sorry there isn't any cake," Joey said, feeling as though he had let them down. "I couldn't bring it on the train."

A constraint fell upon them all, for the two boys were embarrassed that their hopes had been so noticeable and Joey realized that he had blundered badly; he had hurt a pride that he hadn't known they had. He had looked forward to going with them; he had missed Bud as another boy to go around with, although he hadn't admitted it consciously to himself, and they would in a measure have taken Bud's place. Now it was revealed to him that they were different, alien, and he had no key to the difference. He stood looking at them, not knowing what to say next.

"Don't reckon we could handle it anyhow," Claude said suddenly in his funny deep voice. "We had a pow'ful big supper."

"Sure did."

Joey wanted to ask them to help him bridge the gap he had created, but he didn't know how; he gave up. "I reckon we'd better go," he said. "I'll put my things on."

They watched him as he put his good warm clothes on and slipped his flashlight into his pocket, drawing together so that they could talk in their silent, nudging language, and then they all went outside. The wind of the day had dropped and the moon was out; it was cold and clear enough for a frost, and Charley was waiting patiently at the foot of the steps. Joey surreptitiously took two dog biscuits out of the can on the porch and slipped them into a pocket; after they had passed the gate he lagged behind a little and dropped one of them, which the dog picked up and ran off into the field to eat.

They turned west off the road before they reached White's lane and were soon in the woods; presently they came to an old road and followed it. It was narrow, growing into brush, and drifted with leaves; trees stood closely on either side of them, and the bobbing lantern held them in a wavering, coppery circle as they walked. It brought into being a mysterious, limited world, edged with great black sliding shadows and flickering points of light. Charley had disappeared; the two White boys tramped silently along and Joey could find nothing to say to them.

He wished that he could somehow break down the wall that had so suddenly erected itself between them in the kitchen, for he wanted to feel close enough to them to enjoy hunting with them occasionally; he didn't want to hunt all the time by himself, and he knew that he wouldn't enjoy being with them if he always felt like an outsider, as he did now.

As he walked along a step or two behind them, thinking of this, the boys stopped and pushed up their stocking caps; he stopped and pushed up the eartabs on his own. The rolling voice of Charley came to them, mellowed by distance, and they all pulled down their caps again and began to run. They scuttled wildly through the dark woods, stumbling and whipped by branches, until they arrived scratched and blown at the base of a gum tree which the dog was circling with his muzzle in the air. Joey noticed, without really thinking about it, that the dog moved away when either of the boys came near it; staying out of their kicking range was a reflex action with it. He bayed once more and the White boys suddenly began to whoop and dance about. Claude put down the lantern and turned to Joey.

"Shine him!" he shouted. "Shine him!"

Joey didn't know what he meant. He looked up the tree and could see nothing; the lantern's light didn't carry upward very far, and all was blackness and moonshine above him.

"Goddamn, shine him!" Claude whooped.

"Shine him! Shine him!" Odie shouted. "Goddamn!"

Joey stared at them, stunned by the uproar; the suddenness with which they had been informed by a noisy and riotous energy baffled him. They ran up to him, and patted his pockets.

"The frawglight!" they screeched at him. "Shine him with the frawglight! Goddamn!"

At last he saw what they meant, fumbled in his pocket, found the flashlight, and pointed it upward. The bright beam cut across the gloom; it wandered about and settled on a ghostly white shape, clinging to a limb and looking down at them. Its eyes glittered pinkly in the light.

"Whooee! We got him. We got him!"

The uproar ceased as suddenly as it had begun, and Odie said into the silence, "You git him."

There was another silence; the two White boys stared at one another, and Joey said, "It's not a coon, is it? It doesn't look like a coon."

"Possum," Odie said, and turned back to his brother. "Go git him. Hurry up."

"I'm scairt, Odie," Claude said.

"You git him, or I'll bop you," Odie said, and moved toward his brother. Claude fell back a few steps and Odie went after him; while Joey watched, puzzled and uncomprehending, the larger boy suddenly jumped at the other and gave him a punch that knocked him off his feet. He stood over him and drew back one foot to kick; the other scrambled up off the ground and ran to the base of the tree. Joey could see that he was crying now, and then Odie went up to him and hit him again.

Claude cried out in pain, and started to swarm up the trunk of the tree. He reached the lower branches and began to climb, and Joey, still appalled at what he had seen, tried to help him with the light. The boy reached the limb that had the possum on it, carefully stood up, and holding a branch above him with both hands inched out toward it. The possum grinned at him, showing sharp white teeth, and retreated toward the end of the limb.

Odie raised his voice again, shouting, "G'on out! G'on out and shake him!"

Claude inched farther out, and began to move up and down. The limb rose and fell with an accelerating rhythm; the possum started back toward him, changed its mind, and scrambled back out again. It almost fell off several times. Claude increased his efforts and Odie whooped like a lunatic and the limb gave an ominous crack. Claude's face was white and frightened in the darting light, and Joey's stomach crawled with apprehension for him.

The limb let go; Claude hung by his hands and managed to get back to the tree trunk. Charley seized the fallen possum with a snarl, shook it several times, and began to run around the tree with the whooping Odie after him. Claude appeared in the lantern light as though he had got down the tree by magic. They both ran after the dog and fell on him; Claude picked him up roughly by the tail, and Odie snatched the possum out of his mouth by its tail. He held the possum head down, with its head on the ground, and Claude picked up the ax, laid its handle across the possum's neck, and stood on each side of the handle. Odie gave a mighty upward heave; there was a sharp ugly crack as the possum's neck broke, and both boys whooped again. They looked like a pair of bedraggled minor devils at some horrid rite.

Claude stepped off the ax handle and the possum slowly rolled over as it died, grinning. The two boys stood looking down at it and became still. All of the wild energy had gone out of them, and in the coppery light their faces were a little drawn, tired and empty; their shoulders slumped and Claude's face was smeared where he had wiped the tears off it with his dirty hands.

Joey stood in the background, staring at them in their sudden transformation and still hearing, like an echo inside his skull, the crack of the possum's backbone. That chilling sound, the crazy kaleidoscopic scene in the flickering light, the whooping, and Odie's sadistic thumping of his smaller brother showed him that he could never get together with them now. It was not only the incident of the cake that separated him from them; it was an entirely different way of life.

The tensions that had been built up in them by their father and their lives which required the kind of outlet he had just seen were completely beyond his experience.

Odie turned to Claude. "Pick it up," he said. "We got to go home."

CHAPTER SEVEN

Joey slept late the next morning. It hadn't been very late when he got back to the house the night before, and he had first waked at his usual time, but a reluctance to get up and face the world had been in him, and he had gone back to sleep again. In the light of morning the experience of the night before seemed more remote than when he had gone to bed, but he still felt a little queasy about it. When he finally appeared in the living room Mr. Ben had finished his breakfast and was sitting before the stove reading an old magazine, puffing on his pipe. He looked up and grinned.

"Those two run you to death?" he asked.

"No, sir. We didn't go very far. We got a possum. I thought we were going to hunt for a coon."

"They usually end up with possums. That Charley's too smart to tangle with a coon if he doesn't have to. He usually lets them alone unless there's somebody with a gun along. Did you have a good time?"

Joey didn't say anything for a moment. He was afraid that Mr. Ben would think he was a fool if he told the truth, but the affair had puzzled him so much, and been so distasteful to him, that he wanted to share it with someone and talk it out. "No, sir," he said, finally. "I reckon I didn't."

"I wondered if you would."

"They were quiet until Charley treed a possum and got to the tree, and then they began to whoop and holler and Odie hit Claude and knocked him down, and kicked at him, and hit him again and made him climb the tree. Why did Odie hit him, Mr. Ben? He's littler than Odie is, and he was scared."

Mr. Ben took the pipe out of his mouth and looked at Joey for a moment. "I guess I should have warned you that something of that sort might happen," he said. "What else went on?"

"Claude had to go out on the limb and jump up and down. I thought he was going to fall and hurt himself, for the limb broke. And then when they got the possum they put the ax handle over his neck and pulled him up and broke it. His neck, I mean. I reckon I wouldn't have minded so much if they hadn't acted so . . . so . . . I mean, they yelled and jumped around, they were . . . well, they acted like they were crazy."

"So," Mr. Ben said. "I know what you mean. I guess Sam must have been giving them a hard time." He struck a match on the chair and lit his pipe again. "I'll try to explain it to you. In the first place, their lives are different from yours. You have a nice house and nice clothes and your father's good to you. You don't really have many worries. Their father isn't like that. He's a mean sort of man, and having to try to get along without any money on land that's worn out has made him meaner. He's got a grudge on the world, and takes it out on anybody he can. Most people fight him back, but the boys can't. He beats them whenever he feels like it, often for no reason except that he feels like beating somebody, and they have to take it. After they take a certain amount of it, it piles up on them, they build up a head of steam, and they'd blow up if they didn't find something *they* could take it out on, like the possum.. . . . The possum's a sort of safety valve. You see what I mean?"

Joey stared at Mr. Ben, rather appalled at the pictures the old man's words had conjured up. "Yes, sir," he said. "I reckon I do, but why does Odie act so mean to Claude? He was even going to kick Claude."

"Odie's a lot like Sam," Mr. Ben said. "He'll be just like him by the time he's grown up. Sam bullies them both, Odie bullies Claude, and Claude's soft like his mother. I don't know what will happen to him. I wish I could fix it."

"Yes, sir."

The pipe had gone out again and Mr. Ben relit it. "Now, then," he said, puffing clouds of smoke. "I know that the business last night made you feel a little sick and you probably don't ever want to see those boys again, but you will. They live too close, and we have to go over there sometimes, and they'll be over here. They're worked hard and never go anywhere, they have to wear old hand-me-downs and don't get enough to eat, and you're an object of great interest to them. Now that I've tried to explain some things to you, don't you think you can make some allowances and get along with them?" He knocked out the pipe on the edge of the stove. "Incidentally," he said, "a possum's skull's so thick that you can't kill it by knocking it on the head. The way they killed it is the best way."

"Yes, sir," Joey said. He still didn't like the affair of the possum, but he was beginning to understand the rest of it and was already feeling some sympathy for Odie and more for Claude. Mr. Ben had got through to him, although he didn't think he wanted to go possum hunting with them again.

"You'd better have some breakfast," Mr. Ben said. "Charley's outside. I forgot to tell you."

"Yes, sir," Joey said, pleased that the dog was there. "I'll go feed him."

He went outside. The dog was sitting near the steps and his tail wagged slightly when he saw Joey. The boy got four biscuits out of the can and descended the steps and sat down on the bottom one. He wanted to make the dog come to him this time, to have Charley acknowledge that he realized how Joey felt toward him and to show that he trusted him. Now that Joey was able to fully understand Charley's life, from what he had heard about the lives of Odie and Claude, his heart went out to the dog more than ever, for Charley didn't even have the scant resources of the two boys. Even they bedeviled the dog, jumping on him and yanking him about by the tail; he was the most oppressed of them all.

Joey extended a biscuit, crooning, "Come on, Charley, come on, boy. I won't hurt you, you know that. You know it."

The dog cocked his head. He stood up, took a step, and sat down again; it was obvious that a struggle was going on within him. He wanted the biscuit, but like any normal dog he craved affection too, and he had never had any. He had long since accepted the fact that he wasn't going to get it, had done his work and maintained his dignity as well as he was able; now he was being asked to change the viewpoint of a lifetime. He wanted to do it but the habit of caution was so strong in him that he still couldn't quite conquer it. He whined softly, got up and took another step, and sat down again. He had never been so close to Joey before; two more steps would have brought him to the biscuit, but he couldn't make them.

Joey kept talking to him, softly, hoping that this would

be the time that Charley would come all the way, and finally realized that he would not. He knew that Charley wanted to, for his eyes and the set of his ears showed it; another low whine confirmed the impression. He leaned forward as far as he was able without getting up and laid the biscuit on the ground. Charley wagged his tail widely, to show his own feeling, lay down, and stretched out his neck and took the biscuit. This time, however, he didn't go off with it. He ate it where he was, wagging his tail meanwhile. Joey gave him the other three biscuits in the same fashion and sat watching as he ate them, smiling. He knew that he had gained a little more, and decided to go squirrel hunting for a while.

He went back into the house, put on his hunting shoes and coat, got his gun, told Mr. Ben what he was going to do, and went out. He stood for a moment wondering where to go, for he had hunted along the north side of the Pond several times now and wanted to get into new country. He finally decided to hunt between the Pond and the Chickahominy Swamp, for he had never been in that territory and wanted to see what it looked like. He whistled to Charley, and they moved off past the barn and down the path which descended through the woods to the road in that direction. Once on the road he followed it through the avenue of tall cypresses that grew along the south shore of the Pond until he came to the spillway, crossed that, and turned along the stream that came out of the Pond and ended up, miles away, in the Chickahominy River.

Charley moved out, and Joey followed a somewhat southeast direction in the valley of the stream. The country was rather flat and low there, with a good deal of old cypress in it; it had a different feel from the higher, gently rolling land on the Pond's north shore and he wasn't sure he liked it as well. There were occasional thickets of greenbrier, tangled and impenetrable, and a different sort of quietness; presently he began to come to swampy areas that he had to go around, and the greenbrier increased. It was not an open woods; the farther he went the less he could see around him, the shorter his vistas were, and the more he felt closed in. He consciously kept his direction in mind, watching the sun; he had learned that much. He hadn't heard Charley; the dog had been gone for quite a long time, and Joey wondered what had happened to him. He stopped and stood still for a while, listening, with his mouth slightly open.

It seemed to him that he had stood there for a long time, half hypnotized by the silence, when he heard the dog. Its voice was different; instead of the usual rolling bay there was a chop, an excited barking, in it, and it seemed to be moving. Joey was puzzled, for he had heard nothing like this from Charley before. He stood in indecision; he didn't know whether to start for it at once or wait until it settled into something familiar, and while he waited a large dark bird came sailing in from the direction of the dog and dropped into the woods a hundred yards or so in front of him.

It had appeared with such unexpectedness, and dropped into the thick woods so quickly, that his view of it had been fragmentary; nevertheless, he had an impression of dark, barred wings and a snaky neck, a tail spreading and tipped with a lighter color. It couldn't be a hawk, he thought, looking like that. For a moment he was puzzled, and then his heart began to pound. It was a turkey! A wild turkey!

A turkey, and close to him; even now it might be coming his way. He began to shake, and his mind was suddenly full of confusion. All of the methods to kill a turkey he had ever heard whirled around together in his head. He wanted to run toward it, he wanted to stand still, and he wanted to do both of these things at once. There was a greenbrier thicket between himself and the turkey, so thick that he could see nothing. He finally decided to stay where he was for a moment, watching, and just as he decided to do this the turkey came around the right-hand side of the thicket.

His breath caught in his throat, for it was a beautiful thing, shimmering with a dark iridescence, its head moving, taking slow steps. It came a few yards farther and Joey exploded out of his frozen state. His gun came up in a single motion, and he pulled the trigger. Nothing happened; he had forgotten to push off the safety in his excitement, and as he stood there desperately pulling on the trigger the big bird wheeled and with darting quickness ducked behind the greenbriers again. Joey finally realized what the trouble was, and as he started to run shoved the safety forward. He reached the side of the thicket half sobbing with anxiety and excitement, ready to shoot on the instant, but the turkey was gone. The woods were as silent and empty as before.

His feet dragged as he climbed the hill to the house again, and he carried the gun over his shoulder like a stick of wood; all of the pleasure of being in the woods, of being in the world at all, had gone out of his life. He had had that desire of all hunters, a turkey, over his gun barrels, and through his own ineptness it had got clean away. He had acted like the most amateurish of all amateurs, and been so cast down by his defeat that he had given up any further thought of hunting squirrels, of hunting anything, and turned home. He was so disorganized that it was not until he got to the old barn that he recalled Mr. Ben's advice, to the effect that if he ever got into a flock of turkeys and broke them up he was to come home at once and get the old man so that they could return to the spot and call the flock together. He stopped dead when this thought occurred to him, for it was like a revelation from Heaven. All was not lost; there was still a chance. He had not shot and scared them; they would still be trying to get together again, and if Mr. Ben went back with him, with the turkey call, they might still get a shot. "Great day!" he exclaimed, and started to run.

He came running around the corner of the barn, expecting to see Mr. Ben there waiting for him, and instead saw the two White boys sitting on the steps and Charley lying in his usual place in the yard. Charley, with his odd prescience, had known he had to quit and had taken a short cut back to the house; what had brought the White boys was a mystery. They were looking the other way and fortunately didn't see him; he had time to drop to a walk before they realized he was there. He wouldn't tell them about the turkey for the world. It was to be a secret between Mr. Ben and himself, for he remembered what Mr. Ben had said about White and the turkeys Crenshaw had found; he was vexed that the boys were there now, for he couldn't say anything.

Odie and Claude saw him then, and got up from the steps.

"Hi!" they said together. "We thought you'd like to go squirrel huntin', so we came over."

"Hi!" he said and added, craftily, thinking that Mr. Ben could get rid of them somehow, "I reckon I better ask Mr. Ben first. I was going someplace with him."

"He ain't here," Odie said. "He was gone when we come in. They was car tracks in the lane, so I reckon somebody got him and took him somewhere."

All was lost, then, at least for now; the turkeys would

doubtless flock together again before Mr. Ben got back, and they would have to get them another time. He didn't want to go squirrel hunting again, particularly with Odie and Claude, but it occurred to him that if he didn't they might go off and blunder into the place where the turkeys were and either frighten them away, tell their father, or—worst of all—kill one themselves. After his own performance he couldn't bear to think of this possibility. He would have to go with them.

"I'd like to go," he said. "We can go up this side of the Pond."

Both boys began to grin, and Odie walked over to the porch and picked up a shotgun that Joey hadn't noticed before. It was by way of being a museum exhibit; it was a hammer gun, double barreled, so rusty that it looked extremely dangerous, and the stock had been broken at one time or another and wound around with brass wire. The barrels must have been thirty-two inches long, and the entire gun was a little taller than Claude when the butt rested on the ground. It was old, very old, a twelve-gauge. Joey decided to be a long way from it when it was fired, for it was the most untrustworthy-looking gun he had ever seen.

As they started out Joey hoped there would be no performance like the one with the possum, but when Charley treed the first squirrel it appeared that he need not have worried. The two boys seemed to be in a state of grace and without tensions. The dog was at the foot of a huge beech, and as if by agreement the three of them took positions that more or less surrounded it and all stood looking up, each searching his own sector of the tree. Joey wanted to be the one to find the squirrel, but he couldn't see it; he was a little chagrined when Claude gave tongue.

"I see him!" Claude said, in his deep voice. "I done got him cold. Gimme the gun, Odie."

They apparently had an agreement that the one who first saw the victim was the one who got a shot at it, for Odie walked around the tree and handed Claude the gun. Joey watched in fascination as the small boy hoisted the gun, which seemed to dwarf him, and pulled back both hammers. He took a step or two and shot. There was a tremendous roar, flame spouted two feet beyond the muzzle, and the entire forest seemed to tremble; it seemed incredible that Claude wasn't driven two feet into the ground. The squirrel fell out of the tree, Charley grabbed it, and after the usual chase had to give it up. Claude put it into his pocket and grinned at the other two. "I reckon that fixed him," he said, and he looked so small and so triumphant and with it all so droll that Joey had to move off, turn his back, and pretend a coughing fit to keep from laughing aloud.

"That's sure some gun," he said, when he had got control of his amusement. "I thought it was going to knock you down."

"It'll knock me down if I ain't set for it," Claude said. "It's a buster, and that's a fact."

"Yes, sir," Odie said. "You don't keep a-holt of it, it's liable to kill at both ends. You like to shoot it?"

Joey wouldn't have shot it under any consideration. "Thank you, but I reckon not," he said. "I'm used to my gun; I better stay with it. Would you like to shoot it?"

He had never made this offer to anyone before and it popped out before he realized what he was saying, but he didn't regret it. Somehow, because of the incident just finished and Mr. Ben's talk, the two boys weren't odd and dubious strangers any more. He felt differently toward them, and they, because of his offer, felt differently about him. They didn't draw together to communicate secretly with nudges but smiled and nodded.

"Sure would," Odie said.

"Sure would too," Claude said.

They set off again, and the feeling between them held for the rest of the afternoon. The next two squirrels were shot with Joey's gun, one by Odie and one by Claude; they both had a little trouble changing from a hammer gun to a hammerless one with a safety, but they both managed to get their squirrels. Joey saw the next squirrel first and killed it; the fifth one got away from them. It was in the top of a very tall cypress, and after being dusted several times jumped out, spread itself, and half sailed and half fell to the ground. It bounced a foot into the air when it landed and then ran straight at Joey. Odie, Claude, and Charley all knew this maneuver and began to chase the desperate beast as soon as it hit the ground, but Joey had never seen a squirrel do this before. He had a fright; he thought the squirrel was going to attack him, and when he saw the squirrel, the dog, and the two boys all bearing down upon him he froze; he couldn't have moved to save his life.

The squirrel ran between his legs, and Charley was so close behind it and so intent upon it that he ran between Joey's legs too and upset him. The two boys hurdled him as he fell, and the whole pack went roaring on for a few more yards until the squirrel came to a hollow at the bottom of a tree and disappeared into it.

By the time Joey got to his feet again he had realized that the squirrel had only run in this direction because that was the way it was headed when it hit the ground, and hadn't time to look about. He was quickly over his fright and began to laugh. Odie and Claude were laughing too when they came back to him, and they stood together laughing.

"Great balls of fire! We like to run you down!"

"We like to stomp you!"

"I thought I was charged by a man-eating squirrel," Joey said. "Great day, I was scared for a minute. I was too scared to move."

"Charley moved you. He moved you good."

"Sure did."

"I didn't know a squirrel would jump out of a tree like that," Joey said. "I got a little mixed up."

"They'll do it, do you push 'em," Claude said. "He was all the way in the top, he didn't have no place else to go, so he spread out like a flyin' squirrel and turned loose."

"You looked real funny fallin' down," Odie said, and they laughed together again. "I wish we could get a couple more, but we better quit. We get back too late, Pa'll wear us out."

"Sure will."

Odie stuck two fingers in his mouth, gave a piercing whistle for Charley, and they turned back toward the house. When they got there, Charley was waiting in the yard and Mr. Ben was sitting on the porch steps. He had a suit and necktie on and was freshly shaved; he had apparently been to town. Charley looked longingly at the biscuit can, but Joey decided that he had better not feed him with the boys there.

"Sure liked shootin' that gun," Odie said. "She's so pretty and so light it's just like holdin' up a stick."

"Sure did too," Claude said. "Thank you. She kills good, too. Y'all want our squirrels?"

"No, thank you," Joey said. "Don't you want mine?"

"You keep it," Odie said. "We had a right good time. Pa turns us loose, we like to go again sometime."

"I would too," Joey said. "Thank you for stopping for me."

"Sho!" Claude said. "Good-by."

"Good-by," Joey said, and watched them walk around the corner of the house with the dog following them. He turned for a final look and disappeared after them.

Joey sat down beside Mr. Ben. "I wish I could have fed him," he said, "but I thought I better not."

"I think you did the wise thing," Mr. Ben said. "It might hurt their feelings. Did you have a good time?"

Joey told him about the hunt, and about the squirrel that ran at him. "Sure scared me for a minute," he said, "but I did have fun. They weren't like the night of the possum hunt. That Claude was funny when he shot their gun. I thought it was going to knock him down, or blow up or something. I really had a good time with them, Mr. Ben. They're different now."

"Don't count on them always being like that," Mr. Ben said. "The way they act depends on how rough Sam's been on them, and I guess he's had something else on his mind lately and let them be. I mean it when I say not to get too close to them, Joey. You're liable to have another bad time if you do."

"Yes, sir," Joey said, and took the squirrel out of his pocket. It was curled up in death; its small paws were over its eyes, as though it had tried to avoid seeing its approaching end. As Joey stared at it an odd and piercing little pain of regret entered into him. He had a surprising and fugitive wish that he hadn't shot it, which he quickly suppressed; how could he be a hunter and not shoot anything? Nevertheless, he turned away from it; he didn't look at it again. "Will you skin it, Mr. Ben?" he asked.

Mr. Ben nodded, and Joey tried not to think of it any more. To avoid thinking of it he ran over the events of the day in his mind and suddenly remembered the turkey. "Great day!" he said. "I forgot the most important thing. I had a shot at a turkey and got so excited that I forgot to push the safety off." He went into the affair of the turkey in great and excited detail. "I reckon I'd have killed him," he said, suddenly mournful, "if I hadn't been so dumb. Gosh hang it, why did I have to do that?"

"You got buck fever," Mr. Ben said. "I guess almost everybody gets it the first time they have a shot at a turkey." He looked at the sky. The sun was almost down and shadows were long across the yard. "You wait here," he said. "It may not be too late. I'll be right back."

He got up quickly and went into the house, and soon came back with his everyday clothes on, carrying his old L. C. Smith double-barrel gun. "Come on," he said. "If we hurry we might hear them. Take me back where you saw it."

As they hurried down the path behind the barn he explained what they were up to. "It's almost time for those turkeys to go to roost. They fly up in trees for the night and make a lot of noise, and we'll sit there and be still. If they're still anywhere nearby we'll be able to hear them fly up, and then we can leave quietly and come back in the morning early and call them together when they come down again."

"Yes, sir."

"We'll separate, and sit still and listen. Be as quiet as you can when we get near the place."

"Yes, sir," Joey said. The excitement was building up in him again, and although Mr. Ben made pretty good time for his age, it seemed to Joey that they were crawling along.

They crossed the bridge, turned down the stream, and

finally came to the place where the greenbrier thickened and the swampy places began. The sun had dropped by now, although the sky was still light; the woods, the bark of the trees, had taken on a little of the sunset colors of the sky. Joey was by this time in a fever of anxiety and indecision; he couldn't locate the spot, for the woods looked everywhere the same.

"It must have been around here somewhere," he said. "I wish I could be sure, Mr. Ben. I sure wish I could."

"This will do," Mr. Ben said. "I'll stay here, and you go on for maybe a quarter of a mile. Get on a high place if you can, and sit down and be quiet and listen. If you hear their wings beating against the branches when they fly up don't make a sound. Locate it as near as you can and wait awhile. I'll call you when I think we ought to go."

"Yes, sir," Joey said, and went on. He tried to hurry and be quiet at the same time, avoiding stepping on dead sticks or making sucking noises with his boots when the going got swampy. Finally he thought he was far enough from the old man, found a little knoll, and sat down in the leaves. He sat there listening with intense concentration, turning his head this way and that with painful slowness as twilight slowly turned the woods dim around him.

The profound silence stretched out, the trees grew black against the slowly darkening sky, the forest floor about him began to grow dim; Joey longed desperately for the sound of wings, but heard nothing. Finally Mr. Ben gave a "Halloo," and he got up and started back. He was greatly disappointed. Halfway back to Mr. Ben he was startled half out of his skin when a barred owl let go with a volley of blood-chilling hoots in objection to him. He picked up his pace, blundering into bushes and scratching himself; he had to call several times to find Mr. Ben.

"Hear anything?" the old man asked.

"No, sir. Nothing but that owl. Did you?"

"Not a thing. They must have got together somewhere else. Well, some other time."

"Yes, sir," Joey said sadly. Then he brightened. "But I'll get one yet. I got a mind to start practicing on that call, if you'll let me."

"Help yourself," Mr. Ben said. "Another thing you could do is always be still and listen for a while when you're in the woods toward sunset; turkeys roost where night catches them, and you may find some anywhere."

"Yes, sir."

"Well, we'd better go, or we'll be here all night."

They started out, stumbling around, for it was dark now. Joey followed Mr. Ben, holding his gun upright before him to ward off branches and underbrush. The stars had begun to come out, twinkling high above the interlaced limbs over their heads, and far behind them the owl spoke to the night again.

CHAPTER EIGHT

It was raining the next morning when Joey awoke, and he did-n't get up right away. He couldn't hear Mr. Ben moving about and thought that probably the old man felt the same way that he felt himself: satisfied to lie still, warm and comfortable, and listen to the rain on the roof for a while. He fell into a half-dreamy state, and fragments of the things that had hap-pened to him since he had come to the Pond without grownups drifted through his mind; he made a sort of reca-pitulation. He had learned some things. He had been lost in the swamp and been frightened and had found his way out again, and now he would keep track of where he was in the woods; the big bass had shown him an unsuspected meanness in his nature that he would probably manage better when it appeared again. Sharbee and his coon had been another les-son, and Mr. Ben had helped him there; he still wanted the coon but he understood now why it wouldn't be fair to take it. He had learned from the White boys as well. His friends at home were disciplined with an attempt at affection and fair-ness; they had their rages and frustrations, but weren't pushed into such actions as he had seen on the possum hunt. It was the first time he had encountered, and realized, that there were ways of life different from his own and that boys were caught in it.

His mind circled this unhappy thing, and as it did so there came into it the recollection of the dead squirrel with its paws over its eyes and the odd stab of pain it had given him. Why, he wondered, why? It had been fun to shoot it, the excitement had caught him up as it always did; but after he had seen it hiding its dulling eyes, stiff and cold, the scurry of life gone and the triumph of hitting it past, he hadn't wanted to see it again. Why had he felt like that? Was it that death was rather frightening, or was it more?

He couldn't solve it and didn't really want to, for he felt that the question threatened the new pleasures he had found. His mind moved on in its drowsy musing and he remembered a line or two of poetry that he had read. *Magic casements opening on the foam*, he whispered to himself, *Of perilous seas in fairy lands forlorn*. This was mysterious too, for why should these lands be forlorn? Why were grown-up things mysterious? Mysterious, but beautiful too: the singing words, the shifting half-glimpsed images bathed in a radiance of soft, soft golden light. . . .

He awoke sometime later, to find Mr. Ben standing beside the bed; he smiled at the old man. "I reckon I went to sleep again," he said.

"I did too," Mr. Ben said, "but it won't hurt either of us. It's close onto eleven o'clock, and it looks like it might clear, or at least not rain so hard. What will we have for breakfast?"

"Pancakes," Joey said. "We haven't had pancakes for a long time."

"Good," Mr. Ben said, and went out into the kitchen. Joey could hear him starting the fire as he dressed, and when he went to the kitchen himself the fire was roaring in the stove and the dank chill was off the room. They made a great stack of cakes and attacked them in companionable silence; when the time came to wash the dishes Joey saw that their water supply was low, and after the dishes were washed he put on his raincoat, picked up two buckets, and set off for White's.

By the time he turned in at their gate the rain had changed to a slow, soft drizzle which looked as though it would continue the rest of the day. The woods behind the house were half lost in it, misty and changing, and Joey was so interested in looking at them that he walked past the well and suddenly found himself around the corner of the house. There was a little porch there with a roof over it, and beneath it a boy was sitting in a little express wagon looking at him. The boy was small, about as big as a twelve-year-old, and had on an old sweater; his face was normal size, but above it his head swelled to monstrous proportions. It was Horace, the "afflicted" boy that Mr. Ben had told him about.

Joey had a moment of cold horror; he would doubtless have turned and run if he'd been capable of it. He stared at the boy for a long, awful moment, and then the boy's face was lighted by a smile of wonderful sweetness.

"Hi!" he said, in a soft, clear voice. "I reckon you're Joey. Claude and Odie told me about you. I'm Horace."

The boy's fine smile and his soft voice brought with it an immediate impression of intelligence and friendliness; the feeling of horror drained out of Joey and he accepted him. The rigidity left his muscles, and he put the buckets down. His own smile was a little uncertain at first, for he had been quite shocked, but the immense relief that he felt soon made it warmer. He took a deep breath. He said, "I'm glad to meet you, Horace. Mr. Ben told me about you, too."

"Mr. Ben's nice," the boy said. "He's kind."

He smiled again, a smile with an ephemeral hint of melancholy in it; and from the smile, and the words that had gone before it, Joey realized that kind treatment was not always his portion and what his life must be like. For he was intelligent; it looked out of his eyes. Joey knew that he longed for the wide world and all that was in it, and was tied forever to his little wagon and the sandy, empty yard. "Claude told me how Charley overturned you," he said. "I reckon you were surprised."

"I was scared," Joey said. "I'd never seen a squirrel jump out of a tree before, and when he ran at me I thought he was going to bite me."

"I reckon I'd thought so too. Have you hunted very much?"

"Not very," Joey said. "Just since I came down here. I'm not very good yet."

"You like it, so I reckon you will be. I often wonder what it's like to shoot and see something fall down."

A crease appeared in Joey's brow, for this had been the wonder that he had slid away from before he had fallen asleep again this morning, and he came a little closer to it now. It bothered him, and he was afraid that his father or even Mr. Ben would think it sissy if he asked them about it, but Horace was different; Joey felt that Horace would understand him. "Sometimes it's sort of sad," he said, "but when there's another one, you want to shoot that one too. Why is it sad? Why do you want to do it again if it's sad?"

"I don't know," Horace said. "I reckon there's a lot of things people do that make them sad afterwards, and not bad things, either."

"You don't reckon that it's . . . well, sort of sissy to feel like that?"

Horace looked at Joey with a gaze as clear as spring water; he knew what troubled the boy, who was at once sensitive and surrounded and influenced by people who were hunters. Horace, unable to be active, lived in his thoughts; he had often reflected on the baffling question of how a hunter can feel great respect and affection for the creature he kills. He wondered whether Joey would be able to do this or whether he would finally stop shooting altogether. He didn't like killing, but he liked Joey. Joey would have to make his own adjustment in his own time, but meanwhile Horace didn't want him to feel guilty about a thing he so obviously enjoyed. "Sissy?" he asked. "No, I reckon not. I reckon it's sort of nice. You'll never be a mean kind of man if you feel like that." He watched Joey's relieved smile and changed the subject. "You read much, Joey?"

"Read?" Joey asked, lost for the moment. He was still thinking about Horace's answer, which made him feel better; it also made Horace seem older and wiser than himself. "Oh. I like to read. I used to read Tom Swift and books like that, but I don't any more. I like poetry and stuff, and books about real people. Do you like to read?"

"I read books like that, too," Horace said, and they smiled at one another. A fine feeling of friendship, a current of good will, moved between them. "I read them when I can get them."

"I have a lot of books," Joey said. "I can bring some to you. I'll be here again Christmas, maybe. I'll bring some then."

"It would be nice."

"Well," Joey said, "I reckon I better go. Mr. Ben might need the water." He took a quick, secret look at Horace's foot beside the wagon. It lay almost at a right angle to the leg, a useless thing, and a feeling of protest went through him that

Horace should have this additional infirmity; it wasn't fair. "I'll bring you the books."

"Thank you, Joey. I hope you come again."

"I will," Joey said. "Good-by."

"Good-by," Horace said, and smiled brightly at him.

Joey turned away and walked around the corner to the well, where he filled the buckets. The mule had come out into the stable yard; it moved up to the fence along the lane, showed Joey the whites of its eyes, and he gave it a wide berth as he passed it. He thought about his meeting with the crippled boy all the way back to the house, and was considerably sobered when he took the buckets into the kitchen and put them on the table.

Mr. Ben was taking the ashes out of the stove. "See anybody over there?" he asked.

"Yes, sir," Joey said. "I saw Horace."

"You did?"

"Yes, sir," Joey said. "He's nice, Mr. Ben."

"You couldn't find a nicer boy anywhere," Mr. Ben said, and waited for more.

"I walked around the corner of the house and he was there. I was so scared I almost ran for a minute, but I'm glad I didn't. He's smart, Mr. Ben. I like him. I'm going to bring him some books."

"It would be a very kind thing to do. I guess it's almost impossible for him to get many books. His mother helped him some, but he practically taught himself to read."

"I reckon he could teach himself almost anything if he had the chance. It's not fair that he's like that. It's not fair at all."

"No, it's not, Joey, but I wouldn't think too much about it if I were you. Nobody can fix it."

"Yes, sir," Joey said, but he couldn't stop thinking about it. He walked to the window and looked out at the gray and drizzling day, and Horace's fate, so hopeless and so harsh, depressed him. He felt that he had found in Horace a friend different from other boys, like a grownup in some ways but within his reach, and that this friend was so handicapped was dispiriting.

He stared out of the window for a while, and then wandered about the room; finally he saw the turkey call on the mantel and sat down and began to work with it, but the sounds he produced were shrill and off-key. He grew impatient with the call presently; he was still thinking of Horace and wasn't much interested in it. He put it back on the mantel and began to wander about again, touching things as he wandered.

"Joey," Mr. Ben said, after a bit, "take your gun and go for a walk. You'll feel better when you get back."

"Yes, sir," Joey said, with little enthusiasm, but he got his gear together and went out. He didn't feel like going anywhere that he had already been; he didn't feel like going anywhere at all, for Horace's condition, and the bright smile that Horace had given him when they parted, which underlined it, was still in his mind. His feet took him down the path toward the wharf, but part way down he turned off it toward the north and continued in that direction. The woods were old and high, oak and beech interspersed with great ancient pines, and the misty drizzle made them shadowy and mysterious; the litter on the ground was damp and his footfalls made no sound. Being able to move so silently and secretly began to interest him; Horace slipped into the back of his mind, and his spirits rose.

He had wished several times in the past that he could travel through the woods a little above the ground, in just such a silence, and now he was able to do something very like it. Nothing could hear him coming; the animals, unwarned by the noise of his feet in the leaves, would be unaware of him. He slowed his pace and drifted between the trees, stopping frequently to stand still for a while and look about. Silent and slow-moving, he felt almost disembodied; it was as though he wasn't there at all.

The first thing he saw was a squirrel on the ground taking short little jumps and slow steps, pausing to dig small holes in a search for nuts it had buried earlier in the year. Seen so, unconscious of him, it was a captivating animal; several times it suddenly made swift sidewise jumps and skittered about as though playing with an invisible companion. Then, at the edge of visibility, Joey saw something else. There was a flash of wings, and turning his glance that way Joey saw a Cooper's hawk land in a tree. The squirrel's back was toward it and it hadn't seen the hawk, but the hawk had seen it. Joey watched, fascinated, as the hawk dropped down behind the tree, reappeared near the ground, and turning silently in the air glided toward the squirrel behind the cover of a holly bush. As it rounded the holly it put on an astonishing burst of speed. It almost seemed to be a streak as it went for the squirrel. At the last instant before the reaching talons closed on it the squirrel dodged away, dashed for a beech, and leaped up on the trunk. The hawk turned in its own length and pursued it. The squirrel went round and round the tree as it climbed, its claws scraping on the bark; the hawk followed it with marvelous speed and dexterity, but the squirrel managed to stay far enough ahead of it to slip into a hole in the trunk and disappear. The hawk wheeled and flew off; the squirrel's head reappeared in the hole and it raised its voice in a noisy scolding, like a boy pouring scorn on another who had threatened attack with a stick or a stone and been frustrated.

Joey had been so caught up in this swift and deadly incident that he had forgotten to breathe; he took a deep breath now and said, "Great day!" He realized that he was holding his gun and had completely forgotten about it; he had even forgotten about it when he had first seen the squirrel. He was glad that he had forgotten it, for if he had shot the squirrel he would have missed an experience that was much more exciting. He recalled the craftiness of the hawk, the instantaneous reaction of the squirrel, and the swift maneuverings of both of them, and was amazed anew. "Great day!" he said again.

The squirrel had ceased its scolding and withdrawn its head, and Joey, who was feeling very friendly toward it by now, grinned at the hole and went on. The drizzle stopped but the sky remained overcast and gray. His interest in seeing more of the secret lives about him had been sharpened, and he drifted through the misty woods with keen anticipation. He didn't see anything for a while; presently he came to a little clearing overgrown with low brush with a large pile of big rocks in the middle of it. It had apparently been there for a long time; fields must have surrounded it once, and the rocks cleared from them piled there. He stopped at the edge of the clearing and looked at it; while he watched a snaky head appeared in a crack between two rocks and two eyes lit with green fire regarded him. They were baleful and without fear; they seemed to defy him. There was a chittering in the rockpile and a mouse popped out. The head swung and the owner of it, a lean, sinuous brown shape, leaped out, flowed over the rocks, and caught the mouse.

Joey had never seen a weasel before, but he had heard a lot about what bloodthirsty little killers they were. He laid his gun down, picked up a stick, and ran at it. The weasel dodged him with almost contemptuous ease, and carrying the mouse in its mouth disappeared into the rockpile again. Joey ran after it and poked the stick down the crack it had gone into. There was more chittering and several of the snaky heads popped out of other cracks, vanished, then popped out elsewhere. It was like a sleight-of-hand trick. It was impossible to tell how many of them were there; they seemed to surround him, and their eyes all burned upon him with defiance and a chilling hostility. One of the beasts appeared on top of the rockpile as though by magic, bounded toward him, and vanished into another crack almost at his feet. By the time he thought of swinging his stick at it, it had disappeared.

The chittering increased in volume, a thin and hateful screeching that rasped at the nerves, and four heads popped up closer to Joey. It was as though the little savages were preparing to attack him, and a little chill went up his back. He didn't know how many of them were there, he had seen how swiftly they moved, and his imagination suddenly pictured a pack of them bounding out of the rockpile and swarming over him, leaping, screeching, tearing at him.

It frightened him; he dropped the stick, retrieved his gun, and got out of the clearing. He looked over his shoulder several times to be sure they weren't following him, and didn't stop until he was a hundred yards away. He stood there until his heartbeat slowed, for the experience with the demonic little beasts had rather shaken him, and then went on again. He encountered no other animals, and presently came to the top of a low hill. The woods thinned out before him and at the bottom of the hill gave way to a field with a road running along it; a small and somewhat dilapidated schoolhouse sat by the road. The ground around it was pounded hard and

bare and it looked deserted, but just then a woman came out of the door onto the little roofed porch in front and shook what seemed to be a rug.

This was apparently the school which Odie and Claude attended, closed now for Thanksgiving vacation, and the woman was the teacher cleaning up a little. She finished shaking the rug, turned to go in again, and there was a whistle from the bottom of the hill. The woman turned and waved, and a man whom Joey hadn't seen because he had been sitting quietly beside a tree stood up. It was Sam White; Joey was close enough to be sure of that.

The boy was startled to see him there, and to be so close to him; because of the silence of his footsteps in the wet leaves he had almost stumbled over the man. Some things he had overheard, some innuendoes and oblique references, came into his mind. The man had whistled and the woman had waved at him; it indicated that they had met before. In another moment she came out again, shut the door, looked up and down the road, and then crossed it toward White. Joey wanted to run and was afraid to, for she was coming toward him and might see him; she might even call out. If she did this it would bring Sam White's attention to him, and Joey wanted nothing to do with Sam White. Joey had stopped by a thick growth of holly trees and was partially concealed from her; he moved very slowly behind them and crouched down.

The woman came closer. She was not very tall, and she had blonde hair; she was almost pretty, but the almost-prettiness was spoiled by an expression at once avid and wary. She came up to White and looked at him flirtatiously, with her head canted, but when he reached one hand toward her she avoided it with a step to one side. They stood and looked at each other for a moment.

"You ain't very friendly," White said, "movin' out of the way. I reckoned you might be friendlier this time."

"I am friendly, Sam," she said. "I like to talk to you. You know that."

"I reckon you wouldn't be here at all if all you wanted to do was talk."

"That's not true. Why do you say a thing like that?"

"I say it on account of I think it," White said. "Maybe from now on we better talk in the road, or where everybody can see us." The woman didn't say anything; she looked at the ground for a long moment, and White went on. "Maybe," he said, "you want to catch Crenshaw first."

The woman looked at him. "I want to get married," she said defiantly, and added with more calmness, "Every woman wants to get married, Sam. They're nowhere without that."

"You get married, then," White said. "I can wait." He grinned at her. "Well, I got to get back."

The woman took half a step toward him, and stopped. "You're not going to . . . I mean, I always come here to the school for a while on Saturdays. I'm not going to stop coming."

"I'll see you, I reckon," White said, and grinned again. "I ain't liable to quit seein' a woman pretty as you are."

There had been a good deal said that Joey didn't entirely understand, but the half-understood things oppressed him. Besides, they acted as though they were going to part, and he was terrified that White would find him as he turned for home. He half arose from his crouch, not noticing that three shells spilled from his pocket as he did so, and crept away behind the holly trees. He went very carefully at first to make no noise, and then more rapidly. He walked for a quarter of a mile, and as he got farther from them the feeling of oppression lightened; he pushed the experience into the back of his mind.

He didn't want to think about it, and presently was helped by a distraction. He was returning by a slightly different route from the one he had taken to reach the schoolhouse; he had turned a little farther north, and after a bit he came to a belt of young pines. They were about twenty feet high, close growing and thick; there was just enough room for him to move about under them if he stooped a little. The gloom beneath them was accentuated by the gloom of the day, and the ground was covered with their dead needles. There was a feeling of somber mystery about the place, and after he had got a little way into it, a rabbit jumped up in front of him. He could see little of it but its white tail bounding erratically before him, and was too surprised to shoot, but he was ready for the next one. He shot at it but missed, and at the gun's report another jumped a little farther away and by a wild chance fell to his second barrel.

He stuffed it triumphantly into his game pocket and set about looking for more. There were more there; the place was full of rabbits, and his excitement mounted as he moved about in the gloom at a half crouch, keyed up to swift action as the white tails suddenly appeared, danced erratically before him, and vanished. It was the kind of snapshooting, very difficult and fast, with no time to aim, that called for instant response and concentration and made the hunter feel that he was living at the very top of his pitch.

He stopped only when his ammunition was gone. He had three rabbits, and it was beginning to grow dark. Despite his excitement he had managed to keep oriented, and so came out of the pine thicket into the open woods again and set out for the house. The rabbits were heavy in his coat, he was greatly pleased with himself and the day, and had forgotten for the time the scene at the schoolhouse, and Horace as well.

* * *

It was almost dark when Joey climbed the back steps and went into the kitchen. He didn't see the extra lantern on the table; Mr. Ben was just taking a pan out of the stove and turned as he came in.

"Did you see Odie and Claude?" he asked. "They were here to go shooting with you."

"No, sir," Joey said and then remembered. "I didn't see anybody except Mr. White and the school teach—"

He got no farther; Mr. Ben just opened his hands and the pan fell to the floor with a crash, spraying gravy, meat, and potatoes all over everything. He paid it no attention; with one swift step he had Joey by the arm. "Crenshaw is here!" he whispered urgently in Joey's ear. "Don't say any more about that!" He moved away a step or two, and exclaimed in a loud voice, "Ah, damn it to the devil!" Then he went to the living room door and said, "Sorry for the noise, Crenshaw. I dropped our supper. We'll be in as soon as we get it cleaned up."

Joey was still standing in the middle of the floor, collecting himself and wondering what to do next, when Crenshaw appeared in the doorway and looked somberly at him. Crenshaw seemed very big, and a shocked look had taken the place of the diffidence that had been his most noticeable characteristic to Joey before. Joey squirmed to be away from that look, which almost seemed to lay a physical weight on him; to avoid it he turned, reached for a big spoon on the table, and getting down on his knees turned the pan over and began to put the meat and potatoes back into it. He didn't look up.

"I . . . better go along," Crenshaw said. "Y'all won't have any supper, so we better not come."

"Why certainly you'll come," Mr. Ben said. "We'll

scramble eggs or something and be ready after a while. You come later. I'll be disappointed if you don't."

There was a silence, while Joey scraped the spoon around on the floor, then Crenshaw said, "Yes, sir. We'll come, then."

Mr. Ben stepped around Joey and got Crenshaw's lantern, lit it, and gave it to him; they both went out on the back porch, and after a minute or two Mr. Ben came back in again and stood with his back to the door. He looked at Joey without seeming to see him.

"I'm sorry, Mr. Ben," Joey said miserably. "I sure am sorry. I didn't know—"

Mr. Ben's eyes focused. "It wasn't your fault," he said. "Don't worry yourself about it. He stopped in to ask me if he could bring the schoolteacher for a while this evening." He shook his head. "It would have come out sooner or later. Where were they?"

Joey told him, relating their actions and as much of their talk as he could recall. "Then I sneaked away," he said, ending his tale. "I thought Mr. White would find me, and I didn't want to hear any more anyhow."

Mr. Ben nodded, and the line of his lantern jaw grew a little firmer. "I see," he said. "I see. Well . . ." He stood for a moment in thought, and it was apparent that his thoughts were not pleasant. "Well, I'll do what I can. We'll get something to eat, and then you go to bed. It would be better if you weren't around when they get here."

"Yes, sir," Joey said, immensely relieved that Mr. Ben had taken over and that he wouldn't have to face Crenshaw again. "Crenshaw is nice, Mr. Ben. Why would Mr. White do that? I thought the teacher liked Crenshaw; she let him help her move in and he was bringing her here and everything."

"It's complicated," Mr. Ben said. "It's one of those

grownup things that only grownups can fix. Don't spend too much time thinking about it."

"Yes, sir," Joey said.

Mr. Ben got into motion. "Let's clean up this mess and fix some supper. Tom Powers from up the road brought this piece of meat, but we can't eat it now. Just scrape it up and we'll throw it out. What else did you do this afternoon?"

Joey told him while they were cleaning up the floor. He captured again the excitement with the weasels and the rabbits in the pine thicket, and Mr. Ben skillfully asked a few questions as he went along; soon, telling about the thicket, Joey forgot for the time the affair at the schoolhouse and Crenshaw.

Mr. Ben kept Joey interested with hunting talk until dinner was finished, but after the boy said good night and went off to the bedroom, he began to think about White, Crenshaw, and the teacher again. Despite Mr. Ben's efforts to distract his mind from the affair, he remembered the old man's grim expression when he was talking about it and his remarkable presence of mind in letting the pan fall to drown out what Joey was saying. He realized that Mr. Ben was worried, and so he began to worry too. Crenshaw's shocked expression had impressed him; he wondered what Crenshaw was going to do. He didn't think that Crenshaw was going to be diffident and mild, for he obviously had a great interest in the girl, and he had heard enough snatches of conversation at home to know that grownups sometimes got very violent about such things. Joey had seen grownups fight, and the fury of it had frightened him. Would Crenshaw fight White? Would he even shoot him? If he did, would it be his, Joey's fault? The more he thought about it in the lonely darkness of the bedroom the more worried he became.

He began to wonder, being responsible, whether he

would be allowed to come to the Pond again alone if the worst came of it and somebody got hurt, for he was still young enough to find grownups and their decisions often incalculable. What would his father say when he heard about all this? The last thing in the world that Joey wanted was to be put back to coming only with his father; the freedom of being on his own had been wonderful.

After what seemed to be hours of worry he heard the confused sound of voices in the next room. He got out of bed, crept across the room, and put his ear to the door. ". . . glad you could come," Mr. Ben was saying. "I've heard a lot about you from Crenshaw."

"Thank you," the girl said, and there were sounds of everyone sitting down. "I've heard a lot about you too, Mr. Ben. You're famous. All the children tell me about you." Her tone of voice, even to Joey's ear, was a little too effusive; it was like the voices of several of his mother's friends, the ones Joey didn't like very much, when they were talking too loudly and not really meaning all they said. "You've been so kind to all of them, and so helpful," she went on. "You haven't any children of your own?"

"None, Miss Emma," Mr. Ben said. "Only by proxy."

"I think it's a shame," the girl said. "You seem to be so good with them. Don't you think so, dear?"

She apparently asked this of Crenshaw, and Joey got his ear even closer to the door to hear what Crenshaw would say, but he didn't say anything; apparently he nodded, for the girl's voice went on again.

"He's been so strong and silent all evening," she said, "that I'll just talk to you. But I think it's so clever of you to think of being a father by proxy. Are you being a proxy father for the little boy who's with you now?"

"Yes," Mr. Ben said. "I wish you could have met him this evening. He's an interesting boy, but he was tired from a big day and went to bed early. He was up near the schoolhouse this afternoon, hunting rabbits. You didn't happen to see him?"

There was a short silence and things seemed to be crawling around in it; Joey held his breath, and couldn't have moved if he wanted to, but he felt a sudden thrill of admiration for Mr. Ben and his cleverness.

"This afternoon?" the girl asked, and her voice went up just a little. It was not very much, but Joey didn't have his eyes to distract him, and he heard it. "This afternoon? No, I didn't see him. It's vacation, you know, and I wasn't there very long."

"Did you see anybody?" Crenshaw asked suddenly, and to Joey there was no diffidence in his voice this time. It was almost flat, but in the flatness Joey heard, or thought he heard, an odd little note of entreaty.

"No, dear," the girl said, and her voice was under control again. "Should I have? Were you there too?" She apparently turned and addressed herself to Mr. Ben. "Wouldn't you think that if he were anywhere near he would have stopped in and helped me?"

Joey marveled at her duplicity, and hated her for it; then Mr. Ben spoke again. "Maybe he wouldn't want to disturb you," he said, "but there are times when it's better to be disturbed." There was another silence, and then Mr. Ben said, "I'll get us some coffee. It's all ready; it won't take a minute."

Joey heard him get up and walk across the room, and crept back to the bedroom again. He was limp with relief and full of a rather awed admiration for Mr. Ben. He crawled into bed, and almost at once was asleep.

CHAPTER NINE

When Joey awoke he heard Mr. Ben in the living room, got up, and went in there to dress. The old man was setting the table.

"Morning, Joey," he said. "How did you sleep?"

"Hi, Mr. Ben. I was sort of worried in the night."

"I can see why, but there's no earthly reason for you to worry, Joey. None of this is your fault, nothing can happen to you because of it, and I'm glad it happened the way it did. Last night I had a chance to suggest to that . . . the teacher that she had better be careful."

"Do you think she will?" Joey asked. "Crenshaw likes her, and he's *good*, Mr. Ben."

"Yes, he's a good man even if he is a little slow. I think her trouble is that she came from a very small town, no man paid her much attention, and now that she's here and two men are paying her attention it's gone to her head. Probably no one paid her attention at home because they grew up with her and knew what a sidewinder she was."

"What's a sidewinder?" Joey asked. The word intrigued him.

"It's a rattlesnake, but I meant it as a sort of trouble-maker."

"Yes, sir," Joey said. "Sidewinder. Sidewinder." It was a good word, and he said it several more times to himself; it engaged him for a moment, and then he returned to his preoccupation. "What do you reckon she'll do, Mr. Ben?"

But Mr. Ben had had enough of it. "I don't know," he said, "and I don't think you need bother about it. Forget it and enjoy yourself. Let's have breakfast."

"Yes, sir," Joey said, and his heart sank. He had come to the end with Mr. Ben, and knew that there was no use trying to go farther.

"I forgot to tell you," Mr. Ben said as they went into the kitchen, "that I got a letter from your father yesterday. He's coming down to pick you up when you go home. He wants to bring a few things."

"Yes, sir," Joey said, and although he always enjoyed being with his father, he wished that it might have been some other time.

Mr. Ben had taken some eggs out of the cabinet, and broke them into a pan. "I wrote your father back and I wrote a note to Ed Pitmire," he said as he began to beat the eggs. "I wish you'd get the letters on the dining table and take them out to the mailbox so they'll go right away this morning. Mailman will be here pretty soon."

"Yes, sir," Joey said, and went and got the letters and took them down the lane.

Joey put the letters in the box, raised the little red metal flag, and closed the box again. He was very depressed and walked slowly back to the house. Mr. Ben had the scrambled eggs on the table, and they sat down to eat. Joey didn't feel very hungry, but Mr. Ben had a fine appetite and was quite cheerful; it was almost as if a load had been taken off his mind all of a sudden.

"What's your program for today?" he asked. "Charley hasn't showed up, has he?"

"No, sir, he hasn't," Joey said. "I looked for him when I came back from the mailbox." He swallowed some scrambled eggs, not liking them, and then decided to try Mr. Ben out once more. "Mr. Ben, you reckon my father will come down sooner than he thought he would?"

Mr. Ben looked at him, and a small, secret grin appeared on his face. "I don't see why he should," he said. "He's a busy man. He has to work twice as hard now as he used to just to keep you in shells. Do you want to still-hunt?"

"I reckon so," Joey said, but without much enthusiasm.

"You could go back and try those rabbits again."

Joey didn't want to do that; the schoolhouse was that way. "No, sir," he said. "I thought I'd save that and take my father there."

"That's a good idea. Why don't you go with me to visit my traps later this afternoon? We might even hear some turkeys go to roost."

For the first time that morning Joey began to take an interest in life. "Turkeys?" he asked. "You reckon we might?"

"Could be," Mr. Ben said. "We'll be up around the head of the Pond late in the afternoon, easing along quiet and slow, and the chances should be pretty good."

"Yes, sir," Joey said. "I reckon I'll do that. I'll go out this morning somewhere and come back for lunch, and then we can go."

"Good," Mr. Ben said, and they got up and took the dishes out and washed them.

When this chore was finished, Joey went into his bedroom and put on his hunting shoes and got his gear together. While he was doing it he wondered where he would go. He considered paying a visit to Horace and talking to him about his problems; there was no one else he could talk to, and somehow he felt close to the crippled boy. But he abandoned this idea after a moment, for he might encounter Sam White and he shrank from having to talk to the man, of looking into his close-set, inattentive eyes and thinking of him reaching for the teacher and beating Odie and Claude and Charley and the mule. The thought of these things brought a hollow feeling to his stomach; he couldn't do it.

He stood in the middle of the room feeling isolated and lost, and then a recollection of the swamp came into his mind. Silent and still, other-worldly and remote, it suddenly seemed the place for him to go. He nodded, went through the living room and picked up his gun and told Mr. Ben where he was going, took his casting rod from the porch, and went down the hill. The day was windless and quite still; the Pond lay dreaming and flat as a mirror in the sun. He felt better just looking at it, so untroubled and serene, without problems, ready to bear him up and ask nothing of him but that he enjoy being upon it. He stowed his gear in the bateau, got in, and shoved off.

He paddled along a few yards off shore, pausing occasionally to drop his plug between the cypress butts, and caught two nice bass before he came to the close-growing cypresses where the stream emptied into the Pond. Here he stopped paddling for a moment and looked around as though to orient himself, and then went on. The cypresses began to close in around him, like a multitude of columns in a great hall whose lofty ceiling was the blue of the sky darkened by a fretwork of branches; the dark cedar water was the glimmering floor. The feeling came upon him, as it had before, that he was in another world quite different from the open, sunny world of the Pond; it was like the fairy-tale world of children that no grownups nor any hostile thing could enter. He paddled so slowly and carefully that there was hardly a ripple about him.

He recalled for a moment how frightened he had been the other time, and it seemed a far-off thing; he wasn't frightened now. Somehow the experience of getting lost had awakened, in its mysterious way, the sense of orientation, the intangible compass in the mind that some people have, that, even in a country unknown to them, holds them subconsciously in the direction they want to go. He didn't have to think about it; he knew he would get out; his mind was free to listen in the brooding quiet and his eyes were free to watch. The gray drooping Spanish moss grew thicker; the solution to the mystery of what might be there around the next bend continued to elude him.

He recalled the otter and suddenly found himself wishing for it. He wanted to see it again—not to shoot at; the thought of shooting at it never occurred to him—but to watch, unseen, as it moved about its concerns in fluid beauty. He went on for a while longer, silently and in expectation, but he didn't see it. Finally he turned back, still hoping that the otter would appear and bring the movement of life to the great columned hall of the swamp, but it did not.

Mr. Ben had a little upright round sheet-metal stove with a square base, which he set in front of him in the bateau when the weather was cold. He used it mostly to dry and warm his hands after pulling a trap out of the water to take out a drowned muskrat. Joey collected an armful of sticks for firewood while the old man built the fire in the stove; when he had it going he put the stove in the boat, sat down in the stern seat, and they started out.

It was late in the afternoon and shadows were growing long as they paddled up the north shore of the Pond; there was a chill in the air. Mr. Ben had a string of muskrat traps around the Pond, set under water near the entrances of muskrat holes, and occasionally he would head into shore and they would both lean over the side and check the trap. By the time they reached the head of the Pond they had three muskrats, fished up drowned in the traps; the traps had been reset and lowered to the bottom again.

The sun was not far from setting when they started back down the southern shore, and the silence-that comes toward sundown, when whatever wind there is tends to die with the dying sun and the woods prepare for night, held the world. The rhythm of Mr. Ben's paddling grew slower and Joey stopped paddling altogether; Mr. Ben lighted his pipe, and they slid along slowly not far off shore at the head of an oily V of ripples. As they came around a point, missing the cypress knees a little offshore, a sudden flutter and flapping came to them across the water from the next point several hundred yards ahead; a big dark shape flew up into a tree on the shore.

Joey half rose from his seat; Mr. Ben began to back water at once.

"A turkey!" he whispered. "A turkey!" The paddle made a swirling ripple, the water sucked at it, and the old man, digging into the water, got the bateau stopped and slowly backed it behind the point again. "Did you see him?" he whispered. "He's in the tree!"

Joey stared at him, excitement running along his nerves like an electric current. "I saw him!" he whispered. "I saw him, Mr. Ben! What do we do now?"

Mr. Ben was excited too, although he tried to appear blasé. "We'll keep still for a while," he said. "Then we'll cross and go down the other shore."

"Aren't we going to shoot him? Are we just going to let him sit there? Mr. Ben—"

"Shhhhh!" Mr. Ben said. "He won't move again now unless we frighten him. We'll come back early in the morning and just knock him out of the tree." He grinned at Joey. "I can taste him already."

"Are you sure he'll stay?" Joey asked. "Couldn't we sneak up when it gets dark?"

"We couldn't see him, and he might fly off if he heard us coming. He's roosted now; he'll stay there."

Joey wasn't convinced; he was very much afraid that the turkey might move during the night, but Mr. Ben knew more about turkeys than he did, and he finally accepted the old man's decision. They sat quietly, occasionally grinning at one another, as the sun went down and the light faded from the sky. When it was dark Mr. Ben paddled across the Pond and they crept down the far shore.

As they went up the hill in the dark Joey began to think about his father again, wondering whether he had come down sooner than he expected to and would be waiting at the house for them. He hoped not; he wanted with all his heart to have the turkey hanging triumphantly on the porch when his father got there. He could hardly wait until they reached the top of the path to see whether there was a light in the house. There was.

"Somebody's here," Mr. Ben said, and sounded surprised.

Joey didn't reply; he was too cast down. He followed Mr. Ben silently as they climbed the steps and went into the kitchen.

There were footsteps in the living room and then a form

in the doorway, but instead of being Joe Moncrief it was Crenshaw. Joey could hardly believe his eyes. Crenshaw stood in the doorway with his head forward a little, looking rather wildly at them.

"They took her away," he said. "Mr. Ben, they came and brought another teacher and took her away."

"Took who away?" Mr. Ben asked. "Miss Emma? They took Miss Emma? Who took Miss Emma?"

"Yes, sir," Crenshaw said. He looked distraught. "Yes, sir." He started to raise his right hand, and lowered it again in his agitation. "Yes, sir," he said again.

"Well, well," Mr. Ben said. He put the muskrats on the table and started for the door. "Let's go in the living room, Crenshaw. Sit down in there and tell me about it."

"Yes, sir," Crenshaw said, and turned.

Mr. Ben followed him into the living room, and Joey followed them to the door and stood there looking at them. He was so relieved that he felt a little detached.

"Now, then," Mr. Ben said as they both sat down. "Tell me what happened. I haven't got it straight yet."

Crenshaw scrubbed at his face with one hand. "Along about a couple of hours ago Miss Emma came to my house with a man from Williamsburg—I reckon he's the principal there—and said the man got a call on the telephone from the State Board in Richmond to come get her and put her on the evenin' train. They said they needed her right away at the school in Blacksburg. That's where she come from, I reckon I told you."

"I think you did."

"Yes, sir. So he was goin' to take her and put her on the train. She was cryin' a little, she said she liked it here, and she didn't want to go, but the man said the State Board wanted her to, so she had to do it. She asked me would I pack up her stuff and send it to her, and then she said good-by and they took off down the road."

"I see," Mr. Ben said. He nodded his head several times; Joey could read nothing in his face.

Crenshaw's hands stirred restlessly in his lap. "Mr. Ben, I liked her right good, I was thinkin' of askin' her to marry up with me, and now . . ." His voice died away; he sat looking at Mr. Ben with an expression at once lost and protesting. "You reckon they can do that? Take her away, I mean, and put her back in Blacksburg? I liked her right good, like I say. . . ."

"They've done it," Mr. Ben said. "They can put her in any school where they need her."

"Yes, sir, I reckon they can," Crenshaw said, and a hopeless note came into his voice. "Could be I might never see her again. I don't know how I'd ever get all the way yonder to Blacksburg. I ain't much for all this travelin'. I never been on a train." His big body slumped in the chair and he shook his head several times and stared at the floor in front of him.

Mr. Ben stood up and moved closer to him and laid a hand on his shoulder. "Don't take it so hard, man," he said. "I'm sure it will all turn out. You can write to her, and after a while if you still want to see her you can go up there." Crenshaw shook his head again, but didn't look up. "You say the man brought another teacher with him?"

"Yes, sir. She's pretty old, and got a face like a hatchet. I reckon she'll stay with the Perkins for a few days and then move in." He gave a long sighing breath and then slowly stood up. "Well . . ." he said, and looked unhappily around the room. "I reckon if they want to do it, they can do it. I just had a mind to ask you."

"I wish I could help you," Mr. Ben said, "but the State Board has the say with the teachers."

"Yes, sir, I reckon it does." He stood there for a long moment. "Well, I better go. I sure thank you, Mr. Ben."

"Stay and have some dinner with us. It would cheer you up."

"I thank y'all," Crenshaw said, "but I reckon I'll go home." He got himself into motion and walked past Joey without noticing him. Mr. Ben followed him into the kitchen, lit a lantern for him, and saw him out the door.

He didn't look too downcast by Crenshaw's troubles when he came back; in fact, Joey thought that he almost had an expression of satisfaction, and that puzzled him. He had felt sorry for Crenshaw himself, although the news that the teacher was gone from the vicinity had brought with it a feeling of great relief. "He was pretty sad, wasn't he, Mr. Ben?" he asked.

"He was indeed," Mr. Ben said. "He'll never know what a great favor . . . but never mind that."

"Sir?"

"He'll get over it," Mr. Ben said and, turning to the kitchen cabinet, got out a can of corned-beef hash and opened it. "You cut up those boiled potatoes we had left over, and we'll make lyonnaise potatoes again." As he worked away to get the hash out of the can he began to sing. "'I was feeling mighty frisky,'" he sang, and did a dance step or two, "'When they caught me with the whisky . . .' Cut them up smaller," he said.

"Yes, sir," Joey said, slicing away and smiling at Mr. Ben's cracked voice and his unusual gaiety. "I didn't know they changed teachers that fast."

"They don't, usually. This was a sort of accelerated case, you might say." He put the hash in a frying pan and collected the potatoes from Joey. "Gentlemen, sir, that's what it was. You'd better set the table."

"Yes, sir. I reckon Mr. White will be a little surprised."

"Indeed he will, if he's not already. If those boys come around in the next couple of days it might be just as well if you had something else to do. They're going to sweat for it."

"Yes, sir, I reckon you're right. I won't go out with them." He stood with the knives, forks, and spoons in his hand, feeling very sorry for Odie and Claude.

"Hash is getting ready," Mr. Ben said. "How's the table? We ought to eat and go to bed early. We've got to get up long before sunrise."

"Yes, sir," Joey said and got into motion. The turkey had slipped into the back of his mind with all the other things that had been going on, but now that Mr. Ben had recalled it, all the excitement came back again. The old man came in with their dinner, but Joey found it hard to eat very much. Even if his father came tomorrow they would have the turkey to surprise him with. "Great day!" he said. "I bet my father will be the most surprised man in the whole United States when he sees us with a turkey, Mr. Ben. Can we hang it on the porch, so that he sees it as soon as he drives in?"

"That's where we'll hang it."

"Yes, sir." Joey wiggled in his chair at the very thought of pointing the turkey out to his astonished father. He ate a few more forkfuls, and then couldn't sit still any longer. He got up and found the turkey call and sat down again, but although he tried it all sorts of ways, he couldn't get the right notes out of it. Finally, somewhat crestfallen, he put it back. "I reckon I just never will learn to work it," he said. "I do everything you do, but . . ."

"Well, you won't need it anyhow," Mr. Ben said. "At least, this time. But I'll put it in my pocket when we go. Aren't you going to eat any more?"

"No, sir, I reckon not."

"We'll wash the dishes then and go to bed."

They washed the dishes, and Mr. Ben got his old alarm clock, wound it, and set it for four o'clock. Joey undressed in the living room, said good night to Mr. Ben, and went into the chilly bedroom and crawled into bed. The bed was cold; they had forgotten to heat their bricks, but he didn't want to get up again and wait for a brick to get hot. He curled himself up, hugging his knees, and presently grew drowsy. As he fell asleep he was thinking of the turkey, of it falling from the tree, and hanging on the back porch for his father to see when he stopped behind the house.

Mr. Ben had touched off a small fire in the living room stove; it took some of the night's chill off the room, but not all of it. Still half asleep, Joey shivered with cold and excitement as he dressed in the wan light of the single lamp.

"Put plenty of clothes on," Mr. Ben said. "It's cold out, and it'll be colder on the water. I'll get my gun."

Joey fumbled with buttons and yawned and stumbled about, but finally he was dressed; Mr. Ben came back from his room with his gun. "I'd better shoot him," he said. "I'm not too sure your twenty-gauge will talk to him loud enough. I've got some BB shells that will burn him good. . . ." He felt in his pockets, looked surprised, and said, "Well, I had them. I'll go find them." He went off again, and Joey could hear him walking around and poking into things; finally he returned, and they blew out the lamp and went outside.

It was very dark; the stars glittered brilliantly, and the cold made them catch their breaths. Joey hunched himself up inside his clothes, and they started down the path. Gradually Joey's eyes became accustomed to the dark, but his shivering didn't stop; if anything, it increased as the great moment drew nearer. They reached the wharf, untangled the bateau's chain with great care, climbed aboard, and shoved off. A cold and ghostly mist trailed over the water, almost as high as the gunwales, occasionally swirling head-high, hiding the surface. It gave Joey the feeling that they were moving through the clouds, detached from the earth.

He picked up his paddle and helped Mr. Ben as they slid along the dark and umbrageous shore now hidden, now revealed by the slow swirls of the mist. The exercise warmed him a little, but when they came opposite the point where the turkey was, Mr. Ben whispered to him to put his paddle down and turned for the other shore. The cold moved into him again, his excitement increased, and his teeth began to chatter; they sounded as loud to him as a circus band, and he found a handkerchief in his pocket and wadded it up and bit down on it.

They slid silently up to the point; the bateau lost way and stopped several feet from the shore. Now that they were under the turkey, or under where it should be, waves of tremors followed one another through Joey. He was entirely concentrated on the darkness above him. His eyes tried to make out the bulk of turkey, but it was still too dark to see very much. He forgot the mist and the cold and didn't even notice the small movements of the bateau as Mr. Ben held it in position with twists of the paddle, but he could hear the uneven thumps of his heart.

Time crawled by, and almost imperceptibly the sky began to pale. Nearby twigs and branches slowly took on shape and texture and the eye moved higher as the tide of darkness withdrew, and then two rounded shapes, not one, about ten feet apart in the tree, could be seen against the paling sky.

Joey stared at one and then the other, puzzled, for they had heard and seen only one turkey fly up. It seemed impossible that another had joined it, for they had stayed until after dark; then it came to him that one of the shapes must be a squirrel nest. He turned to Mr. Ben, who was also staring up the tree. Mr. Ben felt the movement and dropped his glance to look back at him, and it was evident from the old man's expression that he was confused too. He didn't know which shape was the turkey; he had put the paddle down and picked up his gun, but he held it across his knees in indecision and shook his head. He sat for a moment longer, half raised the gun, and lowered it again, then he looked up at the sky.

He looked at Joey again and shook his head once more. He couldn't make up his mind, and it was growing light more rapidly now; any instant the turkey might awake and launch itself from the tree. The nervous tension had built up inside Joey until he could hardly contain himself; he felt that he was going to explode and apparently Mr. Ben felt the same way, for he suddenly swept the gun up and pulled the trigger.

There was a shattering roar and the bateau bucked from the recoil; leaves and sticks flew from Mr. Ben's target, and Joey had a confused and heartbreaking impression of the other shape suddenly sprouting great wings and vanishing from the limb. It was gone instantaneously, as though by a trick of magic; the limb was empty, leaves and sticks were raining through the trees, and the echoes of the shot were still bouncing thunderously around the Pond.

Mr. Ben slowly lowered the gun, laid it gently on the bottom of the bateau, and picked up his paddle. He didn't look at Joey, and Joey, after a quick and stricken look at him, turned and picked up his own paddle. Without a word they headed toward the wharf.

CHAPTER TEN

They were almost through breakfast before Mr. Ben had very much to say. He had been pretty silent, and so had Joey; in their great disappointment they had passed things hurriedly and kept their noses mostly in their plates.

Mr. Ben pushed his chair back a little and cleared his throat. "Well," he said. "Honest confession is good for the soul. It was my fault, Joey, and I'm sorry."

"Yes, sir," Joey said automatically, and then added, "I mean, no, sir, Mr. Ben. I don't reckon it was. Nobody could tell which was which."

"I should have been prepared for something like that, and I wasn't. If I'd let you take your gun, and if we'd both shot at once, we'd probably have the turkey now." He shook his head. "With turkeys it's always the unexpected that happens, and they react so fast you don't get a second chance."

"Yes, sir. He sure got out of there fast."

"He sure God did," Mr. Ben said. "Bang! Swish! Gentlemen, sir, it was Hey, Betty Martin! and he was gone." He shook his head and grinned ruefully. "Maybe if we'd sat still until he woke up, he might have put his head up and looked around before he flew. Well, if the sky fell down we could all catch larks. We just got excited and went off half cocked."

"Yes, sir, I reckon we did. But," Joey said sturdily, "I'd have done the same thing you did. I would have shot at the same thing. The squirrel nest looked more like a turkey than the turkey did."

"You're a generous and forgiving soul, Joey, and I appreciate it." He grinned at Joey, and Joey grinned back; some of the pain of the great disappointment withdrew into the background. "What are you going to do today?"

"I thought maybe if Charley . . ." He got up and walked over and looked out the window, but there was no Charley in the yard. "He's not there," he said. "You reckon anything's happened to him? Maybe Mr. White . . ."

"I don't know," Mr. Ben said. "I doubt it, somehow. That dog's had a lot of practice taking care of himself. Sam might have him shut up, but I think he'll get here sooner or later. Maybe tomorrow."

"Yes, sir, I hope so." He sat for a moment in thought. "I reckon I'll just go still-hunting today." He stood up and got the turkey call and worked on it for a while, but without very much success. "You reckon I'll ever learn how to do it?"

Mr. Ben held out his hand and Joey gave the call to him. The old man showed him how it was done. His calls fell into the silence of the room as though a turkey itself were there; but when Joey took it back and tried to imitate them, what came out was scratchy and shrill and he knew they would send any turkey in hearing the other way as fast as it could go. He finally gave up and put the call back again.

"I reckon I just can't do it," he said, "and it looks so easy."

"It's not easy when you're in the woods and excited and so cold your hands shake," Mr. Ben said. "I've had trouble that way myself. I wish somebody would invent one that can't make a wrong sound no matter how much you're shaking, but I never saw one like that."

"I wish they would too. I reckon if a turkey was really there and I was trying to call him, I'd shake too much to work your call. I like to shook myself all over the bateau this morning, and if I'd had a call I bet it would have sounded more like a beagle than a turkey." He began to take the dishes off the table and Mr. Ben joined him. They decided to stack them up until they had more to wash, and Joey went into the bedroom and put on his hunting gear and went out.

He hadn't been in the country about halfway up the southern shore of the Pond yet, and so he took the bateau and paddled there. He landed near the beginning of the cutover section which had been lumbered several years past; it ran almost half a mile toward the head of the Pond and was covered with a tangle of brush, young trees several feet high, and the decaying litter and tree tops that lumbermen leave behind them. His father had told him there were quail there, but it was hard going; he decided to stay in the bordering woods for a while and still-hunt, and walked around until he was on a little hillside where he could see for a hundred yards or so around him, then sat down.

After wriggling about for a bit he found a comfortable position and relaxed; the silence settled around him. He knew that nothing would happen for half an hour or so, for if there were any squirrels in the vicinity they would have hidden themselves when they heard him coming and remained hidden that long to be sure that he had passed. If they had hidden in a place from which they could see him they would not move for a much longer time than that, unless he was immobile and they forgot he was there, so he became immobile and listened for the first stir of life, for claws on bark or footfalls in the leaves. His eyes roved about but he kept his head still, and as time drew out, his thoughts drifted from one thing to another.

He thought of Bud and wondered what Bud was doing and whether Bud ever thought of him; he had missed his friend in the odd moments when he wasn't engaged with turkeys or schoolteachers or some other adventure. So many new things had happened to him at the Pond that they had preoccupied him, but Bud was still in his thoughts; Bud's absence left a lonely place when he had time to think about it. He wondered if his father would come today instead of two days hence and hoped not, for he loved his new independence. He thought of the sudden departure of the teacher and was very glad it had happened, though he really didn't understand any of it; the teacher's actions or why Sam White had been there to meet her when he had a family of his own and Crenshaw had no one. He wondered if all grownups did incomprehensible things like that, and why; he couldn't imagine his father doing it, or his mother.

He had to shift his position a little, and as he did it his eye caught motion; he was immediately back in the woods again. A squirrel was coming down a tree trunk sixty feet away, head first, slowly circling the tree. Joey waited until it was on the side away from him and raised his gun, but the squirrel didn't reappear. It had dropped to the ground, and he could hear it in the leaves. A game of hide and seek began, with Joey holding his breath and following the sound and the squirrel moving slowly about but managing to stay out of sight. It moved farther off and then began to move back again; after what seemed hours it suddenly appeared in a clear space between two trees and Joey shot it.

The squirrel fell over, twitched a moment, and lay still.
Joey retrieved it. He felt a little as though he had taken an
unfair advantage—he didn't feel as triumphant as he should;
but he lost this feeling when he recalled the breathless suspense of following its movements by ear and trying to locate
it. He moved on to another part of the woods and killed another squirrel. At the third place he wounded one and it got
away from him. He thought it was dead after the shot and
walked over to get it, leaving his gun leaning against a tree,
but when he had nearly reached it the creature revived. Its
back was broken and it couldn't use its hind legs; it pulled itself along by its forelegs, eluded the stick he swung at it, and
managed to drag itself into a hollow tree.

He didn't like any of this. The sight of it desperate and
crippled and the thought of it dying slowly and in pain considerably diminished his enthusiasm. He left the place and,
after wandering rather unhappily about for a time, sat down
again. He was of two minds about shooting another squirrel
now, and besides, in the stillness of the woods, he began to
feel drowsy. He had got up very early; his head began to nod.
He leaned the gun against the tree behind him and fell asleep.

Sometime later he awoke, and as his eyes reluctantly
opened a sight confronted him that brought him wide awake.
His legs were stretched out in front of him and a squirrel was
sitting on the toe of his right shoe with its forepaws folded
on its chest, staring at him with great curiosity and trying to
decide what he was. He managed to control a start of surprise
and dropped his eyelids most of the way; his mind began a
frantic scurry, searching for some way to get a shot at it. He
couldn't find an answer. His gun was behind him, and at his
first motion to grab it the squirrel would be gone. He forgot
the last, crippled squirrel; he wanted this one, and as his ex-

citement and frustration built up, the squirrel suddenly jumped from his right foot to his left one and faced him again. It twitched its tail several times and gave the whining bark that squirrels give when puzzled. He could have reached out and touched it with his hand, and to have it so close and be unable to do anything about it was finally too much for him. He tensed himself and rolled, making a grab for the gun; the squirrel jumped straight up in the air and landed running; he knocked the gun down and had to scramble about for it, and when he finally had it he jumped up and tore through the woods after the squirrel. A trailing vine caught his foot and he fell full length. He had pushed the safety off on his gun in his excitement, and when he hit the ground the gun went off and cut a widening swathe through the underbrush.

He lay there for a moment, half frightened by the discharge of the gun—which he realized might well have killed him if it had been jarred from his hands and fallen pointing in his direction—and half ready to burst out in laughter at the ridiculous scene which had just taken place. He finally did laugh, at the recollection of the barking squirrel practically in his lap and his own mental gymnastics when he was trying to find a way to deal with it, but beneath the laughter was the sober realization that he had been silly and careless with the gun.

He decided that he had done enough squirrel hunting for the day, got up, and went back to the bateau. He had slept for several hours and the sun was well down in the west, and as he paddled down the middle of the Pond he saw two ducks in the distance against the sky, high in the air. As he watched them they swung and began to drop; they were coming down to the Pond. They scaled down and grew larger, dropped below the trees to the west, and, flattening out a few feet above the water, still came toward him. He put the paddle down and picked up the gun. They came on swiftly; they were going to be almost over him, and as they came into range he swung and shot. One duck began to rise but the other was hit; it took a long glide and struck the water several hundred yards behind him with a splash. He had a fine feeling of triumph, for it was the first fast-flying bird that he had ever shot, the first time he had solved the problem that fascinates shot-gunners until their shooting days are over; the swift and complicated decision of how to hold, swing, lead, and fire so that the target and the shot charge reach the same place at the same instant. The triumph of hitting a squirrel in a tree was very minor compared to this.

He reloaded and put the gun down and turned the bateau toward the duck. It was swimming around, but had a broken wing and was unable to fly; he would have to shoot it again. As he got close to it he put the paddle down and picked up the gun, but the duck dove out of sight and was out of range when it came up again. When he caught up with it, it dove again, and this went on until the duck began to weaken and make shorter and shorter dives. When he was sure that it would come up within range he stood up in the boat to shoot at it, and stepped on the empty shell that he had dropped when he reloaded the gun.

The shell rolled under his shoe and he lost his balance and went over the side. It happened so quickly that he wasn't conscious of doing anything, but his reflexes saved him; if he had gone to the bottom with his hunting gear on he would never have come up. As he fell he dropped the gun on the bottom of the bateau with one hand and grasped the gunwale with the other. He went under the length of his arm and the cold water stabbed him and took his breath, but he was pulling himself up again before he realized that

he had hold of the gunwale. His head cleared the surface, and although his heavy clothes were soaked and much heavier because of it, he managed to get one foot over the gunwale and roll himself aboard. While he was doing it the bateau heeled to the waterline and shipped considerable water, but rolled sluggishly back once he was on the floor.

He hadn't had time to be frightened yet and was too cold to think about it now. The wet clothes gripped him like a freezing coat of mail. He began to paddle, and with the shipped water sloshing about at every stroke finally reached the wharf, fished the gun out of the bilge, and stumbled dripping up the hill with his teeth chattering like castanets.

Mr. Ben was on the porch and helped him get his clothes off; the old man toweled his back while he toweled his front, rolled him in a blanket, sat him in a chair in front of the stove, and shook up the stove to heat the breakfast coffee. When his teeth stopped chattering and he began to get warm he told the old man what had happened.

"Well," Mr. Ben said, "everybody has to meet the fool-killer sooner or later, and you were one of the lucky ones. He wasn't really after you, he just wanted to show you what he could do, but he might be feeling mean next time."

"Yes, sir," Joey said.

"The water's about thirty feet deep where you were, and it's a long walk to shore. You'd better throw empty shells overboard after this."

"I reckon I'd better," Joey said. "I bet my clothes weighed a ton after they got wet."

"It looks to me like you were born to hang," Mr. Ben said, "and I think it would be just as well to let your father find that out in the fullness of time. If we tell him about this caper he'll worry every time you're here. Or maybe he wouldn't even let you come again by yourself."

"Yes, sir," Joey said, considerably chastened by the thought. "I reckon he won't be here until day after tomorrow. You won't tell him, will you, Mr. Ben?"

"No," Mr. Ben said. "After you get warm, now, you ought to put your gun by the stove to dry out and then take it apart and oil it."

"Yes, sir," Joey said, and remembered dropping it with the safety off. The fool-killer had really shown him twice, but he didn't intend to tell Mr. Ben about that. He fell to thinking of that, and of hitting the duck, and the freezing, greedy embrace of water as it closed over his head. It had been quite a day, and now that he was warm and safe and Mr. Ben wasn't going to tell his father, he nodded and drowsed for a while in the chair.

Charley was in the yard the next morning, sitting by the foot of the steps. When Joey went out to welcome him he looked thin, and he was wary; he wagged his tail slightly, in an apologetic way, but kept his distance. It was pretty apparent that he had had a poor time in one way or another, and Joey was outraged. He was generous with the dog biscuits, and while Charley ate them he went in and got his gun.

He decided to go up the north side of the Pond, for there had always been squirrels there before, and he started out across the big field. The dog, which moved a little stiffly, trotted quietly along behind him with his head and tail low and showed little enthusiasm, but when they came to the edge of the woods his head came up and he seemed to feel better; he began to move with something like his usual spirit and was soon out of sight.

Joey couldn't find the first squirrel; there were several round holes in the trunk of the tree and it had apparently gone into one of them. He had brought a dog biscuit along in his pocket and gave it to Charley and they went on. The second squirrel was somewhere in a tremendous beech and very hard to find, for its fur was almost the same color as the bark. Joey moved around and around the tree, searching the branches, until his neck ached from looking up. He was sure it was there, for he could find no hole for it to go into, and after an interminable time and several more circuits he finally spotted it flattened on a limb halfway up the tree.

One shot brought it down and Charley got it; as Joey started to chase him he stopped, raised his head and cocked his ears, dropped the squirrel, and moved off. This was a surprising development; Joey pulled up in mid-stride and looked in the direction that the dog had looked. Sam White was leaning against a tree a few yards off, looking back at him; Joey didn't know how long he had been there, for both he and Charley had been so concentrated on the squirrel that they hadn't noticed him come up.

Joey jumped; he was startled, and then a cold fear took hold of him. He realized at once that it wasn't a chance meeting and that White wasn't hunting; he didn't even have a gun with him. He had a little stick, and as he looked back at Joey he tapped his overalled leg several times with it. His close-set eyes, which had seemed so remote and disinterested when Joey had met him by the well, saw Joey now. The remoteness was still in them, but it was different; the eyes were remote and fixed on him at the same time, and Joey had a fleeting thought of the eyes of the weasels in the rockpile.

The fear that was in him, incoherent and confused, compounded of the things about Sam White that he had heard and seen and thought about, stiffened him for a moment. It seemed to him that everything within him was drawing together, tensing, to burst explosively and throw him into action and flight.

White reached into his pocket, brought out three twenty-gauge shells, and held them in his open hand for Joey to see before dropping them on the ground. "I found these here where you had been sittin'," he said. "Don't nobody shoot a little gun like this around here but you. I don't aim to have young-uns spyin' on me." He licked his lips. "Don't go try to run," he said.

"No, sir," Joey whispered, and swallowed; the sound of it was loud in his ears.

He couldn't run now; all volition went out of him, his skin crawled as though evil things were moving about over it, and he was fast to the ground. White, in no hurry, continued to look at him and seemed to be considering. He raised one hand to his narrow chin, and Joey could see the black rims of his nails. Somehow this seemed to be worse than anything else about him.

Tension wound itself tighter in Joey, and still White remained where he was; the stick tapped his leg again. An observer might have thought that he was savoring the boy's fear and prolonging it; actually he was trying to decide what to do. He was a man of precarious balance; he had contrived to bring this meeting about and in his first blind rage had intended to beat the boy and perhaps hurt him badly, but now that the boy was in front of him he was having some second thoughts. The quickness with which the teacher had been removed indicated that the affair had got out of the neighborhood; there was more power behind the move than he could cope with, and he had had time to think about it and begin to fear it. The fear of this power filled him with rage and frustration, but it also brought a strengthening conviction that things would go very hard with him if he defied it. He was approaching that dangerous point at which he was so keyed up that a spasm of the nerves was just as liable to send him one way as the other, when there was a rustle in the leaves loud enough to break into the intense concentration of both of them. Sharbee came up.

"Good day to y'all," Sharbee said in his soft voice and stopped a few feet away. He had an old, single-barreled gun with him and held it easily; he smiled at Joey and then looked at White with his odd, amber eyes and didn't smile at all. "I heard the dog, so I reckon I come along and see what luck y'all have."

Joey had never been so glad to see anybody; a feeling of relief washed over him that was almost painful in its intensity. Sharbee was shorter than White, and slighter, but he seemed much bigger at the moment. Although he stood easily he seemed, somehow, with his air of a wild creature, to be ready for instant action. He was formidable.

White had been standing motionless through all this, and and now he moved. He raised one hand, took off his old battered hat, and wiped his forehead with the back of the hand. He closed his eyes as he did it and an expression flitted across his face that seemed, strangely enough, to be one of relief. He put his hat on again and opened his eyes. "Hi, Sharbee," he said, and they could hear him let out his breath. "I heard the shot and came along to see what happened too."

"Yes, sir," Sharbee said.

White stood for a moment longer and looked around. "I ain't huntin' today," he said. "I'm lookin' for a good sassafras tree. I reckon I better get along."

He moved off. When he finally disappeared Joey suddenly sat down in the leaves; all the strength had gone out of his legs, and there was a horrible emptiness in his stomach. He tried to speak and couldn't; he choked up and tears came to his eyes. Sharbee moved closer to him and stood by.

"I walks along a way with you," he said softly, "but don't you worry no more. He glad he didn't; he be all right now."

Joey finally regained his self-control, rubbed the tears out of his eyes, and got himself to his feet. "I was so scared," he said shakily. "I'm sorry I was so scared. I sure thank you . . ." He had never heard anyone call a black man "Mister," and he hesitated for a moment. "I sure thank you, Mr. Sharbee."

"Yes, sir," Sharbee said. "You is real welcome."

Joey smiled at him; the black tide of fear was ebbing fast, and he felt like himself now. He got his gun, which had been leaning against the beech, and they started to walk.

"I sure am glad you came along," he said.

"Yes, sir," Sharbee said. "I reckon I didn't rightly just come along."

"You didn't? How were you there?"

"Well, sir," Sharbee began, and looked a little embarrassed. He walked along a few steps, looking at the ground, and then decided to go on with it. "Well, sir, I reckon it was the coon. I know how you liked him, and I was right glad you didn't bring me the cash money. Did you do it, did I have the cash money in my hand, I reckon I might have give him up. I thank you for that. I got to studyin' on it, and the only way I see I could thank you enough was to watch you and see don't nothin' happen."

Joey stared at him.

"Yes, sir," he went on, "I knows what goes on in the woods. I always knows. I don't rightly like to mess in with folks, but it might have been a right bad thing."

Joey was much moved by this revelation; he didn't know what to say. He stood looking at the man who had saved him from a beating or worse, all because Mr. Ben hadn't let Joey take him the money for the raccoon, and he was at once ashamed and extremely grateful to both of them.

Sharbee stopped. "I reckon I turn off here," he said. "Like I say, you be all right now."

"Mr. Sharbee," Joey said. "Mr. Sharbee . . ." Words failed him; he put out his hand, and Sharbee took it. They shook hands quickly, and Joey had the impression of a hand hard and strong but light, delicate, and wild as the raccoon's hand on his ear; the amber eyes looked deep into his own, and then Sharbee was moving off easily through the woods, with the air of a wild creature about him, as though retreating to a place of safe concealment again.

CHAPTER ELEVEN

Joey didn't go anywhere the next morning; his father was due, and Mr. Ben thought that he might appear sometime before lunch. They didn't get up very early, and as they ate breakfast Joey started several times to tell the old man about White and Sharbee, but finally decided not to. He hadn't mentioned it the afternoon before when he had come home, for he had an implicit belief in Sharbee's statement that White would never bother him again and he was afraid that Mr. Ben would be so enraged that he would get his shotgun out and go looking for the other man. He shrank from the trouble it would cause, or that he thought it would cause. For the first time in his life he had known real fear; he had dreamed about it in the night, and now he wanted to forget about it. It was already receding, being pushed into the background by his mind's protective devices, and it didn't seem nearly as frightening in the light of the new day.

After breakfast he got out the turkey call and practiced with it for nearly an hour, but the proper sound still eluded him. He finally put the call away and wandered out onto the back porch. Charley was there, looking better than he had looked the day before, but he was still wary; Joey put dog biscuits on the ground until he couldn't eat any more.

It was nearly eleven o'clock when his father drove up. He had Bud with him, and there was a big black and white setter in the back seat. Charley took one look at the entourage and, as the setter made hostile noises at him from the car, he turned with dignity and trotted around the corner of the house. Joey ran down to the car; he was surprisingly glad to see them. Bud's freckled face was split by a wide grin, and Joe Moncrief eased his long length out of the Model T and took Joey by the shoulders.

"You're looking fine, boy," he said. "I'm glad to see you all in one piece. Your mother doubted that I would."

"Hi, Dad," Joey said. "Hi, Bud. Dad, are you going to stay? For a couple of days, I mean?"

"We have to go back tonight," Joe Moncrief said.

"Is that your dog? Did you buy him?"

"I borrowed him. I thought we might stumble into a couple of coveys of quail while we were here."

Mr. Ben came out of the house and joined the rest of them.

"When Pitmire got your letter and called me," Joey heard his father say to him, "I got going right away with the State Superintendent. I play poker with him. The report I got back later seemed to indicate that they got going too. Is everything fixed?"

"Everything's fine," Mr. Ben said. "I'll tell you about it later."

They began to talk about duck decoys, and Joey stopped listening to them; he hadn't made very much out of the talk of getting going and the State Superintendent anyhow. Bud had got out of the Model T by that time, and they stood smiling at one another, pleased to be together again.

"We got duck decoys in the back," Bud said. "Your

father thought maybe some ducks would be in here sometime and he could get shots at them. Have you caught that big bass?"

Joey had forgotten the bass, and the question came as somewhat of a shock to him. He looked away and searched around in his mind for a way to evade the subject, and then he remembered Mr. Ben saying something about confession being good for the soul and faced up to it. "I caught him," he said, and Bud's face fell. "But I didn't keep him. I put him back."

Bud's face lighted up again. "You put him back? You crazy or something? Why did you put him back, for gosh sakes?"

"Because I wanted to, gosh hang it! He was my fish; I reckon I could put him back if I felt like it. I bet if you caught him you'd take him home and holler to have him stuffed, and stick him up somewhere to catch dust. . . ." He was quoting his mother now. "To catch dust, and everything."

"Shucks," Bud said. "How big was he?"

"I cut the paddle to show," Joey said. "When we go down to the wharf you can see—"

"Joey!" his father said. "Get the decoys out of the back, and you and Bud take them on the porch."

"Yes, sir."

He opened the rear door and the setter jumped out and licked his face and began to trot around. There were two guns in cases in the back, and he and Bud took them into the house and then came back and stacked the decoys.

"I'd sure like to try and catch him," Bud said, when they were finished with the decoys. "You reckon your father would let us go down and try? What did you catch him on? I'd sure like to try him."

"I caught him on my Kalamazoo frog. Let's go ask him."

They ran into the living room where Joe Moncrief and Mr. Ben were laughing together about something.

"Dad, could we go fishing? Bud wants to try to catch the big bass. Could we, Dad?"

"Didn't you catch him? Even with the frog?"

"Yes, sir," Joey said, and a big smile spread over his face. "Yes, sir, I caught him."

"How's Bud going to catch him, then?"

Joey looked back at his father and writhed inwardly. "I . . . I put him back."

"You put him back?"

"Yes, sir."

"Well, I'll be damned," Joe Moncrief said and glanced at Mr. Ben. Mr. Ben raised his eyebrows and said nothing. "Well, I'll be . . . Why don't you wait until after lunch? We'll have it pretty soon. Late in the afternoon would be better anyhow."

"Yes, sir. I reckon it would."

Before they had lunch Joey showed Bud the Kalamazoo frog, but he didn't think that confession for the soul necessitated telling how he had come by it. He explained how it worked, and they plotted the bass's downfall. Then they were called in to lunch, and while they ate their sandwiches Joe Moncrief asked if they had run into any turkeys. Joey's glance slid toward Mr. Ben; it seemed to him that it was Mr. Ben's turn for a confession.

Mr. Ben's mouth was full of sandwich; he looked around the table, swallowed, and grinned. "Well," he said, "in a way."

"In a way?" Joe Moncrief asked.

"Let's say in a manner of speaking," Mr. Ben said and launched into the story. While Joe Moncrief sat back in his chair and Bud listened with rapt attention, eyes round and mouth half open, he described with gestures their cold trip through the swirling mist, their bafflement, and their defeat.

"Gentlemen, sir," he finished up, "that varmint just disappeared, and I'd already said grace over him and eaten twice my share and was mopping up the gravy."

"That's what comes from eating too much," Joe Moncrief said, after he had finished laughing. "But maybe you'd already taken a spoonful of bicarbonate to help digest him."

"I was going to take it when we got back," Mr. Ben said.

"I had another shot, Dad," Joey said, and told about the turkey Charley had sent his way. "And then I forgot to push the safety off."

"Everybody I know has got buck fever at his first turkey," Joe Moncrief said. "I'm sure you'll do better next time. I'm going to take the setter out for a while this afternoon. Do you two want to go? It's about time you got broken in on wing shooting."

Joey looked at Bud. The prospect was an interesting one, but he felt that Bud should decide; he owed Bud a chance at the bass.

Bud, being the perfect guest, looked from one of them to the other. "You say," he said finally.

"Can we do both?" Joey asked. "I mean, go with you for a while and then go fishing?"

"I guess so," Joe Moncrief said. "We don't want to be too late starting back, though. Go with me until about four, and then you can have half an hour to fish. How's that?"

They both agreed to this with enthusiasm, and went off to put Bud's gun together. Recalling Bud's feeling about squirrel shooting, Joey asked him whether he really wanted to go after quail.

"I don't mind shooting birds," Bud said. "I don't feel the same way about them. They're like chickens. You reckon we can hit a quail?"

"I hit a duck," Joey said, "and when I went to get him I fell overboard. I sure was scared." He told Bud about the water closing over his head and hanging on to the gunwale.

"Great day!" Bud said. "Wasn't it cold?"

"I like to froze. Don't tell my father about it, either. Mr. Ben said he wouldn't tell him. He said the fool-killer was teaching me not to drop shells in the boat. I bet I won't do it again."

The setter began to bark in the yard, and they both went to the window. There was a four-wheeled wagon there, unpainted and in the last stages of dilapidation; two oxen were hitched to it with a remarkable set of harness contrived of rope, baling wire, and old pieces of leather, and an old, grayhaired black man was just pulling them to a stop. He was sitting on a plank laid across the sides; one of his hands was bandaged in materials of various colors, as though every old scrap around the house has been utilized. The boys went through the living room and the kitchen to get a closer look at such a curiosity; Joey's father and Mr. Ben were already in the yard, and the man got down, took off his battered hat, and bowed to them.

"Hello, Eph," Mr. Ben said. "I guess you've come for the three dollars I owe you."

"Yassuh, I was passin' by, so I think I jus' come in." He bowed to Joe Moncrief and then to the two boys again. "Gentlemens, good day to y'all."

"Good day to you, Uncle," Joe Moncrief said. "What happened to your hand?"

Eph began to chuckle. "Well, suh, I done made a mistake. Yestiddy, I reckon. Yassuh, yestiddy. I see somethin' run in a hollow log and it seem like a rabbit, so I reckon I get he out. I reach my hand in and he bite me."

"A rabbit bit you?"

Eph chuckled. "Yassuh, he bite my finger. I reckon I done put my finger in he mouth, so I reach in the log again and he bite another finger, and before I get it out he bite my thumb too. Whooee!" he said. He held his bandaged hand up and shuffled comically about in a pantomime of surprise and consternation. "I bleed all over that log. I reckon I have that rabbit in the pot, I ain't ever hear of a rabbit bitin' a man, so I reach in again and he bite all the fingers I got left. Then I got me a stick and poke it in yonder and he come out. Lawd, Lawd, that rabbit, he a mink, and he come out right at me and I get out of he way quick." He jumped to one side to demonstrate, and then slapped his thigh with his good hand and cackled with laughter. They all laughed with him; the two oxen swung their heads and regarded the group solemnly until the laughter died away.

"So you didn't eat him," Mr. Ben said.

"No, suh, he like to eat me."

"I don't think he'd have tasted very good anyhow," Mr. Ben said. "I'll get your money for you, Eph."

He went into the house, and the two boys walked over to look at the wagon. There was a dead turkey lying in the back of it, a wild turkey, dark and beautiful even in death. They stared at it, fascinated; Joey extended one hand and stroked it, and then turned toward his father. "Dad! Dad! He's got a wild turkey in here!"

Joe Moncrief walked over and looked into the wagon. "He has, sure enough," he said and turned to Eph. "Where are you taking the turkey, Uncle?"

"I roost he last night and shoot he this mawnin'," Eph said. "I reckon I take he to Mr. Pitmire, and trade he for a leg of ham meat."

"Dad!" Joey said. "Dad!"

"Wait a minute, now," Joe Moncrief said. "I've got the same idea. I'll take him off your hands," he said Eph. "I'll give you a piece of paper to Mr. Pitmire that will tell him to give you the biggest ham in the place and charge it to me. How about that?"

"Yas, *suh!*" Eph said, and his face was split by a wide grin. "The biggest leg of ham meat in the store be right smart ham meat." He came over and picked up the turkey by the legs; Joey, dancing about with impatience, received it and bore it up to the porch. While he and Bud were admiring it and hunting for a piece of string with which to hang it up, Joe Moncrief went into the house to write the note. He and Mr. Ben came out together and gave Eph the money and the note, and the old man climbed back onto the wagon, got the oxen into motion, turned them around, and still bowing and taking off his hat he drove around the corner of the house. They could hear the ungreased axles squealing and creaking all the way down the lane.

"We'll tell your mother we shot it ourselves," Joe Moncrief said, grinning, "and see how long we can fool her. I'll make you a bet it won't be too long."

"I bet it won't either," Joey said, remembering a number of times that his mother had astounded him with feminine insights that had seemed little short of clairvoyant. "I bet it won't be more than two days."

"Maybe one," Joe Moncrief said. "Get your guns, now. We'd better get started."

They admired the turkey again and stroked it and grinned at one another, then got their guns; the three of them, with Joe Moncrief in the middle, went around the house and out into the big field in front. The setter, which had been capering around them, moved out and began to quarter the ground at a gallop. Occasionally he would pause and look at Joe Moncrief, who would direct him off in another direction with a waved hand.

The knee-high dried brown grass was a little rosy in the long rays of the afternoon sun, and the setter was pretty moving through it; Joey had seldom felt happier. Although they would soon be going home, away from the Pond, they had a turkey to take with them, he had made peace with Bud, and it was exciting to be going after quail. He scarcely felt the ground beneath his feet, and when the setter slowed down, crept a few feet, and stiffened into a point with its tail high, he ceased to feel it at all.

"Ah!" Joe Moncrief said. "Remember your safeties, now."

Still in line, they reached the setter; he rolled an eye at them, and they were past him. Joey, scarcely breathing, brought his gun to the ready. They took two more steps; there was a roar and the air was full of birds. Few men ever become hardened and blasé to a covey rise, and it was Joey's first one. Although he knew what was going to happen, it was a big covey and the roar of it, the hurtling birds that seemed to fill up every square foot about him, shook him up. His gun bucked twice against his shoulder but nothing happened; not a bird dropped, and then, seemingly almost at once, they were far out of range. Joey was astounded; he stood for a moment with his mouth open and then looked at his father, who was lowering his gun.

"Get one?" Joe Moncrief asked.

Joey shook his head. "No, sir. I don't see how I missed them all."

"You didn't pick one out?"

"No, sir. They were so thick—"

The setter came in with a bird, Joe Moncrief took it, and

the dog went out again. "Got a double," Joe Moncrief said. "Look, there's a lot of air around each one of them. You pick one out next time." He turned to Bud, but Bud just shook his head; he had done the same thing. The setter came in again, Joe Moncrief pocketed the bird, and said, "Now you can take turns on the singles."

They went on. The setter pointed again presently, and Joe Moncrief sent Bud in to take the shot. It was a difficult one; the bird went off to the left, and Bud shot behind it both times and missed it. On the next point it was Joey's turn. He was luckier; the bird went straight away, and although he shot too quickly the first time and was under the bird he took more time on the second shot and hit it squarely. The setter fetched it, and Joey, immensely proud of himself, stood and grinned at his father.

"That's my boy," Joe Moncrief said, and solemnly shook hands with him. "Now you're a quail hunter, but if you still want to fish you'd better take off."

Joey was burning to stay with the quail, but Bud looked at him with such entreaty that he couldn't refuse. "I reckon we'll go fishing," he said, and his father nodded understandingly. "Next time you go . . ."

"Trot along," Joe Moncrief said, "and pack up your gear if you beat me back."

Bud's eyes bugged out when Joey showed him the cuts he had made on the paddle. "Great day!" he whispered. "Great day in the morning. It hardly seems like there could be a bass as big as that. Oh, Joey, you reckon he'll bite on it again?"

There was so much longing in his face, such an anguish of hope and yearning, that Joey's heart went out to him; he was glad now that he had put the bass back. Bud wanted the bass even more than he had wanted it; Bud was more of a fisherman than he was, and would be all his life. "I sure hope so," he said, like an older boy, and took charge of things. "Don't even make any noise getting in the boat."

Bud nodded solemnly; he seemed almost like a boy in a dream, and had already yielded the direction of the affair to his friend. They crept into the bateau like two Indians making an escape from under the guns of enemies by night. After they had shoved off Bud turned and grinned shyly at Joey. "I'm scared," he whispered.

Joey smiled back at him, and after they had got out a little way stopped paddling. "Try it now," he whispered. "Before we get there. Jerk it a little."

Bud made several casts. The first time he jerked the rod tip too quickly, but after several casts he settled down and everything was fine. The bateau moved over the dark water like someone on tiptoe, with hardly a ripple; the cypresses slid closer. Bud half rose once, and Joey whispered, "Not yet."

They were nearly under the tip of the longest limb when Joey breathed, "Now."

Bud stood up slowly, brought the rod back, swung it forward, and sent the frog on its way. It hit the water at the exact spot where the bass had broken on their first day, and before Bud could move it, the monster came up again in a slashing rise and took it down. Bud struck him, the rod arced to a semicircle, and the bass came up again and ran over the surface for five yards on his tail, wildly throwing spray that glittered like diamonds in a path of sunlight slanting through the trees.

This time the bass didn't go to the bottom and bore down and sulk; he fought all the way, shattering the water until his strength was gone and he was brought in and Joey netted him. When he was in the live box, filling it, the two boys sat and stared at him almost in awe. Bud was shaking and his breathing was as irregular as though he had run a hard race; presently he looked up at Joey and smiled.

"Great balls of fire," he said and gave a vast sigh. "We caught him again." He was still holding the rod; he looked at the bass for a long moment, put the rod down, and leaned over and picked up the net. He stood up again and started to edge the net into the live box.

"Bud?" Joey said. "Bud, what are you going to do?"

"I reckon I'll put him back in too."

"You're not going to keep him?" Joey asked, unbelievingly. "You mean you're not going to keep him?"

Bud shook his head and paused with the net. "I reckon I just don't want to kill him. You don't care, do you, Joey? You put him back. If you'll give me that frog," he said, "I could hang that up in my room instead."

Joey looked at him, recalling the Sears catalogue and his maneuverings with it and how he had felt when he threw the bass back himself. All that was gone now; he had made it up; he was very glad that Bud had caught the fish and fixed everything and was going to put it back. "Okay," he said.

Bud made a scoop and dumped the bass over the side. As before, it lay in the water a moment while they both looked at it and then swam slowly away.

"Thank you, Joey," Bud said. "I reckon I'll never catch such a good fish ever again."

"You're sure welcome," Joey said. "I reckon I won't either." He picked up the paddle, and as he did so the duck that he had hit two days ago and forgotten in the press of events, which had been hiding with its broken wing among the cypresses, grew too nervous to stay still any longer and came out beating the water with its good wing and kicking with its feet. It passed them splashing water wildly in its erratic course, and Joey, quickly exchanging the paddle for his gun, shot it. It was a wood duck drake, the most beautiful duck on the continent.

They climbed the hill, Joey carrying the duck and Bud carrying the paddle with the cuts on it. Near the house they met Joe Moncrief, just getting in from his quail shooting.

"Where's the fish?" he asked.

"Bud caught it, Dad," Joey said. "But he put it back in too."

Joe Moncrief looked from one of them to the other and seemed a little puzzled. "I'll be damned again," he said and shook his head. "A man learns something new every day."

It was growing dark when they all went out to get into the Model T. The turkey, the duck, an assortment of squirrels, and the quail and Joey's pile of gear were put on the floor in the back, the setter climbed into the rear seat and curled himself up, and Joey shook hands with Mr. Ben. It seemed that he had been there a long time; a lot of things had happened to him, and it was a sort of wrench to be leaving the old man.

"I sure thank you, Mr. Ben," he said. "We had a good time, didn't we?"

"I never had better company," the old man said. "It brought back a little of my long-departed youth to have you around. Come again when you can."

"Yes, sir. Maybe I can come Christmas. Don't kill too many squirrel nests, Mr. Ben."

"I'll go easy on them," Mr. Ben said. "Good-by."

"I'll be down for a couple of days next week," Joe Moncrief said. "I'll see you then."

He cranked the Model T, they all waved, and drove out of the yard. They turned through the gate, coasted down the hill, and crossed the spillway with the headlights making an illuminated tunnel through the trees. As they made the short turn to start up the next hill the lights picked up an animal crossing the road, and Joe Moncrief braked the car. It was a bobcat, stumpy-tailed, big-footed. It turned its head toward them, its eyes glowed fiery and green in the lights, and then with a lithe bound it was gone. With its pale fur and swift, fluid movement it had almost seemed like a ghost. The Model T had stopped; Joe Moncrief reversed and swung the lights into the woods, but they didn't see it again.

"Dad!" Joey exclaimed. "Dad, it was a wildcat!"

"It sure was."

"I didn't know there were any real wildcats here."

"There are probably several of them," Joe Moncrief said, "but I doubt you'll ever see one again."

CHAPTER TWELVE

The turkey was eaten with exclamations of pleasure over its inimitable flavor. If Joey's mother entertained doubts as to who had shot it she contented herself with a small and secret smile; and Joey went back to school. His teachers wondered occasionally, when they had time, what he was daydreaming about and gave him a little leeway, for they all liked the boy. He gave Bud the Kalamazoo frog and the pair of them hung it on the wall in Bud's bedroom, and they were in and out of one another's houses again. They played desperate and argumentative sandlot football and made forays in the evenings after dinner with other members of their gang to round out their collection of barrels for the Christmas bonfire, for there wasn't much time left; the holidays were approaching with disconcerting speed.

In the midst of these comings and goings Joey was at first as often absent-minded at home as he was at school; he was back in the somber pine thicket with the rabbits popping up in front of him or paddling silently as a shadow over the dark swamp water among the cypresses. He was watching the weasels in the rockpile again, or the swift dash of the Cooper's hawk, hearing the barred owl as the stars brightened in the night sky, or standing in the sunny quiet of the winter-bare woods watching and listening for something that as yet he couldn't define or imagine but that was in reality a realization of his place and purpose in the world around him. As he felt isolated from the grown-up world and the reasons for grown-up actions, he felt more an observer than a participant in this world and its mysterious life and wanted to be more a part of it.

Anyone who could have looked in on these reveries would have been struck by the fact that he didn't shoot anything in them. He didn't realize this himself; possibly he would have sooner or later if the approach of Christmas hadn't engaged him more as the days followed one another. His parents were a little put off by his desire to get back to the Pond; it apparently interested him more than Christmas did and this didn't seem altogether normal to them. He had talked several times to his father and mother about going to the Pond during vacation, but so far they hadn't given him an answer; they had put him off by asking whether it wouldn't be too cold, or implying rather than saying outright that they thought he was turning into a sort of hermit and should stay home and play with his friends for a change or that they would like him home with them this time.

"Why, for gosh sake?" he asked. "After Christmas vacation I'll be home with you all the time. There aren't any more vacations, and I can't get to go. Please, Mom."

"We'll have to see," was all his mother would say.

"Mom! I'd rather go than hang around and play a lot of dumb football and stuff. I've *got* to go, Mom."

"We'll have to see, Joey. I'm sorry I can't be more definite, Joey."

"But, Mom, I promised to bring Horace some books, and everything." He had told her about Horace.

"You could mail him a few today, and take him some more if you go down. It's nice of you to think of him."

"Yes, ma'am. He can't go anywhere. And, Mom?"

"Yes, Joey?"

"Mom, there's a man there named Sharbee. I'd like to take him a present, Mom."

"Who is he, Joey? I don't recall you've mentioned him before."

"He has a pet coon," Joey said impenetrably. "Mr. Ben took me to see him."

She looked at him, realizing that there was more than was apparent to her, but he avoided her eye and she knew she would get little more out of him. "Is he nice?" she asked.

"He's a black man, Mom. He lives in the woods, and he's real nice. He's good, Mom, and awful poor."

"I'm sure he's good, honey, if you say so," she said, and wanted to put her arms around him. He seemed so young and vulnerable and out of reach; she longed to help him over all the rough spots she could but knew that, barring accidents that would enable her to look into his life, she wouldn't be able to. "Did he help you in some way?"

"Yes'm," Joey said. "Mom, I . . ."

His voice died away; he wasn't going to talk about it. "Well," she said brightly, "how about a warm sweater like the one we gave to Mr. Ben?"

"That would be okay."

"I have to go downtown this afternoon, and I'll try and get it then. How big is he, Joey?"

"He's a little bigger than I am. Mom, it would be nice if I could take it to him. I don't think he'll get any Christmas presents, and if I could take it to his house—"

"Please, not now, Joey. You'd better go find the books

you want to send Horace and we'll wrap them up so that I can mail them when I go out."

"Yes'm," he said. He stood looking at her for a moment beseechingly, and then turned and went upstairs.

She went into the kitchen, where Mary had the three Christmas fruit cakes on the table and was pouring a little whisky over them.

"I get them out and they seem a little dry," she said and looked up. "Why you look sad? Ain't nothin' happened, has it?"

"I was thinking about Joey," Mrs. Moncrief said. "He wants to go back to the Pond, and I feel he's so far away down there, and a lot of the time there's no one to watch out for him."

"Mens is always far 'way, one way or 'nother."

"He wants to get a present for a black man who lives in a little house in the woods. Something must have happened that he's grateful for, and I wish I knew what it was."

"That Mr. Ben, he know that man, I reckon."

"Yes, Mr. Ben took him there."

"That man be all right then, Mr. Ben take him there. Yes, ma'am. Maybe Mr. Joey get in a tight, and that man help him get out. He got to find out things, Miz Moncrief, but he be all right. He be all right with Mr. Ben and that man. Yes, ma'am, he lucky. Last place I work, the butler take the boy to a camp meetin', and they was all rollin' around on the floor and callin' on Jesus. Scared that boy good, if it didn't do nothin' else. Lawd, Lawd!" She shook her head and then began to laugh.

Mrs. Moncrief had to smile, and began to feel better.

Christmas came, with presents for everybody; the house was decorated with holly, ground pine, and mistletoe that Mr. Ben had sent up in a big box, and the tree in the living room glowed with fragile ornaments. There was a good deal of coming and going among the adults, eggnog and fruit cake, candy and cookies; Joey got ten dollars in cash, a .22-caliber repeating rifle, an assortment of clothing and outdoor gear, several books, and other miscellaneous objects. The hand of his father was apparent in the outdoor gear and the rifle, and he showed Joey how to operate it.

"Seemed about time to start in with a rifle to shoot squirrels," he said. "A shotgun's too easy. Now that you're a quail hunter, maybe you'd begun to feel that yourself."

"Yes, sir," Joey said. He was, as a matter of fact, working around in his own way to the same conclusion. "It sure is a swell gun, Dad." He aimed it at a stag in a picture on the wall, said "Pow!" under his breath, and put the rifle down and caressed it. "You reckon it's good for turkeys, too?"

"It has a lot more range than a shotgun, that's for sure. There are a couple boxes of hollow-point long rifle shells that ought to be just the ticket if you get within reach of a roosted turkey. You'd have to be awful fast to get one out of a blind or running on the ground with it."

"Yes, sir. If I could only go down to the Pond in a couple of days I could try it out."

Joe Moncrief gave him a lopsided grin. "I know what you mean," he said, "but we have a small problem. Not so long ago you were pretty little, and your mother and I had to watch out for you all the time. To me, you're growing up; you've got to learn how to take care of yourself, but your mother is still afraid you'll get in trouble and she won't be there to help you. Mothers are that way, Joey. They have a harder time turning loose."

"Yes, sir," Joey said, and his spirits sank. He felt the gun again, running his hand down the smooth barrel.

"We've talked about it," his father said, "and I'm on your side as much as I *can* be. I can't promise anything, but maybe something will turn up that will help. Don't give up yet."

"No, sir, I won't," Joey said, and his spirits rose a little. All wasn't lost yet, and hope buoyed him up. "I'd sure like to go. Can I go out to the fire for a while?"

"Sure," his father said. "Give my greetings to the chivalry of Hanover Avenue."

"Yes, sir," Joey said, and went upstairs to get his firecrackers. They were an integral part of Christmas, just as they were a part of the Fourth of July in the North. He got them out of his bureau drawer and went down to the corner where two of the stolen barrels were flaming nicely and five or six boys sat around on boxes, talked about their Christmas presents, and fired off an occasional firecracker. Bud showed up in the course of an hour or so, and Joey took him home to show him the rifle. They went to Bud's house to see his presents, returned to the fire, and so the day went by. Nothing to forward the cause of getting to the Pond appeared, but Joey was still hopeful when he crawled into bed; after his mother kissed him good night and turned out the light he was back at the Pond again with his new rifle, stealing silently through the woods or sitting quietly in the bateau waiting for turkeys to roost as the sun set golden behind the intricate tracery of the bare trees.

He awoke next morning acutely aware that there were ten dollars to be spent. He wasn't due to watch the fire until four o'clock the next morning; he had the whole day to spend waiting for the miracle that would open the way to the Pond, and decided to go downtown. He got permission and around ten o'clock visited the fire for a while and then caught a jitney at the corner. The jitneys were a fairly recent phenomenon, mostly Model-T Fords that men drove over a route to the middle of town and back; they took people downtown or brought them home for a nickel, and were closer than either of the two streetcar lines that served Joey's part of Richmond.

Joey rode to the corner of Ninth and Broad Streets, which was in the shopping district; he had a milkshake in a drugstore and strolled west on Broad Street, looking into shop windows and several times going into stores. The streets and stores were full of people; there were all sorts of bargains now that Christmas was over, and although the two five-dollar bills were burning a hole in his pocket he could find nothing that he wanted to buy. The trouble was that his mind wasn't really on buying anything. He was just marking time; he stood about, staring at this and that, going off into periods of absent-minded immobility and getting into everyone's way. People stumbled into him and went off mumbling to themselves, and presently he grew as wearied with them as they did with him and decided to go home. He crossed to the north side of Broad Street, which held the cheaper stores where the black people did their buying, to catch an outbound jitney, and as he stood on the curb waiting for one to come by he suddenly thought he heard a turkey calling. This brought him back to his surroundings as though a bucketful of cold water had been thrown over him. He started and looked around.

The clear, plaintive yelping went on; it had not been inside his head, and every note was perfect. His eyes searched swiftly among the dungaree-clad men moving past him for someone with a call like Mr. Ben's, but he couldn't find anyone; in another moment he had more or less located the sound, and saw an old man leaning against a store front with one hand in his pocket. He had been told many times not to talk to strangers, especially downtown and more especially on the wrong side of Broad Street, but this was an emergency. He went up to the old man, and another yelp or two confirmed the location; the sounds were certainly coming from the pocket.

"Have you a turkey call?" he asked. "Is it yours?"

The black man looked at him. "Yassuh," he said politely, and taking his hand out of his pocket opened it and revealed a small wooden cylinder about four inches long and two inches in diameter with a pencil-sized stick protruding from one end of it. As Joey stared at it, fascinated, the old man pushed the stick down and as he let it come up again a beautiful note fell on the air.

"Great day!" Joey said. "No matter how cold you get, it wouldn't make any difference."

The man suddenly smiled. "Tha's right, tha's right," he said. "You talks like a real turkey hunter." A sudden and wonderful rapport appeared between them. "It ain't like them box calls that don't work when you's a-shiverin' and a-shakin'. Nossuh! It ain't and tha's a fac'."

Joey began to tremble; he had to have it. "Do you want to sell it?" he asked, and held his breath for the answer.

The man looked down at the call and back at Joey again. "Well, suh," he said. "Well, suh." He frowned in thought while Joey almost danced about with longing and impatience. "I have to make me another one, and maybe I don't get it right. I like right well to 'commodate you, but . . ." He shook his head. "I ain't sure."

Joey saw the call getting away from him; it was unbearable, and suddenly he grew quite calm and crafty. He recalled what Sharbee had said about cash money. He reached into his pocket and brought out one of the five-dollar bills and stretched it out between his fingers.

The man looked at it and his eyes opened wider. "Fi' dollars," he breathed. "Fi' dollars." Several other men, seeing Joey holding the bill, stopped and stared. The old man looked around at them and made an abrupt gesture. "Git along!" he said. "Leave me and this gennelman be." The others drifted off, and the old man muttered to himself; Joey, on pins and needles lest the interruption interfere with the impression that the five-dollar bill had obviously made, extended his arm and put the bill into the old man's free hand. His fingers curled around it, and he slowly held out the call. Joey took it; the world was his. He pushed the plunger down gently several times, and the notes came out fine and clear.

"I sure thank you," he said.

"Yassuh," the man said, and fingered the five-dollar bill. "If you didn't talk like a turkey hunter, I reckon I wouldn't done it. You push it easy, and it'll be all right. Not too often, now. Turkeys get scared when it's done too often."

"Yes, sir," Joey said, forgetting himself a little in his euphoria. He thought that he'd better get away from there in case the man changed his mind. "Good-by."

"Yes, suh. Thank you."

They grinned at one another, and Joey quickly turned away. He walked to the next corner and caught a jitney there. Halfway home he couldn't refrain any longer, and pushed the plunger four times in rapid succession; the jitney driver gave a great start and almost ran onto the sidewalk. He righted his Model T with a mighty wrench.

"Great God, boy," he said. "You got a turkey in your pocket? You keep that thing quiet, or we'll be up a tree."

"Yes, sir," Joey said, beamed at him, and kept his hand wrapped lovingly around the call the rest of the way home.

Joe Moncrief was genuinely impressed with the call; he said it was the best one he'd ever seen, and was a little put out that Joey hadn't possessed sufficient presence of mind to get the old man's address so that he could get several more of them.

"I reckon I didn't think of it," Joey said. "I was so scared I wouldn't get this one that I forgot. Maybe we could find him again tomorrow."

"I doubt it," Joe Moncrief said. "It sounds to me like he's from the country somewhere; he didn't know what to do and just stood there working his call and wishing he was home. No city man's going to stand on a corner and do that."

"Yes, sir. Dad, now I've got the call I ought to go down and try it. Maybe we could have another turkey for New Year's Day. Dad?"

"The situation is still obscure," Joe Moncrief said. "Let's hear it again now."

Joey pushed the plunger; the yelping call echoed through the house. Joey's mother had long since given up and gone somewhere else, and Joey and his father hunched over the call, grinning delightedly at one another in pure admiration, like two violinists listening to a Stradivarius. Around nine o'clock Joe Moncrief sat back. "I hope we can get down there together before the season's over," he said. "I think you'd better go to bed now. Four o'clock will be here pretty soon."

"Yes, sir," Joey said. "I sure hope something happens tomorrow."

"I hope so too. Good night."

"Good night, Dad."

He went upstairs, put the call on his bureau where he

could see it first thing in the morning, and finally got himself undressed and into bed. He thought about the call as he grew drowsy; visions of turkeys regaled him, and presently he fell asleep.

His father, yawning and rumpled, shook him awake at four; presently, yawning himself and feeling as though the surrounding world was off a little in the middle distance, he went to the fire. The neighborhood looked different at that hour, empty and closed away, the houses secretive and dark; not a light showed anywhere except the arc light hanging on its pole at the corner. The boy on duty, alone and nodding in the cold, flat illumination of the arc light, had let the fire go down until it was almost out. Joey, shivering in the chill, put a fresh barrel on the embers and woke the other boy up.

"Man, sir," the other boy said, staggering to his feet, "my bed's lonesome for me. I feel like I been sleeping in a grave-yard. So long."

"So long," Joey said, and watched him stumble half awake around the corner and disappear.

Joey sat down on a box; the barrel he had put on caught fire and he edged up closer to it to get warm. The sparks from the burning barrel rose glowing toward the stars, and Joey, half hypnotized and half asleep, watched them in their courses. Time drew out; somnolently he put on another bar-rel, and after an hour or so another boy named Paul Ransom appeared. Joey, as well as most of the other gang members, didn't like him very much; occasionally he got into the sort of mischief that was a little beyond the borders of discretion and so brought them to grown-up notice; but the vigil had been long and lonely and Joey had got bored with it. At that hour he would have been glad to see anybody, and Paul was carry-ing a four-foot length of metal rain gutter.

"Hi!" he said. "What's that for?"

"I got a skyrocket," Paul said, "and this is to set it off in."
He put the rain gutter on the ground; the rocket lay in it,
sleek, quiet, full of wild power that could be awakened by a
spark. They both stared in fascination at it.

"We're not allowed to have rockets," Joey said finally, but
he was already wavering.

"I know that, you goof. I stole it in a store."

They stared at it again, each seeing the hurtling rush of
the thing on a trail of fire, the splendid burst of color in the
sky. They looked at one another, then looked all around.
They were alone, all alone.

"You reckon it will go right?" Joey asked.

"It's got to go right with this gutter."

Joey knew better, but he couldn't help himself; the time
had come to speak up, to withdraw himself from the enterprise and try to talk Paul out of it, but he didn't speak. He
looked at Paul again; they both grinned, and Paul propped
the rain gutter at an angle against a box. He took a burning
stick out of the fire, knelt, and gingerly applied it to the fuse.

The fuse sputtered and caught; sparks raced up it as the
two boys drew together and held their breath. The fire in the
fuse seemed to die, and then there was a fiery roar. The initial
thrust of the rocket tipped the rain gutter, and as they
watched in horrified fascination the rocket took off, roared
across the street, and vanished roaring into the second-floor
window of the house across the street. Glass shattered, the
rocket burst in a wildly dancing shower of red, blue, and
green lights, and the window curtains caught fire. It was a
magnificent and awesome sight.

The two boys vanished as if by magic. Joey, like a hunted
animal, had no thought but to get safely to his lair. He tore in

the front door, slamming it behind him, and galloped thunderously up the stairs. He had no sooner reached his room than his father dashed in from the hall with his hair standing up and his revolver in one hand. He pulled up at the sight of Joey, stared for a moment, and relaxed.

"What the hell . . . ! What is it? Joey?"

Joey found his voice. "Dad?" he quavered. He wished the floor would open up and swallow him.

"Why did you come in here like a troop of cavalry at five o'clock in the morning, scaring us half to death? *What* is it?"

Mrs. Moncrief's head appeared around the doorframe; her eyes were wide with fright. Joey looked at her and quickly looked away.

"Joey?" his father said sternly.

"Dad! Paul had a rocket, and it went in Murtrie's window."

"A rocket!"

"Oh, Joey!" his mother said.

"Go back to bed, Irene," Joe Moncrief said. "I'll take care of this." Her head disappeared, and just as Joe Moncrief started to speak again there was a great uproar of clanging bells and thundering hooves in the street. They ran to the window; the fire engine was going by, and the driver was already beginning to pull up the big horses, leaning back against the reins.

Joe Moncrief turned from the window and laid a long, considering look on his son. "Well," he said, after a moment, "you sure managed to create a little excitement to start off the day. Was there anyone there but you and Paul?"

"No, sir," Joey answered.

"I see." He stood for a long moment with his brow creased in thought. "I think you'd better be out of town for a few days. Get your gear together, and I'll take you down to catch the early train. I'll call Ed Pitmire later." He turned and went out the door, then stuck his head back in. "Don't forget the turkey call," he said, and disappeared once more.

The fire engine went by again as Joey finished packing; the horses were walking this time and the bells were silent. The blaze in the curtains had been quenched, and the engine was returning to the firehouse. There were lights up and down the block, people were moving about, and Joey remembered Sharbee's present and five more books for Horace at the last moment before he and his father went out the back door.

CHAPTER THIRTEEN

Mr. Ben came out of the kitchen when they drove up, looking considerably surprised. He had been shaving; he held his straight-edge razor in one hand, and his face was still half covered with lather.

"Got an escaped convict here for you," Ed Pitmire shouted, as he killed the engine. "A fugitive from the law. You reckon you can hide him for a while?"

Joey sat grinning delightedly at Mr. Ben as he came down the steps and walked over to the car, and he grinned back. "What's the charge?" he asked.

"Burnin' half the town down," Pitmire said. "Anyhow, that's the way I heard it. Richmond's in ruins, or it would be if they left him there. General Sherman couldn't done better. I'll help you unpack," he said to Joey and climbed out. Joey climbed out the other side and ran around to shake hands with Mr. Ben.

"I'm glad to see you back," Mr. Ben said. "What's all this about?"

"There was a little fire," Joey said. "I'll tell you about it when I carry my stuff in. I'm sure glad to be here, Mr. Ben." He began to move back and forth between the car and the

porch, carrying his gear and the food that he had bought at
Pitmire's store; Pitmire helped him, and when the back of the
Model T was empty, cranked the engine and got behind the
wheel.

"I've still got coffee, Ed," Mr. Ben said.

"Can't wait," Pitmire said. "Liza got to get to Williamsburg and buy a hat. She's goin' to a christenin'." He waved,
turned the Model T, and as usual narrowly missed carrying
the end of the house away. When the echoes of his rattling
charge down the hill had died away they sat down on the steps
for a moment.

"Now, then," Mr. Ben said. "Before I finish this shave,
tell me about the fire."

Joey told him about the rocket and the narrow escape he
had from staying home. "The fire engine came, and everything," he ended up, "and my dad took me to the depot and
we had to wait for the train."

"Clearly the hand of Providence was in it," Mr. Ben said.
"I told you that you were born to hang. Well, I'd better get to
my shaving."

He went into the kitchen, and Joey began to carry the
things inside. As he walked back and forth through the house
he smiled with pleasure at being there again, and breathed
deeply of its remembered smell of woodsmoke and gun oil,
kerosene, and the mixed and ghostly masculine emanations
of tobacco and damp woolen clothing hung over the stove to
dry. It was faintly sour, like dry oak leaves dampened by rain—
an outdoor, wonderful smell without face powder or cologne
or anything scrubbed or female in it, dusty and casual, and
when he had laid out his clothes and gear he took the turkey
call into the living room. He peeped around the doorframe,
saw Mr. Ben just drying his face, and pushed the plunger

down twice. The old man whirled around and walked quickly into the living room. "Gentlemen, sir," he said, "that's it."

Joey gave it to him to look at, and got the new rifle to show him. The old man tried the call several times, nodded his head in appreciation, and examined the rifle; as they talked Joey walked to the back window and looked out. Charley was in the yard, sitting in his usual place near the bottom of the steps, with his eyes on the back door.

"Charley's here," Joey exclaimed. "Excuse me, Mr. Ben." He went out onto the back porch and greeted his friend; the dog flattened his ears and wagged his tail. He was looking a bit better, and as Joey went to the biscuit can he came a step or two closer to the steps. Joey sat on the bottom step with a biscuit and waited for him, and after sitting with his head cocked for a long moment, assaying the situation, the dog got up, moved within reach, and, stretching out his neck, daintily took the biscuit and ate it there without moving off. He ate three biscuits, standing there. This was much better than last time, but when Joey moved a little, thinking to pat his head, he moved off out of reach but with an expression that was almost apologetic; he seemed to imply that he wanted Joey to pat him and was sorry, but he wasn't quite ready to allow it yet. All this indicated progress and Joey was pleased with it; it seemed to him that it showed more than cupboard love, that the dog wanted to be friendly and trusting with him. "You wait here," he said, and went into the house and changed his clothes and got his rifle. He saw Sharbee's package and decided to take it to the little house while he was hunting, and perhaps see the raccoon again. He told Mr. Ben where he was going and set out.

After a bit it occurred to him that he hadn't targeted the rifle yet. He hadn't even shot it; there hadn't been time. He found a fairly open place in the woods and hacked a blaze on a pine tree with his belt knife, leaving four square inches or so of bark in the center as a bull's eye, and shot at it a few times. This showed him how to line up the sights and where to hold. Charley came in to see what he was shooting at and went out again; presently he began to bay, but when Joey got to the place he found that the squirrel was in a pine tree, and he couldn't see it.

There was no answer when he reached Sharbee's cabin and knocked on the weathered door; Sharbee wasn't home. He searched around in his pockets, found the stub of a pencil, and wrote, "Merry Christmas from Joey Moncrief" on the wrapping paper and propped the package against the door. He thought of waiting for a while, for he wanted very much to play with the raccoon again, but the desire to try the new rifle on game was too strong and he turned toward the Pond. He had lost track of Charley and walked for a long way before he heard the dog again. This time the squirrel was in a big oak, and after Joey located it he was soon made aware of the great difference between spraying the immediate vicinity of the quarry with several ounces of shot and hitting it with a single bullet. After making the bark fly several times but missing the squirrel, he began to grow impatient with the rifle and wish he had brought the shotgun instead. When the squirrel jumped up, ran about the tree (during which time he was powerless to hit it), and finally popped into a hole he was ready to give up the rifle forever.

He left the tree disgruntled and mumbling to himself, greatly disappointed with his new weapon. He almost turned back to exchange it, but he was near the head of the Pond by this time; it was a long way to the house and he decided not to go. After walking for a time he sat down in the leaves to wait for Charley's bay, for he didn't know where the dog was and thought he might have been moving away from him. He had leaned the rifle against a nearby tree, and as he sat looking at it he began to like it all over again. It was beautifully made for its work, clean-lined and efficient, and he recalled his father saying that it was time he began shooting squirrels with a rifle, that a shotgun was too easy. It *was* pretty easy, he admitted to himself; there certainly had been infinitely more satisfaction in hitting the quail or the duck or a bounding rabbit in the pine thicket. They had been difficult, moving swiftly and demanding a coordination as swift and difficult, and when he had almost instantaneously solved such a problem as they presented it was something to be proud of. There was no such problem about hitting a motionless squirrel with a scatter gun, and he had to admit that hitting them that way was not nearly so much fun as it had been at first, when it was a novelty.

As he sat there turning these things over in his mind he made the adjustment of moving from the status of pot hunter to the status of sportsman, who does things the hard way in a sort of game with himself and gives the quarry as much chance as he can. He didn't do it by a logical progression of thought or all at once, for he was pretty young, but he was well on the way. When he heard the dog's rolling bay in the distance, he picked up the rifle with new enthusiasm; when he reached the tree, found the squirrel, picked the best position, shot with care, and brought the squirrel down with one shot, he was proud of himself. He felt that he was close to joining the select company of Daniel Boone and the other frontiersmen who had shot the long rifle and either "barked" their squirrels or shot them only in the head. He knew that it would take a lot of practice to do that, but he intended to manage it.

He took the squirrel from Charley, who went off at once, and it seemed to him that he had hardly put it into his game pocket before a great snarling suddenly arose in the direction of the Pond. It was obviously a fight and he ran toward it, hurried on his way by a loud, chilling scream of rage that made the hair stir on his head and certainly hadn't come from Charley. As he approached the shore he saw the dog and some large, dark creature that he couldn't immediately identify rolling about wildly in desperate battle. They were so entangled, and their movements so swift, that his eyes could scarcely follow them; their darting heads and the white flash of sharp teeth blurred on his sight, and their snarling frightened him. In an instant when they separated Joey saw that the other animal was the otter, and then they leaped together again and rolled off the shore into the water.

It was soon apparent to Joey, staring at the two fighting animals and the flying water, that Charley was now at a serious disadvantage. The otter was more at home in the water than he was on land. He appeared and vanished, he struck from any direction, and now that he was in his element he showed no inclination to break off the fight and escape. The distance between the fighters and the shore began to widen, and Joey suddenly realized that the otter intended to get the dog out of his depth and drown him.

"Charley!" he screamed. "Charley!"

The dog was too engaged to hear him, but turned his head toward shore and tried to leap toward it; the otter rolled and vanished, struck from below, and pulled him under. His head emerged again; his eyes were wild and he was choking, but he was pulled under the second time. Joey didn't have time to think, but he knew that the dog he wanted to love him, that had tried to apologize for not loving him sooner, was in terrible trouble. He jumped into the water. It came almost to his armpits and the bottom was soft and oozy, and when he reached them and as the otter rolled to the surface again he swung the rifle and hit it across the back with the barrel. It turned, snarling, stared at him for an instant with burning eyes, and sank away. Charley came up again, desperately flailing at the water; Joey grabbed him by the collar and half swam and half walked ashore.

He was trembling and felt as though he had run for miles; the cold of his soaked clothing bit into him. Charley, who had lain for a moment as though dead, swayed to his feet and, with head and tail hanging, coughed up water. When he was through he stood looking at Joey for a moment and then moved shakily over and licked the hand that Joey extended to pat him.

The loyalties of boyhood are blind and unthinking and complete in their season, and Joey's loyalty to Charley was as blind as most. It had had a confused and intricate beginning, compounded of the excitement over his first killing of game and the feeling of guilt about killing and violence impressed upon him by his mother; he had turned to the dog, which had started it all, because the confusion of feelings made him lonely. He had wanted the dog's affection as a support, a kind of vote of confidence, and the dog had been unable to give it. The reason why the dog had been unable to give it had enlisted Joey's sympathy, made him more determined to win its reluctant affection, and bound him more tightly to it.

He didn't ask himself how the fight had started or whether the dog was to blame for it or why there had been a fight at all; such questions never occurred to him. The otter had come close to killing his friend, and so the otter, which

had once so engaged him that he had asked Mr. Ben not to trap it while he was there, had become his enemy. His rescue of the dog, which had brought Charley to accept him at last and lick his hand, was the final confirmation of his delusion.

He knelt and put his arms around Charley, crooning to him, and the dog relaxed against him with a sigh. They stayed that way for a long moment, savoring their pleasure and relief and the bond that was now between them. Presently Joey grew aware that Charley was shivering, and then that he was shivering himself. His teeth were chattering and his soaked clothes struck into him with an iron chill. "Have to go," he said between his clicking teeth, and stood up. "Come on, boy."

He started for the house with the dog at his heels, trotting occasionally until he was out of breath and then walking again. As he began to warm up from the exercise, he thought at first of his new relationship with Charley, and then he got around to the otter. He began by hating it, a direct and simple emotion, and then he thought of its vengeful scheme to get Charley into deep water and drown him. The longer he dwelt upon this the more malicious and evil the otter seemed to him. Once in the water it could have broken off the fight and gone away, but it hadn't done that—it had stayed and plotted murder; and as he turned this over in his mind he grew sure that it would always be a threat to his friend, it would lie in wait for him, and so he would have to kill it.

By the time he reached the house he was fixed on this idea, and was already beginning to plan a campaign to do in the otter. He gave the dog several biscuits, went into the house, and rubbed himself warm with a towel and put on dry clothes. When Mr. Ben came from the outhouse behind the barn he found the pair of them sitting together and Charley taking biscuits from Joey's hand; Joey's other arm was around the dog.

"Gentlemen, sir," he said, pausing nearby, "it looks as though you finally did it."

"Yes, sir," Joey said. "I rescued him from the otter."

"What did he tangle with the otter for?" Mr. Ben asked. "I thought he had better sense."

"It tried to drown him," Joey said, and told Mr. Ben what had happened. "It really tried to drown him," he ended up, "and it wasn't fair."

The old man had heard him out without interrupting, and then spoke up. "Maybe he got between the otter and the water, and wouldn't let it pass. If he did, he had it cornered, in a way. Any animal will fight when it's cornered, Joey."

"Yes, sir. But after it wasn't cornered it kept right on. It schemed against him, Mr. Ben. It's mean. I reckon it aims to kill him if it can, and I'm not going to let it. I'll go after it and get it first."

This was said with such determination, with such an oddly grown-up air, that Mr. Ben was rather startled by it. It didn't seem like Joey at all. "What?" he asked. "Are you really serious about this?"

"Yes, sir."

"You'll have to spend all your time at it. I doubt if there's an animal in the country harder to catch up with. After all, Joey, the fight might have been as much Charley's fault as the otter's. Have you thought of that?"

"Yes, sir."

"So," the old man said. He saw now what the state of affairs was, and gave up argument. "*Delenda est Carthago,*" he said, and added, "You'll have to get up early in the morning to get that one."

"Yes, sir, I will. What does *Carthago* . . . what was it? . . . mean, Mr. Ben?"

"It means 'Carthage must be destroyed,'" Mr. Ben said. "An old Roman got a bee in his bonnet about Carthage, and ended up all his speeches in the Senate by saying it."

His mild irony was lost on Joey. "Yes, sir. I reckon I'll learn it. Could you say it again, please?"

Mr. Ben's expression didn't change; he repeated the phrase several times until Joey knew it, and when Joey asked him if he knew the Latin word for otter he had to admit that his Latin was too rusty to supply it.

"I don't really need it," Joey said. "I'll know what I mean when I say it. *Delenda est Carthago.*" He got up and brought several more biscuits for Charley, and pointed out to Mr. Ben the several cuts that the otter had scored on the dog. When Mr. Ben started to move closer to examine them, Charley got up and moved off a little; his trust in Joey was not going to be extended any farther. It was strictly a private affair between Joey and himself.

"It's a good thing for his own sake that he's not going to love the world from now on," Mr. Ben said. "So you're going to concentrate on the otter, are you?"

"Yes, sir."

"Are you going to take Charley along?"

"I reckon not," Joey said. "It might catch him when I wasn't near enough."

"I think that's wise," the old man said. "But how about the new turkey call? I thought you were going to spend your vacation hunting turkeys."

"I reckon I'll just have to wait until I get the otter, Mr. Ben. If I roost some while I'm looking for him, then maybe we could go."

"Good enough. I'm going around to see to my traps in a little while and you can come along if you want to hold off your crusade until the morning."

Joey had been thinking of starting his hunt that afternoon, but the afternoon was getting on and he wouldn't have a great deal of time before darkness came down; besides, now that Mr. Ben had invited him to visit his traps with him he felt that he should go. For some reason Mr. Ben wanted him along, and the old man had been so good to him, and left him so much freedom to do as he wished, that Joey was glad to defer to him. "Yes, sir," he said. "I reckon I'd like to go."

He gave the dog another biscuit, talked to him a little more, and then they went down the hill, started a fire in the boat stove, and pushed off. An overcast was slowly spreading across the sky and the wind had dropped; the water was still, with a faintly oily look, and reflected the gray, wintry trees along the shoreline with a mirrorlike fidelity. The bateau slid silently along at the head of its oily ripple, and they didn't say very much to one another. The first few traps didn't yield anything, and, seemingly suspended between the gray water and the gray sky, they both fell into different preoccupations. Joey sat quietly in the bow with his gun on his lap, watching the shoreline and gathering himself in his mind for the morrow and the days that would follow when he would think of nothing but the otter and his pursuit of it; a feeling of melancholy had descended upon Mr. Ben. He had enjoyed Joey's enthusiasms and the feeling that had grown between them, the hints he could give the boy and the few sticky moments—like that with White and the teacher—that he had been able to smooth over. A good deal of the time his life was a lonely one, without very much in the future any more, and being a sort of mentor had been a pleasant experience. He knew that this was going to be taken away from him, at least for a while and perhaps for a long while; for the boy had suddenly withdrawn and changed, given over his careless and shifting explorations for a vendetta based upon a misconception. This disturbed the old man for it seemed too unboylike, too adult and concentrated, and he wanted Joey the way he had always been. Too many people in his life had suddenly changed, a quirk of personality hitherto unsuspected had taken them away from him, and he was depressed by the thought that it could happen again.

They were nearing the head of the Pond by that time, and Joey suddenly turned to him and pointed toward the shore. "It was right over there," he said. "Mr. Ben, will you lend me your alarm clock when we get back?"

"Yes," the old man said. "You're welcome to it."

CHAPTER FOURTEEN

It was still dark when the alarm clock shook Joey awake, and the room was very cold; he got shivering into his clothes with the help of his flashlight, went into the kitchen and lit the lamp, and ate a few slices of bread and butter. There was a basket of persimmons on the table, and he ate several of them. They had found the basket at the back door when they got back to the house the previous evening; all of the persimmons had been carefully selected and were perfect, and the basket was a homemade one beautifully plaited out of twigs. It had apparently been left by Sharbee, as an acknowledgment of his Christmas present.

After a moment of indecision Joey decided to take the shotgun and went out the back door. It was still dark, and there had been a light dusting of snow during the night. It would help him, for if it hadn't fallen the only procedure open to him would have been to sit somewhere along the shore in the hope that the otter would eventually pass by. Now he could make a circuit of the Pond to see whether he could find its tracks, which might give him an idea of its movements and the places that it liked to land. If it had been moving about after the snow fell he might find something. He went down the hill and started at the dock.

The evening before, after dinner he had talked with Mr. Ben about the habits of otters, and he knew now that his chances of even seeing it again were very remote. Mr. Ben had told him that it probably had a den somewhere along the shore or on the edge of the swamp with an underwater entrance, that it probably didn't stay around the Pond all the time but periodically made a circle of possibly twenty miles around the little ponds and streams in the vicinity, and that he wasn't at all sure that it ever came ashore twice at the same place. If it caught a fish, the old man had said, it would come ashore to eat it, and there might be a few bones or some dung with fish scales or crawfish shells and claws in it, but who knew whether it would visit that spot again? When he set traps for an otter he set them in these places, but he only caught an otter about once in five years or so. It was easier to find a small needle in a large haystack, said Mr. Ben, than such an animal.

On top of this, Joey had no assurance whatever that his enemy was still about; it might have started on its swing around the country right after the fight, in which case it wouldn't be back until after he had gone home. If the weather grew a little colder and the Pond froze, it would also go away to work the streams that stayed open. Thus briefed, Joey was well aware of what he was up against, but he was not discouraged. Just as he was convinced of the rightness of his crusade, he was convinced that it would be successful. He moved along the shoreline slowly and carefully, foot by foot, often pausing for long periods to sit quietly and watch. It was nearly noon by the time he reached the head of the Pond and the beginning of the swamp, and the overcast that had covered the sky looked as though it might break up and let the sun through to melt the snow. If this happened it would leave him with over half the shoreline unsurveyed for tracks, and he realized he had better put off his still-hunting pauses until some other day.

He picked up his pace and started on his circuit around the borders of the swamp, and here his difficulties began to multiply. Many small streams ran out of the swamp and meandered all about and he thought he should follow most of them for a way; trees were insecurely rooted in the wet ground and every storm had uprooted some of them. The area was a tangled nightmare of windfall timber; he had to crawl through or over it or make wide detours, and the swamp covered a much greater area than he had expected. He found tracks of foxes and minks, possums, squirrels, rabbits, and raccoons, but nothing that looked like the otter's. The short winter day began to draw toward an end, earlier than usual because the overcast still covered the sky, and he had to turn back with most of the swamp's edge unexplored.

It was dark when he got back to the house, and he was tired to his bones. There was a stew keeping warm on the stove, and as he came into the kitchen Mr. Ben was just coming from the living room pulling on his coat.

"I was just going out to see where you were," he said. "It's pretty cold to sleep in the woods without any supper. You'd better let me know about where you're going to be after this."

"Yes, sir," Joey said. He pulled a chair close to the stove and sat down wearily to take off his hunting shoes. After he got them off he sat for a moment wiggling his toes and soaking up the stove's warmth; the smell of the stew made him realize how hungry he was. "Yes, sir."

The old man stood looking at him for a moment with his forehead creased, lantern-jawed, stooped a little, with the lamplight laying a silvery sheen over his one day's growth of gray stubble. "You didn't have any lunch either, and I doubt much breakfast. You're going out again tomorrow?"

"Yes, sir, I reckon I will."

Mr. Ben took his coat off, hung it over the other chair, and began to dish up the stew. "No more of that," he said, coming closer to an order than he ever had before. "If you're going on with this caper you'll take time to boil a couple of eggs for breakfast, and we'll pack a couple of sandwiches before we go to bed. Let's eat, now."

"Yes, sir," Joey said. He got up stiffly and followed Mr. Ben into the living room. The first mouthful of stew was the best thing he had ever tasted in his life, and as he sat there chewing it he looked at Mr. Ben and realized that the old man had been worried about him. It brought him back momentarily from the concentration that had been enclosing him; he was rather abashed that he had not given a thought to the old man, who had always been thoughtful of him. "I'm sorry, Mr. Ben," he said. "I'll write down where I'm going and leave it on the table every day."

"A lot of things can happen to anybody alone in the woods," Mr. Ben said. "What would your father and mother think of me if you were to get into trouble out there and I didn't know where you were?" Joey didn't say anything; he wasn't at all sure that his father—and certainly not his mother—would let him do what he was doing. "A lot of people would think I ought to be locked up for letting you do this at all," Mr. Ben went on, echoing Joey's own thought, "but people and even boys have to settle things for themselves, and you've had one experience with the fool-killer. You'd best think of it once in a while. And if you get into trouble shoot three times. I'll listen particularly just as it's getting dark."

"Yes, sir," Joey said humbly. "I will." He smiled at the old man and began to eat again. He finished his stew, and as he sat there, with the good warm food inside him and the grateful heat of the stove on his back, he began to nod. Fragmentary recollections of the woods powdered with snow, the windfalls he had crawled through, and the sustaining excitement of expecting to see the otter at any moment drifted through his mind as he fell asleep. Mr. Ben got him to his feet, steered him into the bedroom, covered him up, and wound the clock without waking him.

The overcast had held through the night and the temperature hadn't changed; the snow was still there the next morning, and Joey went up the other side of the Pond. The usual tracks were about, a delicate and fascinating record of the comings and goings of many creatures, but the otter's wasn't among them. As Joey rounded the last point before the cut-over section, however, he saw well ahead of him, near the water, a dark shape against the snow. It was too far away to identify and the morning was too gray to give it color, but it seemed to be crouched and eating something; being so close to the water Joey thought that it must be eating a fish. Excitement took hold of him and he wondered how he could get near it. His best chance seemed to be to angle back into the cut-over and stalk it, so he took that course after picking out a high tree on the other side of the Pond to give himself a mark of location.

He moved as fast as he could with quietness, but the cut-over was a tangle of blackberry vines and brush and old tree-tops that were dry and crackly. He was afraid that the animal would finish its meal and vanish before he got in sight of it; the stalk seemed to last forever and he hurried it, and either his impatience or the light breeze (which he had forgotten in his preoccupation) betrayed him. When he came over the last little rise and could see the place, the object of his stalk was gone. He was bitterly disappointed, and when he reached the spot he found the rather doglike but narrower tracks of a fox leading away from it. The creature had been a fox after all, but it had been eating the remains of a fish; there were a few bones and a tail still there. Fox tracks were all about and practically covered the area, but when he got down on one knee and searched about among them he found one different pawmark; five-toed, almost round, and a little over three inches across. It could have been made by nothing but the otter.

The otter had been there, then; it had brought the fish ashore, left some of it, and the fox had found it. That Joey hadn't frightened off the otter itself lessened his disappointment, and the fact that it was still there and hadn't left the Pond as yet was most encouraging to him. He continued to search about among the tracks and finally found, sandwiched between two of the fox's, another that looked like the otter's but was smaller. This was a puzzling thing, but finally the answer came to him; there must be a young otter there too.

"Great day!" he said to himself. "A little one!"

This would make it better, he thought; it would be easier to find two than one. The little one wouldn't be as wary, and if he could only get it . . . A number of wild schemes began to run through his mind, most of them too impractical to be considered for very long, but one remained. If he could only get the little one and hang it up near the water somewhere, it would attract the other, and he could watch the place until the other came.

This plan was the measure of his delusion; that it was ruthless and cruel didn't occur to him. He stood up, feeling now that he had a more potent weapon, and continued on his way. He found no more otter tracks along the shore, and came to the swamp again. This side of it was like the other, full of blow-downs and detours, and buoyed up by the new plan he grew careless; he hurried too much and finally, in climbing over one very bad tangle of fallen trees, slipped on a snowy branch and fell through the confusion of trunks and branches. It was a bad fall and half stunned him. When his ringing head began to clear he tried to stand up; hot pain shot through his left ankle and he found that it wouldn't support him.

He lay still for a time while the pain diminished, and fear built up in him. There was a flutter of wings over his head, and he looked up to see a big red-tailed hawk on a branch above him. The snow it had disturbed in landing drifted down around him; it gripped the branch with sharp talons, and its cold, impersonal eyes assayed him as possible prey. At his movement it jumped from the branch and flapped off, but for a little time its hungry eyes still seemed to be boring into him. He shivered. If he had broken his ankle and couldn't walk he was in a bad situation; although he had left a note for Mr. Ben, it merely said that he was going up the south side of the Pond and around the swamp, and that was pretty indefinite. There was a great deal of country they would have to look for him in, and it was difficult country. Mr. Ben would have to get other people, and that would take time; he wouldn't start to do any-thing until dark or later, and he, Joey, would be alone and cold and uncertain.

He was afraid, but as he thought of these things his first blind fear began to diminish. He wasn't in unoccupied coun-try and out of reach; sooner or later they'd find him. His tracks were in the snow, if it held; he could crawl; he could shoot his gun to help them locate him; he would be making a great nuisance of himself. These things were bad, but if he had to give up the search it would be worse. Tears of frustration and anger at his own carelessness came into his eyes, and, grasping two of the branches above his head, he pulled himself up. The ankle hurt, but not as badly, and after putting weight on it gradually and moving it a few times he found that it would work. It wasn't broken after all, and after he crawled out of the blow-down and hobbled carefully about for a time it stopped troubling him.

His relief was great and he went with more care; he realized that a much worse thing could have happened to him. Late in the afternoon he came to a large creek flowing into the swamp, and judged that it was the main one. When the otters left the Pond for their periodic swing around the country, he thought, this would probably be the creek they would use; if he hid somewhere along it, if he could stay there long enough, he would probably see them sooner or later. He wanted to explore it further, but although the overcast was breaking up and daylight would last longer than it had yesterday, the afternoon was waning and there wouldn't be time. He estimated that he was more than halfway around the swamp so he continued on to be sure that there wasn't a larger creek between this one and the place where he had turned back yesterday, and so went on to the house down the northern shore.

It was after dark again when he got back. Mr. Ben had left the kitchen door open despite the chill to be more sure that he would hear the gun if Joey had to shoot it. He closed it when Joey came in, put more wood on the fire, and got his back to it. "Any luck?" he asked.

"No, sir," Joey said wearily. "Not yet." He went on to his bedroom to change his boots and leave his gunning coat. As he sat pulling his boots off he thought of telling Mr. Ben about his plan for the little otter and his plan about the creek, and decided not to. At any other time he would have done it, but this time he would not. He had grown closed away and secretive, and proud of his plans—which, indeed, were very logical and mature for his age, and not like him. Nothing that he was doing now was like him.

The next morning he left early and went up the southern shore to see if the otters had landed again at the place where he had found the fish. They hadn't, and he went on to explore the creek. It had cleared in the night and warmed up enough to take most of the snow away, and after the sun got up it melted what was left. The snow had lasted long enough to show him that the otters were still about, or had been two days ago; it had fallen at a propitious time for him, and seemed to indicate that luck was with him. Buoyed up by this, he went at his exploration of the creek with enthusiasm and finally came to a place where there was a waterfall. It was only four feet high, for there was little surface rock in that country, but it was high and vertical enough to cause the otters to come ashore to get around it; one bank was precipitous, too steep for them to climb, and the other was gently sloping. This was where they would come out when they passed, and he decided that this was the place to wait and waylay them.

There was a pine thicket to hide in within gunshot, and he set about clearing a field of fire in front of it and making himself a comfortable place to sit; when all this was done he sat down and composed himself to wait.

He got up even earlier the next morning to be at the place at first light, and stayed there until the edge of darkness. No otter came past that day, or the next, or the day after. He began to wonder whether he had been wrong in his plan, but he stayed; he had an odd conviction that sooner or later he would see them. As the days followed one another, as he sat immobile in his hiding place or moved from the house to the place and back to the house again in the half-light when most of the wild creatures were returning to their dens or emerging from them, he saw more of their lives than he would have seen in a year of hunting. They weren't game in his mind now; he didn't think of shooting at them for fear of frightening or alerting the otters, and began to see them differently. Before, they had been targets, somewhat like animated but wary mechanical figures clothed in fur or feathers, to be outwitted, knocked over, and put into his game pocket; now they slowly turned into personalities with mannerisms and idiosyncrasies all their own.

He first noticed this in a solitary old raccoon which lived in a hollow in a big beech not far from his hiding place. It was a very large raccoon, and the first time he saw it it came ambling up the creek from its nocturnal wanderings early in the morning, pausing occasionally to turn over a stone in the creek bed. When it did this its paws, so much like little hands, seemed to have a life of their own; they felt all about while the old raccoon sat hunched, apparently not interested in them, and looked all about. As it came nearer it climbed out of the creek bed, walked a few steps, and turned back to the creek bed again. There was a light-colored stone near the falls; it went straight to that, felt all about beneath it, and left the creek bed again. When it came opposite Joey it stopped, turned its black highwayman's mask toward him, and froze. Although Joey hadn't moved and there was no wind, something told the old raccoon that an alien presence was there. It sat for a time, apparently weighing the mysterious intuition;

several times it tensed as though to dash off, and relaxed again; finally it turned without haste, moved to the beech, climbed it, and disappeared into the hollow. Thereafter, when Joey was there, it paid little attention to the pine thicket. Oddly enough, it never investigated the thicket further but always avoided it; but no matter how it approached the beech it always made a detour to feel under the light-colored stone. During the day it occasionally came out of its hollow and sprawled over a limb to take a sunbath; it was company for a few of the long hours and fun to watch.

Several other raccoons wandered through the territory, but they all went through an elaborate series of maneuvers to investigate him; several deer passed, delicately moving and pretty, but only one of them was aware of him. That one startled him half out of his skin by approaching unheard and snorting loudly when it finally identified him. None of these animals stampeded off in fright after they had placed him but quietly withdrew; in some unfathomable way they seemed to know that he wasn't dangerous.

Others never knew he was there: a mink, dark and quick and lethal-looking as it worked the creek; two flying squirrels living near him that he often watched in the gloaming swooping down swift and shadowy between the darkening trees; a terrified rabbit and the bounding, sinuous weasel that pursued it; several hunting owls that went over him like ghosts in the dusk. A possum almost walked across his legs one day and rolled over, grinning, to play dead when he moved. After a while it cautiously came back to life and died again when it saw he was still there; it went through this amusing performance several more times before it decided that he was harmless and went off, looking distrustfully back over its shoulder.

There were long periods when the woods were silent and empty. Between these empty and silent hours, however, he saw more than most people because he had more patience and more time, and in these hours he thought about the livelier ones.

The play of life about him, the clean and simple reasons for the actions of the creatures that he watched, their acuity and their moments of stress or calm or playfulness, brought him closer to them as time went on. He wondered about the enigmatic sixth sense that seemed to make them less assiduous in avoiding him than they had been before and made a start toward understanding it; unconsciously he was moving into a sympathy and concord with the animals around him, but he had a way to go yet. His feeling about the otters disturbed it, and if this feeling began to soften, he would remember the fight or Mr. Ben would mention that Charley had come look-ing for him and he would hate them again.

He sat on, through several storms, through sunny days and cold, gray ones; more than half of his long Christmas vacation went by. Mr. Ben worried but didn't interfere; perhaps the old man saw something waiting to emerge but not very apparent yet from a few things that Joey said about the animals that he watched. It was a strange time, detached and set aside from the usual tenor of his life, and sometimes he realized this himself and in a remote way wondered about it. Sometimes it was like being in a dream, like someone else watching a boy named Joey who was doing a queer thing; sometimes he felt that something more substantially based than himself was watching and waiting for the time when it could approach and free him from the dream.

He sat on, half hypnotized in the silent and brooding

woods, having rationalized his affair to himself as older and supposedly wiser heads before him had rationalized their pogroms, wars, and Inquisitions.

There came a morning when he awoke a little before the clock, with a feeling different from other mornings, a premonition that this would be the day. When he switched on the flashlight he could see his breath and shivered as he dressed, but the shivering was physical and not from anticipation; inwardly he was quite calm. He went into the kitchen, and when he lit the lamp everything looked cold and flat and otherworldly despite the shadows and the soft light; the kitchen looked different too, and somehow increased the surety that was in him. It was as though some apperception, coming from the restlessness within the dark den under a bank, coming across the leaden water, had reached him and told him that the otters would move out. He had to hurry, for he had a long way to go; he left without eating breakfast or taking the sandwiches that had been made the night before and put in a bag on the table.

When he reached the head of the Pond there were streaks of dusty crimson in the sky, glowing and diffuse; the woods were emerging from the night. They had brightened when he came to the boundary of the pine thicket, and then he heard the first spitting snarl. It dropped to the long, menacing moan with which fighting cats had awakened him in the night at home, and suddenly rose to a screech that made his hair stand up. The sounds came from near the waterfall; he half raised his gun and began to run through the pines. The thick carpet of fallen pine needles deadened his footsteps, and through an interlaced screen of branches he saw a shape bound forward and back again; the snarling went on.

He stopped at the thicket's edge and had the otters before him, the big one and the pup half grown, and the long-legged snarling bobcat. The pup was confused and frightened; it made several false starts and retreated, and the big one, whose back was claw-raked and bleeding, leaped to head it off and drive it around the waterfall and into the water and then turned back to the bobcat again. The bobcat moved with extraordinary quickness and seemed to be everywhere at once; its paw strokes were so fast they blurred on the eye, but the big otter, despite the disadvantage that its short legs imposed, always seemed to be between the pup and the cat that wanted it. The old otter caught the cat at the end of a bound, took the punishment, and dealt his own; the cat didn't like it, broke away, and stood several yards off with its face contorted with fury.

The violent action had held Joey spellbound; the sudden quiet freed him. He had always hated cats, those eldritch disturbers of the night, and to see the otter drive it off suddenly filled him with such admiration that he almost shouted encouragement. The otter stood for a moment, black and bloody; then, obviously ready to carry on the fight, it took several steps forward. The bobcat moved back two steps, snarling. Joey didn't think; he swung the shotgun up and fired at the cat.

The cat fell over backwards; the otter turned its broad whiskered muzzle toward Joey, looked at him without fear, and then turned again and drove the pup before it around the fall and into the creek.

Joey stared for a moment at the place where they had been, and then at the dead bobcat lying a few yards away. He took a deep breath and expelled it in a sigh, like someone waking from a long and troubling dream. He lowered the gun and looked around, and it was only then that he saw Sharbee standing near him. Sharbee had come through the pine thicket too, and one sweeping branch half concealed him; he stood with his old gun under one arm, his pale amber eyes fixed broodingly upon Joey, and suddenly he smiled.

"I was powerful afraid you was about to kill him," he said, "and the little one, too. After all that long time waitin'."

"I reckon I almost did," Joey said. His mind ran back, over the fight and the search in the snow, the hours he had waited in the thicket; all of it seemed very long ago and almost as though it had happened to someone else. "I reckon I almost did," he said again, and suddenly felt light and free. Then he remembered the feeling that had come upon him sometimes, that someone was watching him. "Did you know?" he asked.

"Yes, sir," Sharbee said in his soft voice. "I watched you, like I did before. I had to be sure," he said and nodded.

"It was the fight," Joey said, feeling that he had to explain himself, "when he tried to kill Charley."

"Yes, sir," Sharbee said. "It the little one. He have to watch out for that. One time they go away, and when they come back the she one gone. I reckon somebody catch she." His voice changed a little. "They is the best. They happy and pretty; they right peaceable does everything leave them be." He smiled again, more to himself than for Joey, and the boy could see that he knew their lives and loved them.

"I reckon I made you worry," he said. "I'm sorry, Mr. Sharbee."

"It all worked out," Sharbee said, "like you was meant to help them. I thank you, again, and for the Chris'mas gif. You a real good boy, Mr. Joey. Come spring I get a little coon. You come see me in June. I have him then." He smiled again, raised his free hand, and stepped back; Joey could see him moving through the shadows of the pine thicket, and then he was gone.

Joey walked over, picked up the bobcat by its hind feet, slung it over his shoulder, and started for the house.

Charley was lying in the yard, looking rather forlorn. When he saw Joey he stood up and trotted to meet him, wagging his tail in welcome. He thrust his nose into Joey's hand and then he smelled the cat; his hackles rose, and he circled the boy to investigate, saw that the cat was dead, and then trotted along beside Joey looking as pleased as though he had killed the beast himself. Mr. Ben came out the back door carrying a basin of water to throw out. When he saw Joey he put the basin down.

"Hi, Mr. Ben," Joey said, and moved his arm to get the cat off his shoulder and hold it up. "Look."

He walked to the steps, dropped the cat to the ground, and sat down. Mr. Ben came down the steps and sat down beside him, looking at the cat. They both stared at it for a moment, then Joey turned toward Mr. Ben.

"There was a little one," he said, "and the bobcat tried to get it, and the big one fought it. He was wonderful. You should have seen him, Mr. Ben."

"And you shot the bobcat."

"Yes, sir. Somebody had caught the mother and the big one, the father, he's raising the little one. He sure is a fighter, Mr. Ben. I reckon Charley tried to get the little one too, but I didn't know that then."

Mr. Ben didn't ask him how he knew all this. "You've got it settled, then," he said.

"Yes, sir."

"Good," Mr. Ben said, and a smile began on his face. "I'm glad that's over. It's been lonely without you."

"I reckon it has. I felt sort of funny too, but I just had to do it. I'm glad I did, Mr. Ben."

"So am I," the old man said. "I wondered sometimes, but I thought you'd better do it your own way. I'll skin that cat and you can have a rug made out of it."

"Thank you, Mr. Ben. I reckon I better feed Charley now."

"I fed him," the old man said. "I doubt if he can hold any more."

They smiled at each other and sat staring in companionable silence at the bobcat; soon Joey's head began to nod. He was suddenly so sleepy that he couldn't hold his eyes open; an overwhelming desire to sleep, to forget the emotions that had caught and driven him, the long, long hours and the catharsis at the end, washed over him like a strong and rising tide. He staggered up and began to climb the steps; halfway up he paused. "Charley," he mumbled. "Charley." The dog heard him; it got up and came after him and followed him into the house. It hadn't been in a house for a very long time and was wary, but it stayed beside him, and when he dropped into the bed, already asleep, it lay down beside the bed with a sigh.

CHAPTER FIFTEEN

It was late in the afternoon when Joey awoke, and the house was very quiet. Charley wasn't in the room, and Joey thought that probably Mr. Ben had let him out and he had gone home. He had a dim recollection of the dog close beside him as he came into the house, and that pleased him; they were really friends, and wouldn't have been if there had never been a fight. He lay there still a little drowsy, listening for Mr. Ben's footfalls, but could hear nothing; probably the old man had gone out to see to his traps. He remembered them sitting on the back steps looking at the dead bobcat, slab-sided and collapsed-looking with the breath of life gone out of it, so different from itself when it had been pouncing about with a demoniacal expression in its agate eyes, full of vitality. What if it had found the otter in a trap, fast and encumbered and helpless, as the hawk had found him when he lay half stunned after he had fallen through the blow-down?

As he thought of this, of the hawk's impersonal but pitiless eyes, he shuddered; no creature was ever free from the shadow of a violent death. Yet they didn't dwell upon it; they went calmly about their lives and played happily when the

mood was on them, like the two little flying squirrels in the
dusk between the flights of hunting owls or the solitary old
raccoon with the light-colored stone. The raccoon knew that
there was nothing under that stone, and had known it for a
long time.

As these things drifted through his mind he felt very close
to the animals he had watched; not hating any of them any
more took away the last barrier between them and himself.
He wanted to know more about them, to share—if only as an
observer—in their lives. They were as interesting and varied
(and much less complicated and unaccountable) as people,
and made no demands upon him. He wasn't ready for the demands of people yet.

His mind drifted back to the fight and the things it had
brought him: Charley's trust, and the long hunt and the
things that had come of it. Why, after all his plans and the
long wait, when he had his enemy the otter under his gun,
hadn't he shot it instead of the hungry cat? Perhaps he should
feel as though he had done a silly thing, and yet he didn't; he
felt light and free, as though the thing he had done was right.
Besides, he had been a hunter, and now there was an intimation of a reluctance to hunt in him; it was a puzzling and disturbing thing.

His forehead creased as he searched for a clue to these
riddles, and presently he dozed again. When he awoke it
was a little past twilight, and the room was growing dark.
There still wasn't a sound in the house. He got up and
walked through the living room into the kitchen, but they
were dark too; Mr. Ben wasn't about. He lit two lamps,
shook up both stoves, and put more wood into them, for
the house was getting cold. Mr. Ben had never been this
late at his traps, and Joey began to worry about him. He

239 ar TH POND

wandered around the house, wondering what he ought to do; he had almost come to the decision to go down to the wharf with his flashlight and take out one of the other boats when he heard footsteps on the porch and ran into the kitchen. Mr. Ben was just coming in the back door and grinned at him.

"Turkeys!" he said. "I roosted some turkeys up near the cut-over!" He was in high spirits and thumped the three muskrats he was carrying down on the table. "Must be eight or ten of 'em. This time I bet we'll eat turkey."

For a moment Joey was cross at Mr. Ben for worrying him, but his relief was so great and the news so exciting that he quickly got over it. "Great day!" he said. "Eight or ten? Are they close to the water? Can I take my gun this—"

"They're not close enough," Mr. Ben said. "We'll have to wait until they fly down and call them. Let's get our dinner started. I could eat a bear." He took off his coat and sweater and put the frying pan on the stove. "Open some of that canned hash," he said, bustling around. "I'll get the potatoes sliced up." He sliced the potatoes while Joey opened the cans, dumped everything into the pan, and began to stir it around. "Gentlemen, sir," he said, "the air was full of turkeys. It looked like bargain day."

"I thought something had happened to you," Joey said. "I was about to come and see. I never thought of turkeys. What will we do, Mr. Ben?"

"We'll get up early and go back to the cut-over and hide, and when we hear them fly down we'll call. Hand me the plates."

Joey handed him the plates; he filled them and they took them to the table. They were both hungry and attacked their dinner, but as Joey ate he imagined the procedure as

Mr. Ben had sketchily outlined it: the hiding and waiting in the dark, daybreak, the uncertainty and suspense. The more he pictured it the more exciting it became. He could hardly wait to finish his dinner; when the last mouthful was gone he went into the bedroom and brought back the new call. Looking at Mr. Ben he pushed the plunger down, and the faultless, yelping note filled the room. They grinned happily at each other.

"That's it," Mr. Ben said. "You couldn't do it better if you had feathers on. That old man knew his business." He stood up. "We'll wash the dishes, and then you better head for bed. I've got to skin those rats, but I won't be long behind you. As long as you've already got the clock, set it for four and wake me up."

"Yes, sir," Joey said, and got up to take out his own plate. He had forgotten for the time the questions that had puzzled him; he was impatient for morning to come. He was afraid that he wouldn't be able to get to sleep, but five minutes after he had climbed into the cold bed he was dead to the world.

The morning was cold, and this was its coldest hour; there was heavy frost on the ground and the stars glittered frostily. Joey pulled his head down into his collar and watched the vapor of his breath float sluggishly upward. They were only at the wharf, and he was shivering already.

"Holy Lazarus!" Mr. Ben said, untangling the old trap chain that held the bateau. "I wish I could light the stove. Talk about Greenland's icy mountains . . ."

As it had before, the chilling mist was trailing languidly over the water, and they climbed aboard the bateau and shoved off into it. For a while their progress was as cheerless as passage in Charon's ferry across the gloomy

243 ~ THE POND

Styx, but after a bit their exertions warmed them and their eyes grew accustomed to the darkness. Two ducks that had been sleeping on the water got up quacking and pattering across the surface, but they couldn't see them; they were only disembodied and temporary distractions in the mist. Soon after that Mr. Ben swung the bateau, and presently they reached the other shore. Joey crawled over the bow and carried the old sashweight the length of its rope, laid it carefully on the ground, and waited for Mr. Ben to join him.

It seemed to him that they walked for miles through the frosted brush, working their way around old treetops that reached out like monstrous spiders; unseen briers came out of nowhere and raked and clung to them. Mr. Ben finally found a place that suited him. It was below the top of a little rise and, so far as Joey could see in the gloom, gave them a down-hill view into a small, fairly flat and open grassy clearing. After they smoothed out a sitting place and removed everything that might crackle, Mr. Ben went off and returned with an armload of brush to which dead leaves still clung and arranged it as a low blind in front of them.

They sat down to wait. Joey could feel Mr. Ben shivering against him, and shivered in return. Dawn stole into the sky and Joey got his call out; the world about them slowly emerged from night. The woods at the edge of the cut-over grew clearer, and the frost sparkled on the brush on the higher spots as the first sunlight touched it; presently they heard the dry rattle of stiff feathers on branches as the turkeys began to launch themselves and fly down. Joey had been shivering with cold; he shivered harder now with excitement and anticipation. His hand tightened on the call, and Mr. Ben whispered, "Not yet."

An age went by, and there was an end to the flapping; the turkeys were all down. Mr. Ben's restraining hand was on Joey's arm. He waited a little longer, and then whispered, "Now. Three times."

Joey was terrified that he would do it wrong, but the call worked perfectly. There was an answer off to the right. Before Joey could push the plunger again Mr. Ben's hand was on his arm once more, gripping harder than Mr. Ben had intended. "Wait!" he whispered. "Wait!"

Joey was nearly frantic; he wanted to call at once, to talk to the turkey that had yelped and might even now be standing indecisive and ready to turn away, close at hand in the concealing brush. The hand gripped and held and finally fell away. "Once," Mr. Ben whispered. "No more."

Joey called once and put the call down and picked up his gun. He remembered this time, and laid his thumb on the safety; he wasn't going to be caught that way again. He sat frozen, staring through the little opening in the brush piled before him. One moment the clearing was empty and the next there was a big gobbler in it, a materialized lean shape, black and touched with metallic iridescence, magnificently wild and beautiful with its snaky head high and darting quickly this way and that.

"Shoot him!" Mr. Ben breathed.

Joey jumped up and, holding on the turkey's neck between its darting head and its body, fired both barrels at once. The recoil knocked him over backwards, but as he went he saw the turkey go down. He scrambled up and hurdled the brush; the turkey was flopping wildly about, and he ran after it. Another darted out of the brush in front of him and leaped up and flew over his head, and just as he fell on his turkey he heard Mr. Ben's gun roar.

He was first back to the blind, and then Mr. Ben came in with his bird and dropped it beside Joey's. They grinned triumphantly at each other; they laughed in their pleasure and shook hands.

"Great day!" Joey said. "Great thundering balls of fire! We did it, Mr. Ben! We did it!" He couldn't stop talking; he was too full of his triumph over the wariest of creatures, of relief from the awful tension and suspense. "When I saw him out there . . . Great day! I bet my father will sure open his eyes. I bet I'll never forget it, Mr. Ben."

Mr. Ben put a hand on his shoulder. "I don't think you ever will either," he said. "Neither will I. You ought to write your father and ask him to bring that box of bicarbonate next time he comes." He grinned again. "Well, the prayers of the righteous availeth much, that's for sure. As one old turkey hunter to another, I salute you, and I'd admire to have you join me for breakfast."

After a fine leisurely breakfast they gutted the turkeys and hung them on the screened porch where their impressive appearance would surely stun any casual passer-by. When they had finished this pleasant chore and were surveying their handiwork with great satisfaction, Charley trotted into the yard.

"Now, I take it, you'll be off after squirrels," Mr. Ben said.

"I don't reckon I will," Joey said, and after he had said it was surprised. It had popped out before he thought, but as he considered it he wasn't sorry. Somehow, he didn't want to kill squirrels, or any four-legged thing, any more; the desire was gone. For a moment he felt a curious regret, remembering the first ones and the fierce wild excitement of it, and then he was sure. "I just don't want to do it," he said. "It's funny, Mr. Ben."

"I don't think it is," the old man said. "You learn about yourself as you go, and," he went on, taking a long look back into the past, "sometimes it takes too long."

"Yes, sir," Joey said, missing the regret in the old man's voice. "I reckon you thought I'd never quit going up there."

The old man smiled. "I didn't mind."

"I bet you did. Last night when you were so late I worried about you, and that was only once."

"Well, we're even now," Mr. Ben said. "And if you're not going after squirrels, what are you going to do with this day so auspiciously begun?"

"I don't know," Joey said. He felt a little lost, as though he had come to the end of something and was waiting for whatever was going to take its place to begin. He moved restlessly inside his clothes; Mr. Ben put a hand on his shoulder, and they turned away from the turkeys and walked out onto the open part of the porch. Charley came up the steps; he pushed his nose into Joey's hand, Joey stroked him, got four biscuits from the can, and they all sat down on the steps together for a while as Charley ate the biscuits. "I don't know what I'll do," Joey went on, resting his hand on the dog's back. "I wish Bud was here." He stared in front of him for a long moment. "When I was waiting up on the creek I sort of got to liking all the animals, Mr. Ben. Birds are different. I reckon I can still shoot birds sometimes, but . . . Maybe I'm like Sharbee. I reckon I'd just like to watch them and know all about them and everything."

Mr. Ben nodded. "You could do it, boy," he said. "There are more people all the time and things will get crowded, and the people will want to get away from it once in a while and go places where it's quiet and the woods still grow and the varmints still live in them. They're going to need somebody like you to tell them about it and help run it. You can learn a lot more in college and be ready when they need you."

Joey hadn't begun to think that far ahead and the idea was new to him, but it sounded fine; it sounded just like the thing he wanted to do. "Great day!" he said, as the beauty of it took hold of him. "You reckon I could? You reckon my father would think it was all right?"

"I'm sure he would."

"I'll sure ask him."

"I'll ask him too," Mr. Ben said. "You've got the bulge on him now with that turkey, but I'll put in my two cents anyhow."

Joey turned to the old man who had been so good to him and a great glow of gratitude and affection filled his heart; his smile was a little tremulous. "Thank you, Mr. Ben," he said, and afraid that he would show too much emotion quickly stood up. "I reckon I'll go see Horace now. That's what I'll do. I never did take him the books I brought."

Mr. Ben stood up too. "You do that," he said. "Stop for the mail on the way, and give Horace my regards."

"I will," Joey said. He went into the house and got the books, and with Charley beside him went out the lane. He stopped at the mailbox and found a letter from his father in it. As he walked up the road he tore it open. It read:

Dear Joey:

I'm sorry, but I'll have to cut your vacation short. Everything's fixed about the skyrocket, and I have to go to New York for a week and your ma's worried about having you so far away while I'm gone. Maybe I'll be there to get you before you get this letter, or anyhow soon after you do. Maybe I'll bring Bud and his cousin from Atlanta with me for company on the ride. You and I can come down again before the season's over. I bought the setter.

Love,
Dad

He folded the letter and put it in his pocket, and for once was not too cast down by the prospect of leaving the Pond. The feeling of being at a loose end that had come upon him awhile ago made it not too much of a wrench this time, and he wanted to talk to his father about the future that Mr. Ben had suggested. Besides, his father said they could come a little later; they could hunt turkeys and bring the setter and hunt quail. All this sounded exciting, and his mind was busy with it as he turned off the road and walked up White's lane. When he was nearly to the well, he dropped the books. One of them was *Peter Pan in Kensington Gardens*, and he had picked it out especially because he thought the wonderful Arthur Rackham illustrations would delight Horace for a long time. It fell on its spine, and one of the plates came out and the light wind carried it through the fence.

Not remembering, Joey climbed the fence and ran after it. In the middle of the enclosure he was suddenly aware of a queer high sound and the quick pounding of hooves and looked startled around to see the mule with its yellow teeth bared and its ears laid back coming for him. He turned to run and tripped himself and fell down. It was a terrible moment; he saw the running mule come swiftly closer and couldn't seem to move, and cried out. The mule reared, between him and the sky, and a black shape leaped over him and Charley had the mule by the nose. The mule screamed and went back on its haunches, leaped sideways screaming, and ran around the enclosure shaking its great head, whipping the dog about. When it reached the fence it reared again, flailing at the dog with its front hooves. Joey was on his feet; he ran toward them, and his wild glance finding a piece of fence rail on the other side of the fence, he scrambled over the fence and grabbed the rail and beat at the mule with it. There was a confused shouting and Sam White appeared behind the mule with a pitchfork, which he jabbed into its rump. As the mule wheeled, one of its forefeet caught Charley in the head, and he fell beside Joey and lay still.

Joey was on his knees beside the dog; the mule swung away and White climbed the fence and knelt next to the boy. It was evident to Joey that one of Charley's forelegs was broken; there was a shallow cut on his head and his eyes were closed, but he was breathing.

"Goddamn mule!" White said. "I wish to God I could afford to shoot him. You reckon that dog's all right, outside of bein' knocked out?"

"It looks like his leg was broken," Joey said, stroking Charley's side and wishing desperately that he would open his eyes.

"Goddamn mule. We wouldn't eat much meat, wasn't for that dog. I reckon I better tie his leg up."

"Isn't there a vet?" Joey asked. "If there's a vet you ought to take him there."

White looked at him. "I can't afford no vet," he said, in a flat tone. "Not for a dog."

"My father would pay him," Joey said. "Please take him to the vet, Mr. White. It was my fault. I forgot about the mule and went in there and it came after me, and if it hadn't been for Charley . . ." He had been surprisingly calm until then, and suddenly he began to shake. "Please take him," he pleaded. "My father will pay anything that it costs. Mr. Ben will tell you where to send the bill."

White stared at him for a moment, his remote eyes intent for once. "I will, then," he said finally. "You stay here with him while I get the machine."

He stood up and hurried to the barn; soon he came down the lane in his old Model T. He stopped it and got out, and he and Joey picked Charley up and carried him over and laid him on the floor in back. Joey wanted to go along, he was anxious to see what the vet could do, but White wouldn't have it. "I reckon you better not," he said and drove off.

Joey stood watching him go. He was pale and still shaking from the fright he'd had, from the feeling of being in a nightmare with the mule rearing over him and unable to move, but he wasn't thinking of that. His mind was on Charley, hurt and still with his eyes closed and his leg dangling; maybe he was going to die, or would always be lame. Joey couldn't stand that thought; his fists clenched and his eyes blurred with tears.

"Joey," a voice said. "Joey?"

Joey started and looked around. Horace had come up in his little wagon, steering with one hand and turning one of the rear wheels with the other; it had been hard work to get through the sandy soil, and sweat stood out on his bulging forehead. "You aren't hurt, are you, Joey? I heard the sounds but my mother and Odie and Claude are out getting running cedar for the florists and there was nobody to push me. Are you all right?"

"I'm all right," Joey said, wiping his eyes. "It was Charley. The mule hurt him, and your father took him to the vet." He had stopped shaking now. "I was bringing you the books."

"Is Charley hurt very much?"

"I don't know," Joey said. The books were still scattered where he had dropped them, and he gathered them up. "He has a broken leg, I think, and he was unconscious. Oh, Horace, I hope it's not bad."

"I hope it's not too. I like him. Did you like him, Joey?"

"I wanted to be friends with him and he wouldn't be, and then I helped him get away from the otter and then he was friends. He helped me get away from the mule."

"Helped you?" Horace asked. "Joey, did you . . . ?"

"I dropped the books and a page blew in there and I forgot and went after it. And then the mule came after me."

"Oh, Joey," Horace said. "Oh, Joey. Didn't you know, didn't they tell you?"

"Mr. Ben told me. He said your father . . . he said . . ." He stopped in confusion.

Horace looked at the ground. "Yes," he said, in a low, shamed tone. "That's right. Everybody knows it. And Charley too, and . . ." He shook his swollen head, and when he looked up his eyes were bright with tears. "I wish it hadn't been you, or Charley."

Joey was greatly moved by Horace's tears, by the boy's melancholy life and the things that his fate had prescribed for him; he was so moved that he wanted to get down on his knees and put his arms around Horace to comfort him, as one would comfort and defend a child against the frightening shadows that lay in wait in the world. He almost did it, and then the emotional moment passed; something within him, self-conscious and masculine, held him back. It confused him for a moment, bringing a brief regret. He looked at Horace, who seemed to realize what he was feeling; they gazed at one another with rueful smiles, and Joey put the books in the wagon.

"Thank you, Joey," Horace said. "And thank you for the books."

"I hope you like them, Horace," Joey said. He felt that he should go, now. "Shall I pull you back?"

Horace nodded, and Joey pulled the little wagon back to the place where he had first seen the boy.

"Will you ask your father to let us know, when he gets back?" he asked.

Horace nodded again and smiled, that smile of surpassing sweetness that Joey still remembered from the time before.

"I'll send more books," Joey said. "Good-by."

"I'm glad I know you, Joey," the boy said. "I hope you'll be happy in your life." He smiled again, and bowed his head; much moved, Joey stole away.

Almost three hours later, as Joey and Mr. Ben were sitting on the steps, Sam White drove in. He didn't get out of the Model T, and they walked over to the car.

"He come to on the way," White said. "The vet said he reckoned he'd be all right. He put a thing on his leg, and he's goin' to keep him a few days."

Joey felt almost lightheaded with relief; he had been dreadfully worried. "I sure am glad," he said. "I was afraid he was going to die, or be lame."

"Wouldn't have been no account lame," White said. "I told the vet that. I told him I ain't about to feed a lame dog, but he said it would be all right."

He moved back in the seat, as though to start off, and Joey moved forward. "If he's lame," he said, "if it isn't all right, will you give him to me? I'll keep him if he's lame."

White turned and gave him a puzzled look, as though such a thing was beyond the comprehension of a sensible man. "What for?" he asked, and as Joey recoiled a little added,

"If you want to do it, okay. I got to get back." He nodded, turned the Model T around, and drove around the corner of the house.

Mr. Ben looked at Joey and shook his head; they walked back to the steps again, and paused at the bottom step.

"Mr. Ben," Joey said. "Mr. Ben?"

"Yes, Joey?"

"I'd like right well to have Charley anyhow, whether he's lame or not. I'd be real good to him, and he wouldn't be hungry or get hurt or anything. I sure wish I could have him, Mr. Ben. You reckon if my father went to Mr. White . . ."

Mr. Ben slowly shook his head. "Sam would never sell him," he said, "as much as he could use the money. It might take him years to find another dog as useful to him, and he knows that. Besides, I'm not sure Charley would be happy in town, as much as he likes you. He has a sort of pride in his work; it's part of him, and he wouldn't be the same without it."

"But, Mr. Ben—"

"He'd be like the Indians," Mr. Ben said. "They had a pretty hard life, but it suited them. When it was taken away from them, even if they were made more comfortable, some of them sort of fell apart and got lazy and dirty and didn't care any more."

"Yes, sir," Joey said sadly, and then brightened. "But he'll be all right. The vet said he would."

Mr. Ben nodded, and they said no more. Now that they knew Charley would recover, and that racking anxiety was gone, their great relief brought a lassitude upon both of them.

"I reckon I better go pack up," Joey said presently. "My father sounded like he was in a hurry."

"I'll lend you a hand," Mr. Ben said.

They climbed the porch steps and went through the house and into the bedroom and slowly began to get Joey's things together. Into their mutual lassitude a gentle pensiveness had fallen, for they were going to miss each other. Presently Joey paused in his laggard efforts and looked at the old man's bent head; a small lump came into his throat. "I reckon I've been pretty lucky to have a Pond," he said, after he'd swallowed it, and then, "I sure thank you for everything, Mr. Ben."

"You're welcome, Joey," Mr. Ben said, without looking up. "I think I should be the one to thank you. Don't let it be too long before you come back again."

Whatever Joey was going to reply was interrupted by the rattling arrival of a car in the yard. They both got up and went to the window. The Model T was just stopping. Joe Moncrief had already seen the turkeys; he pointed at them and opened the door and jumped out. Bud and a girl, a pretty, dark-haired girl of thirteen, appeared from around the other side of the car and ran to join Joe Moncrief; they all stood pressing their noses against the screen to see the turkeys hanging from the ceiling.

The girl, Bud's cousin, was in the shadow of the porch roof now; Joey had seen her for only a moment in the sun as she ran around the car, but it seemed to him that he saw her the same way still. A special light, a nimbus, had gathered around her and glowed upon her and set her apart. Joey was confused. Something was happening to him that had never happened before, bringing with it a tingling lightness, at once melancholy and gay, that drew him to the girl within the nimbus and made him hesitate.

"Mr. Ben," he said, turning to the old man. "She's pretty, Mr. Ben."

Mr. Ben had been watching him; Mr. Ben's face held an odd little smile. "Ah, me," he said. "There are new problems and discoveries every day, aren't there? But this one will be more enduring than most." He put his hand gently on Joey's shoulder. "Come along, pilgrim," he said. "We'd better go outside."